THE SHADOW ON MOCKWAYS

THE SHADOW ON MOCKWAYS

MARJORIE BOWEN

Edited and with an introduction by
Gina R. Collia

Published by Nezu Press
Queensgate House,
48 Queen Street,
Exeter, Devon,
EX4 3SR,
United Kingdom.

This edition published 2025

The Shadow on Mockways first published in book form by W. Collins Sons & Co Ltd., 1932.

ISBN-13: 978-1-917113-09-0

Cover: *The Haunted House* by Edwin Edwards (1823-1879). Courtesy of Birmingham Museums Trust.

In the interest of preservation, the punctuation and spelling of the original first edition text have been maintained, and the original formatting has been used wherever possible. Only minor publisher errors and spelling inconsistencies have been silently corrected.

'Miss Marjorie Bowen'
The Bystander, 5 September 1906.

'I have used many names for business purposes, but they were none of them of my choosing and seemed rather to be fastened on me like a series of masks.' - Margaret Campbell, *Myself When Young: By Famous Women of Today*, 1938.

Margaret Campbell
The 'Lady with the Hundred Names'

by Gina R. Collia

Margaret Gabrielle Vere Campbell was born into poverty, in a house belonging to an elderly lady named Mrs Cole, on Hayling Island, off the south coast of England, on 1 November 1885.[1] She was the second child of Vere Douglas Campbell (1853–1906) and his wife, Josephine Elizabeth (née Ellis, 1860–1921); Josephine had been pregnant when she married Vere in the summer of 1884, but their first child, Dorothea, had died in infancy in a London lodging house a year before Margaret was born.[2] A third daughter, Phyllis Gertrude Bowen Vere Campbell, was born in the summer of 1890, when Margaret was four years old.[3] Of Irish descent and 'handsome, intelligent, attractive, a giant in stature', Vere was the third son of Dr Hugh Campbell (1823-1902) and his wife, Henrietta (née Johnson, 1826-1912).[4] Josephine was the third daughter of Reverend Charles Bowen Ellis (1821-1887), a West Indies-born Moravian minister, and his first wife, Priscilla (née Bayly, 1829-1879).[5]

Vere and Josephine Campbell's marriage was not a happy one. Vere was an alcoholic who, though he had always been kind to his daughter, disappeared from Margaret's life almost entirely by the time she was five years old.[6] Josephine, to whom Margaret was never close, was prone to 'hysterical ill-humour';[7] she scolded Margaret frequently, regularly made her stand in a corner with her hands on her head, and repeatedly told her that she 'ought never to have been born.'[8] Though Margaret's very early memories were happy ones, as she got older and became more aware of the people around her—of those who had complete power over her—she found that they 'began to be terrifying', and her mother's 'gusts of rage' bewildered and alarmed her.[9]

> 'I heard shouts, quarrels, echoes of scenes—battles or fights, they seemed to me. I was hustled from one room to another, shut in sometimes for hours together, very much afraid and wondering what was happening. Someone would open the door and push in a glass of milk and a slice of bread and butter, and once, I remember, a rag doll, and tell me to be quiet or to "efface myself," or to "run away and play, there's a good girl." '[10]

Margaret received no formal education as a child. Her mother, an aspiring writer and playwright, attempted to teach her to read and write, but each lesson 'exploded in a scene', which only served to increase her frustration and annoyance towards her daughter; five-year-old Margaret was often slapped on the backs of her hands with a hair-brush or shut in a room without any food as a punishment for 'refusing to spell out of obstinacy.'[11] Eventually, Marion Piggott, the family's nurse-cum-housekeeper, who was always referred to as Nana, succeeded where Margaret's own mother had failed. Nana also 'loved to

Josephine Campbell, *Morning Leader*, 1907.

dilate upon murder cases, even taking her charges to see the house where the dark deed was done', inspiring in Margaret an interest in actual murders and celebrated poison cases that 'began to ferment in that young mind of hers' and, many years later, found an outlet in her novels.[12]

During her early years, Margaret had little access to books.[13] Her family moved from one London lodging house to another, to avoid settling debts, and she made use of whatever she could find to read on the current landlady's bookshelf. When the family moved to Kensington, Margaret began to educate herself with books borrowed from the local library, and when, having been evicted for non-payment of rent, they moved again to lodgings on Vauxhall Bridge Road, she began visiting the National Gallery, the British Museum and the South Kensington Museums.[14]

In her teens, Margaret dreamed of becoming a great artist, and one of her mother's friends suggested that her passion for art should be encouraged as there might be money in it. She applied to attend the Royal College of Arts in South Kensington, but she failed the entrance examination.[15] Then, after several more moves to new lodgings to avoid paying yet more creditors, her mother decided that she should attend the Slade School of Fine Art, which she did from 1901.[16] But her work was regarded as poor by her professors, she failed both of the examinations she took whilst there, she was perpetually embarrassed by her mother's failure to pay her tuition fees on time, and she 'began to be aware of the disability of sex.'[17] As a result, she lived in a 'constant state of depression and terror.'[18] She went without food on a daily basis, was embarrassed by the state of her poor clothing, and she felt that every other student was a better artist than she was. Deflated and despairing, she turned to writing and, as there was no money to buy paper, took to scribbling out stories and notes on the backs of her own drawings.[19]

Following several more house moves, Margaret's family took lodgings in a street off Russell Square, and she managed to get some work carrying out research and fact-checking in the British Museum.[20] By that time, she had nearly finished writing a novel and had completed a number of poems and short stories, but her mother, who had failed to secure any interest in her own writing, attempted to persuade her against pursuing a literary career. In an attempt to force her to focus on her painting and drawing, she sent Margaret to Paris, but she failed to provide enough money to pay for lodgings, let alone tuition costs for art school classes.[21] Despite her circumstances—'I was hungrier then than I had ever been'—Margaret enjoyed her time in Paris, visiting museums and galleries and adding to her knowledge of art and history, but she made no progress in her career as an artist and returned to writing.[22]

When she had been in Paris almost a year, Margaret's mother sent for her to return home.[23] Once back in London, she showed some of her writing to her mother; Mrs Campbell's response was to declare it 'hopeless'.[24] This did not, however, prevent her from sending her young daughter's novel, the swashbuckling historical romance *The Viper of Milan,* to an agent. His response was not encouraging: the story was not believable, he disliked the unhappy ending, and it was 'not the kind of thing… that a girl was expected to write.'[25] Her mother suggested that, as she was a girl, she should write a 'pleasant tale', possibly 'something simple', if she wished to be published, but this proved an obstacle for Margaret; the tales she wanted to write were 'often full of dark and sinister shades.'[26] She wrote to escape the world she was forced to exist in, and by writing of dark subjects she managed, to a certain extent, to rid her mind of her own troubles.[27] Margaret's novel went on to be rejected by eleven publishers, and Mrs Campbell suggested that her daughter find an alternative way of making a living.[28] But it was eventually picked up by Alston Rivers Ltd. and published in 1906, when Margaret was twenty years old, and very much to everyone's surprise, not least of all Margaret's, it became a bestseller.[29]

'Miss Marjorie Bowen',
The Tatler, 12 September 1906.

To avoid possible confusion, as her mother wrote under the name Campbell, *The Viper of Milan* was published under the name Marjorie Bowen, the surname being taken from her grandfather, Charles Bowen Ellis. Margaret later wrote that the decision had not been hers; she had wanted to write under her own name, the pseudonym chosen had been odious to her from the outset, and 'this use of two names unfamiliar and even slightly distasteful to me helped to divorce me from my own work.'[30]

By the end of October 1906, only two months after *The Viper of Milan's* publication, demand for the book was so great that a sixth impression had already been published, and lending libraries were forced to increase their orders for it by the day.[31] And as a result of the success of her first book, 'the literary sensation of the autumn season',[32] Margaret received a cheque for sixty pounds—the money going straight to her mother—and entered into a new contract with the publisher for two more books.[33] Mrs Campbell ceased the little work she had been doing to support herself and her children, Phyllis 'did not believe in work', and Margaret became the family's only breadwinner.[34] However, her income was not quite enough to keep four people, and she found herself 'harnessed to a career of hard work' and forced to 'chase every odd five-pound note in order to keep up with expenses.'[35] Loans had to be repaid, her mother's friends had to be 'helped', and Phyllis wanted singing, dancing and riding lessons; before a year had passed, her earnings had been spent.[36] And nobody was happier for it; in fact, Margaret felt that they were unhappier than they had been before.

Josephine Campbell was bitterly jealous of her daughter's sudden literary success, having failed to achieve any for herself.[37] Critics had questioned why she had bothered to write her novel *The Crime of Keziah Keene*, published in 1889, one calling it 'downright nonsense', another describing it as having 'very little narrative and no plot.'[38] The reviewer for *The Academy* expected it to sink 'into well-deserved oblivion.'[39] And her novel *Ferriby*, published a year after Margaret's first great success, was described as leaving 'an unpleasant taste on the intellectual palate.'[40] Her play *Mizpah Misery*, staged in 1894, was described as 'sorry entertainment', and *The King's Password*, put on in 1900, failed to be 'convincing, satisfying, or even coherent'; it was described by the reviewer for the *Liverpool Mercury* as 'crude', 'artificial', and 'rhapsodically melodramatic', with the occasional carefully-written line 'drowned in verbiage.'[41] After years of trying and failing to make a name for herself, she had 'the galling experience of having to stand aside and be congratulated by foolish tactless people on her "clever daughter".'[42]

Shortly after the publication of *The Viper of Milan*, Margaret's father died; he had been found dead in the street with his wife's address in his pocket.[43] Margaret, with the assistance of her father's brothers, arranged for him to be buried in Kensal Green Cemetery.[44] His wife, though they had been separated for some years, went to pieces and never recovered from her loss, and Margaret, desperate to gain some freedom from her increasingly difficult and volatile mother, returned to Paris.[45] She found that she could write there easily, and she began to make a life for herself, away from the stifling influence of her mother. But Mrs Campbell was not about to let her daughter break away; she followed her to France and insisted she return home.[46]

The Viper of Milan was followed quickly by two more novels, both successful and both issued by Alston Rivers, *The Glen o' Weeping* (retitled *The Master of Stair* for the US market), published in 1907, and *The Sword Decides*, which came out in 1908. These were followed by *A Moment's Madness*, which appeared in the Christmas number of *Cassell's Magazine* in 1908, *The Leopard and the Lily*, issued by Doubleday, Page & Co. in 1909, and *Black Magic: The Tale of the Rise and Fall of the Antichrist* published by Alston Rivers in 1909.

Yet no matter how hard Margaret worked, and no matter how much she tried to please them, her family remained unhappy and ungrateful. With more money coming in, though never enough to meet their expenses, they moved to a flat at 55a Maida Vale, near St. John's Wood, the ground floor of which was occupied by the London and Provincial Bank.[47] Margaret found her new home 'extremely gloomy and depressing'; life there was 'untidy, humdrum, and unsatisfactory', and the 'atmosphere was one of constant nervous hysterical storms and tension.'[48] Additionally, the house was haunted, so much so that Mrs Campbell arranged for an expert from the Society for Psychical Research to stay there and investigate while the family escaped to a cottage in Cornwall.[49]

Phyllis Campbell, *The Tatler*, 4 August 1915.

Phyllis and Nana slept in rooms at the top of the Maida Vale house, and it was this top floor that was the focus of the ghostly activity at first; there were groans, footsteps on the stairs, knockings on the doors, and the sound of someone pacing to and fro.[50] Phyllis refused to sleep in her room and moved to the floor below, and the man-of-all-work, a fellow by the name of Frederic Payne, began complaining that the basement was 'overrun by supernatural creatures.'[51] Lights and water taps were switched on and off, windows were flung open, and Margaret's mother, who had begun hearing scufflings and moanings, saw 'a wheel of light whirl down the stairs.'[52] At first, Margaret saw and heard nothing and did not believe in the haunting, but by the time the Society for Psychical Research was contacted she too had begun experiencing ghostly goings on. One evening, when she was alone in the house and the light was beginning to fade, she opened the door of the drawing room and saw 'a gigantic figure, hooded and cloaked, with very square shoulders, passing into the little room on the stairs that had been turned into a bathroom.'[53] Then, not long afterwards, she awoke in the night and felt 'oppressed by a feeling of unreality.'[54]

> 'There seemed an oppression of something intensely evil, an abstraction and yet something in concrete form. As she

> lay quite still she saw in the air two objects rather like a pestle and mortar or a bulbous-shaped medicine glass, something with a black body and a long neck, lying in a bowl. They were of a blue colour and seemed to be of thickened glass.'[55]

Margaret was later told that the Maida Vale house had once been a private lunatic asylum, that an 'unchronicled tragedy' had taken place within it, and that after the event the doctor who lived there had moved in a hurry.[56] In truth, the house had been a private nursing home, and the tragedy had been the death of a female patient under the influence of chloroform in December 1902, for which the inquest returned a verdict of 'death from misadventure'.[57]

It was at this time, while her mother, sister and Nana were preoccupied with ghostly goings on, that Margaret met Zefferino Emilio Costanzo (c. 1882-1916), a Sicilian who had lived in London for several years.[58] Her family did not like him, and she liked rather than loved him, but he offered a means of escape; he was going back to Italy and might be there for some years, and he wanted her to go with him. And despite her mother's opposition to the match—she opposed the removal of the family breadwinner—Margaret and Zefferino were married in the October of 1912.[59] Zefferino was given a position with a company that was building a railway in the Carrara district of Lucca, and the following year the couple set out for Italy, taking a furnished house in Lucca Reggio, a two-hour train ride from Florence.[60]

For a time, Margaret was quite content in her new life. She learned to sew and, like her new Italian neighbours, kept hens and pigeons, though hers were not for food; she loathed meat and none was allowed in the house.[61] At the beginning of their married life in Tuscany, the couple lived on Zefferino's income; his wife's earnings continued to support the Campbell family in London. But when the railway in Lucca was completed in 1919, Zefferino lost his position and fell ill as a result, and the couple were forced to live on Margaret's income from writing. In an effort to reduce their outgoings, they moved to Florence and took an apartment in a large farmhouse near Santa Margherita.[62] Their rooms were uncomfortable, and Zefferino, who by then had acquired a constant cough, became increasingly violent-tempered; Margaret felt that all her hopes for a new, different life, away from the petty arguments and miseries of life with her mother, had been crushed. Then, on 4 August 1914, they received the news that England had declared war on Germany.

Margaret and her husband made attempts to get back to England, but their efforts came to nought.[63] The banks restricted withdrawals almost immediately; it was possible to get enough money for basic living expenses but nothing more.[64] Food prices increased, there were riots in Florence, and receiving accurate news from, or sending news to, England was next to impossible. In October, now heavily pregnant, Margaret journeyed with her husband to Sicily to his family home; she grew fond of his father and sister, but she detested the island itself, the way of life there and the disputes that everyone around her seemed to be embroiled in.[65] As she had remained the sole breadwinner of her family in London, she had continued to be productive throughout her marriage—she had produced two or three novels per year since the publication of *The Viper of Milan*—but now she had difficulty acquiring paper to write on or the time in which to use it.[66]

Following the birth of her baby daughter, Giuseppina, on 6 November 1914, Margaret became determined to return to England, and she and Zefferino finally began the long and arduous journey three months later.[67] They arrived in London one wintry day in February 1915, and Margaret found her mother and sister much as she had left them.[68] It soon became apparent that there was no place for Margaret's new family with her old one, so she and her husband moved into a farmhouse above the Kentish marshes, taking old Nana with them, and Zefferino took up poultry farming.[69] But during the cold winter months his health deteriorated.

On 19 May 1915, after a very brief illness, Giuseppina, then only six months old, died, and Zefferino was so affected by the loss of his daughter that his health deteriorated further still.[70] In the hope that milder weather conditions would be beneficial, Margaret arranged for them to move to South Devon.[71] She had continued to write—she was, after all, the only breadwinner for two families now—and was receiving an income which, though not quite as good as it had been before the war, was enough to sustain them. But it was shortly after their arrival in Torquay that she received two life-changing pieces of news: she was pregnant for the second time, and her husband would live no more than six months if he did not return to the warmer climate of his homeland. So, in October Zefferino sailed for home while Margaret remained in Torquay, awaiting the birth of her second child, Michael Birillo Vere, who was born the following January.[72]

One month after Michael's birth, Margaret received bad news from her husband; he was more seriously ill than she had thought, had fallen out with his family in Sicily and moved to Tuscany, and he wanted her to go to him with their baby son.[73] It was, of course, impossible to take a newborn baby on such a journey, so she left Michael in England and travelled to Italy alone. She nursed her husband, with very little help from another soul, until his death. Zefferino died from tuberculosis on 5 November 1916 at the Villa

Margaret in a 'Belle Alliance' dress. *The Sketch*, 10 March 1915.

Ceciale, in the sea town of Forte dei Marmi, in Lucca.[74] Margaret returned to England at the beginning of 1917, to her mother and sister, who still very much disapproved of everything she did, and to the infant son who, after so long a separation, did not recognise her as his mother.[75]

The little family left Torquay and moved to Hampstead Heath, and, in the October of the same year, Margaret entered into her second loveless marriage.[76] Arthur Leonard Long (1886-1983) was aware from the very beginning that his wife did not love him—'her story and her feelings had been fully explained'—but the marriage appears to have been fairly successful; it was a 'singular and pleasing union, to end only with their deaths.'[77] Her second marriage produced two sons—Athelstan Charles Ethelwulf was born on 2 Jan 1919, and Hilary Blaix Winch Vere was born on 24 June of the following year—both of whom, along with their half-brother, Michael, Margaret schooled at home until they were eight years old.[78] As with her first marriage, her second was supported by her writing income, and, as she had done since the publication of her first novel, she remained incredibly productive. In December 1921, Margaret's mother died—'a bitter death that was the direct outcome of her frustrated, unfortunate life'—and 'her sister went away and they saw no more of each other.'[79] From then on, she was no longer weighed down by the troubles and temperaments of her mother and sister, and she was responsible for the support of only her own household.

Articles published in the *Weekly Dispatch* in 1930 and *Sydney Morning Herald* in 1932 give us an insight into Margaret's working methods.[80] She used an ediphone, which she found 'an inspiring helper';[81] considering her prolific output, without it, she explained, 'neither my eyes nor my hands would stand the amount of work'.[82]

Margaret at her Kent home with her three sons: Michael (left), Athelstan (right) and Hilary (centre). *The Graphic*, 3 November 1923.

She narrated her story aloud, 'as though she were reading it from a written page'; once the story was completed, she transcribed it to paper, 'developing and colouring characters and scenes' as she went along.[83] She also took inspiration from listening to music; it was while listening to Beethoven's *Leonore* that the story of *Captain Banner*, a three-act drama written under the pseudonym George R. Preedy, first began to take shape in her mind.[84]

Margaret employed several pseudonyms during her career; in addition to her most well-known pen name, Marjorie Bowen, she wrote as Joseph Shearing, Robert Paye, John Winch and George R. Preedy. These appear to have been adopted to set certain works apart from those issued under the Bowen name, and with Preedy and Shearing there was some effort made to conceal the author's true identity for several years. *The Tatler* reported in 1952 that, a few years earlier, 'these pseudonyms were among the most jealously guarded secrets of the publishing world.'[85]

Margaret explained, many years after Preedy, Shearing, Paye and Winch first appeared in print, 'I became bored with the success of very early years. I felt I was living on another's reputation, so changed was I from the girl who had written "I Will Maintain!".'[86] And it's not terribly surprising that she should attempt to cast off the Bowen pen name for a time; it had been foisted upon her at the beginning of her career, and she had always detested it. 'The name Marjorie Bowen has always annoyed me,' she explained to a reporter in 1931, and she had found it impossible to express her 'second individuality' when using it.[87] In addition to the fact that she very much disliked her first pseudonym, she also felt that, when using it, 'her work was not receiving the close attention of the critics and the public', and that there was still 'a prejudice against women writers.'[88]

> 'When I am writing as George Preedy my whole personality definitely changes. The books I write as George Preedy are no effort whatsoever to me, but those of Marjorie Bowen are difficult and cause trouble.'[89]

Margaret wrote two novels as Robert Paye: *The Devil's Jig*, which appeared in 1930, and *Julia Roseingrave*, published in 1933; the former was still being advertised as an exceptionally successful 'first novel' by a new author when Paye's true identity was revealed in the autumn of 1930.[90] *Idlers' Gate* was published under the name John Winch in 1932, and that author's identity was made public the following year.[91]

The first title written under the name George R. Preedy was *General Crack,* published in 1928. The novel was a bestseller and immediately set the literary world speculating about the true identity of this talented new writer; Arnold Bennett, H. G. Wells, and Rafael Sabatini were all suspects.[92] Preedy was, according to the *Sunday Express*, 'the most retiring author in existence'; all efforts to get in touch with him failed, and appeals for him to reveal himself received no response.[93] He was obviously an expert in eighteenth-century history, and his only rival, according to the same newspaper, was Marjorie Bowen, whom they suggested Mr Preedy should meet.[94] The *Daily News* printed stories by both authors—Preedy's 'A Tune for a Trumpet' and Bowen's 'The Globe of Glass'—just days apart, to 'enable readers to make a comparison for themselves'.[95] It then sent samples of the two authors' handwriting to Dr C. Ainsworth Mitchell for 'microscopical examination', to discover if they were produced by one hand, but the good doctor concluded that there was 'not enough material upon which to base an opinion.'[96]

Speculation continued until the next Preedy novel, *The Rocklitz*, was dramatised in 1931. A reporter spotted Margaret, 'huddled, shyly, in a corner', altering Mr Preedy's script at the Duke of York

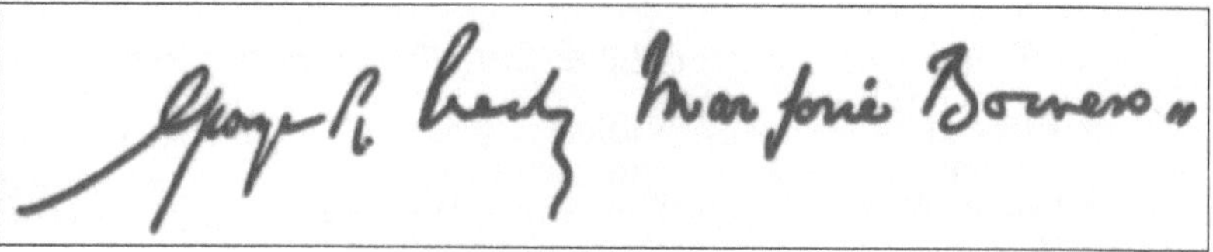

The signatures of George R. Preedy and Marjorie Bowen that were examined by Dr C. Ainsworth Mitchell. *Daily News*, 13 February 1930.

Theatre in London, and the jig was up.[97] 'I was trying to work a hoax,' Margaret explained; 'I wanted to get away from the type of writing done by Marjorie Bowen and to write something different as George Preedy.'[98] Not that this revelation prevented people from continuing to question the Bowen-Preedy connection. The following year, under the heading 'Tales under Two Titles: Bowen-Preedy Riddle Deepens', the *Sunderland Daily Echo* pointed out that, though 'it used to be admitted they they were one and the same person—a Miss Jekyll and a Mr Hyde', *Who's Who* had nonetheless continued to list them as two separate authors, with different biographical details, addresses, and interests.[99]

As Joseph Shearing, Margaret wrote historical novels with a true crime element; these were described as 'evil, sinister, ghostly, strange, baleful, terrible, relentless… and malevolent.'[100] The first Shearing novel, *Forget-me-Not*, was published in 1932, and from the moment of its appearance there was 'a definite and devoted cult of readers of this writer.'[101] Whilst there was much conjecture regarding the author's identity—at first, Mrs. Belloc Lowndes was the prime suspect—it remained a secret for a decade.[102] Joseph Shearing was 'one of the impenetrable mysteries of the day.'[103] It wasn't until 1942, when *Twentieth Century Authors: A Biographical Dictionary of Modern Literature* was going to press, that Margaret finally confessed to the fact that she and Shearing were one and the same person.

In 1939, the autobiography of 'Marjorie Bowen', *The Debate Continues,* was published by William Heinemann under her real name: Margaret Campbell. However, at the time, to make matters more confusing, she was often referred to as Gabrielle Long and Gabrielle Campbell. In 1949, a reviewer suggested that if Lon Chaney was billed as the 'Man With the Hundred Faces', Margaret should likewise be described as the 'Lady With the Hundred Names'.[104] The *Bookseller* considered it necessary to print a glossary of her noms de plume, and the *Evening Despatch* suggested jokingly that it was only a matter of time before Margaret announced she was also 'H. G. Wells, Arnold Bennett, Noel Coward, and Edgar Wallace'.[105] The author herself 'often thought of herself by the name Margaret under which she was baptized, a name borne by many Scotswomen since a royal saint made it popular.'[106]

Margaret achieved a great amount of success during her lifetime; her books sold extremely well for years and several of them were adapted into films and plays: her 1928 George Preedy novel *General Crack* was adapted as the film *General Crack* (1930), starring John Barrymore, her 1939 Shearing novel *Blanche Fury* was adapted as the film *Blanche Fury* (1948), starring Stewart Granger, and another of Shearing's, *For Her to See* (1947), became the film *So Evil My Love* (1948), starring Ray Milland, Ann Todd, and Geraldine Fitzgerald. Margaret was also one of the writers who worked on *Under Capricorn* (1949), the adaptation of Helen Simpson's 1937 novel, directed by Alfred Hitchcock and starring Ingrid Bergman, Joseph Cotton, and Michael Wilding.[107]

Margaret was described as a 'quiet, cultured woman';[108] she was 'a tall, shy, pleasant woman', 'always considerate and punctual for appointments', who, though she made a lot of money from her writing, 'lived modestly' and did 'much of her own housework'.[109] 'There is no vanity in the personality of Marjorie Bowen', wrote the reporter for the *Sydney Morning Herald* in 1932; she was a 'gentle-voiced woman' who was so lacking in self-importance that she answered her own doorbell.[110] Towards the end of her life, she lived quietly in a flat off the King's Road in London, where 'few of her neighbours' knew her 'well enough to point her out and say "That is Marjorie Bowen".'[111] When she was not writing, she had her hobbies; she still enjoyed painting, she was a skilled embroiderer, she particularly liked making dolls, for which she knitted petticoats, and she made many of her own clothes.[112] 'Life without a hobby,' she said, at the Diamond Jubilee Convention of the British Amateur Press Association in 1950, 'would indeed be barren. It is part of the English character to be an amateur and a little eccentric. If we weren't we should cease to be British people.'[113]

In the summer of 1952, Margaret suffered a broken arm.[114] In September, she spent two weeks in Ulster, trying to catch up with work on her novel *The Man with the Scales*, which her publisher had been urging her to finish.[115] She stayed with her friend May Morton, the Irish poetess who in her poem 'Gabrielle', written the previous year, had described Margaret as 'A sword of flame—a mind that probes and flares… A slender willow tree—a form of grace'.[116] With the author herself incapacitated, May took on the task of writing down Margaret's dictation, and the novel was finished while she was in Ireland.[117] It turned out to be the last that Margaret wrote.

On 3 December 1952, Margaret suffered a fall on the parquet floor of her bedroom. She took to her bed and, according to her youngest son, her condition appeared to improve for a while, but on 22 December she collapsed, and she died the following day in St. Charles Hospital, Kensington. She had suffered a haemorrhage due to having fractured her skull during the fall.[118] She was sixty-seven years old. At her death, she left behind more than a hundred and fifty novels and two hundred short stories. She once admitted that she herself was not certain how many books she had written.[119] Sadly, most have never been republished.

Notes

1 *1939 England and Wales Register* for the date.

With regard to her name: the *England & Wales, Civil Registration Birth Index, 1837-1915* and the *National Probate Calendar* record her name as 'Margaret Gabrielle', while the *England & Wales, Civil Registration Death Index, 1916-2007* and the *1901 England Census* have her down as 'Gabrielle Margaret'. Numerous death notices referred to her as 'Margaret Gabrielle Long'. I have chosen to refer to her by the name she chose in her own autobiography: Margaret.

Name of the cottage's owner, see Margaret Campbell, *The Debate Continues: Being the Autobiography of Marjorie Bowen.* London: William Heinemann Ltd., 1939, p. 1. Mrs Cole was most likely Frances Cole, who lived at 6 Clarendon Road and died in the autumn of 1885, just before Margaret's birth, at the age of 79. *See 1881 England Census.*

2 Marriage: *England & Wales, Civil Registration Marriage Index, 1837-1915.* Dorothea's birth and death: *England & Wales, Civil Registration Death Index, 1837-1915.* Location of Dorothea's birth: Campbell, op. cit., p. 1.

3 Born 1890, died 1982. *England & Wales, Civil Registration Birth Index, 1837-1915*, and *England & Wales, Civil Registration Death Index, 1916-2007.*

4 Description of Margaret's father: Campbell, op. cit., p. 50.

According to the information provided to medical directories at the time, Hugh Campbell studied at Edinburgh and Trinity College, Dublin. So far, I have found no record of him having studied at Trinity College. He passed the necessary examinations at St. Andrews in 1863 (see the *Sun*, 11 May 1863, p. 20).

5 *1871 England Census.*

6 Campbell, op. cit., pp. 7-8.

7 Ibid., p. 9.

8 Ibid., p. 7.

9 Ibid., pp. 2-3.

10 Ibid., p. 8.

11 Ibid., p. 11.

12 *Kensington Post*, 7 June 1947, p. 5. In her comments, Margaret refers to her childhood nurse without naming her, but Nana was her only nurse.

13 Campbell, op. cit., p. 11. Marion Piggot is recorded as the family's housekeeper in the *England Census* for 1901 and 1911.

14 Campbell, op. cit., p. 32.

15 Ibid., p. 42.

16 Ibid., p. 64.

17 Ibid., p. 65.

18 Ibid.

19 Ibid.

20 Ibid., p. 70.

21 Ibid., p. 77.

22 Ibid., p. 79.

23 Ibid., p. 83.

24 Ibid., p. 84.

25 Ibid.

26 Ibid.

27 Ibid., pp. 84-85.

28 Ibid., p. 85.

29 Newspaper reports often claimed that *The Viper of Milan* was published when Margaret was just sixteen or seventeen years old, but when it appeared, in August 1906, she was three months shy of her twenty-first birthday.

30 Campbell, op. cit., p. 91.

31 *Daily News* (London), 19 October 1906, p. 4.

32 *Daily Mirror*, 8 September 1906, p. 5.

33 Campbell, op. cit., p. 93.

34 Ibid., pp. 83 and 94.

35 Ibid., p. 95.

36 Ibd.

37 Ibid., pp. 95-96.

38 *Scottish Leader*, 26 September 1889, p. 2, *Ross Gazette*, 5 February 1890, p. 3, and *The Saturday Review*, 28 September 1889, p. 356.

39 *The Academy*, 19 October 1889, p. 250.

40 *Bath Chronicle*, 5 September 1907, p. 6.

41 *Birmingham Evening Mail*, 13 March 1894, p. 4, and *Morning Post*, 29 May 1900, p. 5, and *Liverpool Mercury*, 22 May 1900, p. 8.

42 Campbell, op. cit., p. 95.

43 Ibid., p. 99.

44 Ibid., and the burial register for Kensal Green Cemetery, London.

45 Campbell, op. cit., p. 99.

46 Ibid., p. 100.

47 *1911 England Census.*

48 Campbell, op. cit., p. 102.

49 Ibid., p. 116.

50 Ibid., p. 106.

51 Ibid., p. 107. Margaret remembers that the man-of-all-work was called Palmer. However, according to the *1911 England Census* his name was Frederic Payne.

52 Ibid.

53 Ibid. p. 116.

54 Ibid. p. 117.

55 Ibid.

56 Ibid. p. 127.

57 *Hastings and St Leonards Observer*, 20 December 1902, p. 2.

58 Campbell, op. cit., p. 118. His name is not given in Margaret's account of her life, *The Debate Continues*; in various other sources it is given as Zeffrino Costanzo, Zefferino Costanzo, Zeffirino Costanzo, and Zeffirine Costanza. In November 1918, Margaret's second husband, Arthur L. Long, wrote to the *New York Herald* to correct a piece about his wife's book, *The Third Estate*, and in that he refers to 'Zefferino Costanzo' (see the *New York Herald*, 17 November 1918, p. 43).

59 *England & Wales, Civil Registration Marriage Index, 1837-1915.*

60 Campbell, op. cit., p. 132.

61 Campbell, op. cit., p. 136.

62 Ibid., p. 151.

63 Ibid., p. 156.

64 Ibid.

65 Ibid., p. 158.

66 Ibid., p. 163.

67 *UK and Ireland, Find a Grave Index, 1300s-Current.*

68 Campbell, op. cit., p. 174.

69 Ibid., p. 175.

70 Ibid. Giuseppina Costanzo was buried in the churchyard of St Mary the Virgin, Stone-cum-Ebony, Ashford, Kent, England.

71 Ibid., p. 182.

72 *England & Wales, Civil Registration Birth Index, 1916-2007.* Full name: birth certificate (registered in Newton Abbot).

73 Campbell, op. cit., p. 188.

74 *England & Wales, National Probate Calendar (Index of Wills and Administrations), 1858-1995.*

75 Campbell, op. cit., p. 288.

76 *England & Wales, Civil Registration Marriage Index, 1916-2005.*

77 Campbell, op. cit., p. 290.

78 Birthdates of her sons: birth certificates, *UK, World War II Allied Prisoners of War, 1939-1945. WO 345*, and *England and Wales, Death Index, 1989-2021.* Schooling: *Sydney Morning Herald*, 27 August 1932, p. 9.

79 Campbell, op. cit., p. 291, and *England & Wales, Civil Registration Death Index, 1916-2007.*

80 *Sydney Morning Herald*, 27 August 1932, p. 9.

81 Ibid. A recording device for oral dictation where sound was recorded on a wax cylinder. The machine marketed by the Edison Records Company was trademarked as the 'Ediphone'.

82 *Weekly Dispatch*, 14 September 1930, p. 1.

83 *Sydney Morning Herald*, 27 August 1932, p. 9.

84 Ibid.

85 *The Tatler*, 13 August 1952, p. 13.

86 E.g.: *Torbay Express and South Devon Echo*, 27 December 1952, p. 5.

87 *Weekly Dispatch*, 1 February 1931, p. 11.

88 *News* (Adelaide, Australia), 3 February 1931, p. 9.

89 *Weekly Dispatch*, 1 February 1931, p. 11.

90 *Weekly Dispatch*, 14 September 1930, p. 1.

91 *Liverpool Daily Post*, 30 September 1933, p. 6.

92 *Weekly Dispatch*, 1 February 1931, p. 1.

93 *Sunday Express*, 9 February 1930, p. 4.

94 Ibid.

95 *Daily News*, 15 February 1930, p. 5.

96 *Daily News*, 13 February 1930, p. 7.

97 *Weekly Dispatch*, 1 February 1931, p. 1, and *Daily News*, 2 February 1931, p. 1.

98 *Daily News*, 2 February 1931, p. 1.

99 *Sunderland Daily Echo and Shipping Gazette*, 10 January 1933, p. 6.

100 Stanley Kunitz and Howard Haycraft, *Twentieth Century Authors: A Biographical Dictionary of Modern Literature.* H. W. Wilson Company, 1942, p. 1272.

101 Ibid.

102 *Daily News*, 3 June 1932, p.4.

103 *Daily News* (London), 19 October 1906, p. 4.

104 *Ireland's Saturday Night*, 26 March 1949, p. 2.

105 *Evening Despatch*, 2 February 1931, p. 6.

106 Campbell, op. cit., p. i.

107 Donald Spoto, *The Dark Side of Genius: The Life of Alfred Hitchcock.* Boston: Little Brown, 1983, p. 309.

108 *Derby Daily Telegraph*, 26 February 1931, p. 4.

109 *Evening Standard*, 27 December 1952, p. 2, and *Belfast News-Letter*, 16 March 1953, p. 3.

110 *Sydney Morning Herald*, 27 August 1932, p. 9.

111 *Evening News*, 10 March 1947, p. 2.

112 *Belfast News-Letter*, 16 March 1953, p. 3.

113 *Bromley & West Kent Mercury*, 22 September 1950, p. 4.

114 *Newcastle Journal*, 4 August 1952, p. 3.

115 *Belfast News-Letter*, 16 March 1953, p. 3.

116 May Morton, 'Gabrielle', in *Sung to the Spinning Wheel.* Quota Press, 1952, p. 18. Though the poetry collection was published in 1952, the poems were written the previous year, see *Belfast News-Letter*, 19 November 1951, p. 3.

117 *Belfast News-Letter*, 16 March 1953, p. 3.

118 *Belfast Telegraph*, 29 December 1952, p. 1.

119 *Evening Standard*, 27 December 1952, p. 2.

"All torment, trouble, wonder and amazement, inhabits here."

The Tempest.

CHAPTER I

BEALE said:

"That man over there has a house that would suit me."

He nodded towards one of the little iron tables under the striped umbrellas in the small hôtel garden where two solitary individuals were seated.

Falkland hadn't noticed them before and said so. Beale pulled up his brows and answered dryly:

"The stout chap is Dobree, the American millionaire, the other is his friend, confidant—familiar."

"I don't know much about millionaires," admitted Falkland pleasantly. "This one looks, from here, an odd sort of fellow."

"I don't think any one knows much about this particular millionaire—he's all over the place, got interests in everything, but in a very quiet way—most benevolent and all that sort of thing."

"What is this house you were speaking of?" asked Falkland idly enough.

"He's got many houses, places dotted all over the world—this particular one is called 'Mockways,' on the Welsh border. I saw a photograph of it once. It impressed me a good deal."

"As what?"

"As a very peculiar sort of house," replied Beale thoughtfully. "I always wanted to paint it, seeing the owner here made me think of it again. I'm tired of landscapes and people, I want to do a house, a strange house, and call it, 'Portrait of a Mansion,'—trouble is, to find the model, and, as I said, that man had one that would serve my turn."

"Well, ask him to let you do it," smiled Falkland easily. "I don't see that there ought to be any difficulty."

Beale shook his pleasant dark head.

"Dobree is very difficult, millionaires have to be, he keeps out of any kind of publicity, he hates even to be recognised, he wouldn't like to know that he is known here, but he is."

"What is he doing here?"

Falkland regarded with curiosity the object of this conversation; there were only the four of them in the prim garden dotted with little tables under the orange linen umbrellas. It was late afternoon, hushed, sunny and warm; behind, the white flat front of the hôtel with green shutters and pink flowers at the windows showed the glaring sun, before them, the forest of Bitterne showed dark in the shade; the trees came up to the very verge of the gravelled space in front of the Headfort Arms, that was so small, so quiet and so very exclusive and expensive.[1]

Beale was a painter not unknown yet not famous, who lived in agreeable Bitterne during the summer, and Falkland was his friend who had a little money always well spent, and a little leisure always well employed. Falkland proposed to do great things with his life but did not quite know what; they were both not more than twenty-five and pleasant, lively, and not bad looking.

Falkland could not have found so much to say for Dobree, at whom he gazed curiously across the sunny little garden.

The millionaire had the ordinary appearance of a stout, elderly man, well dressed in riding kit and self-assured, but he was too stolid and expressionless; he seemed to sit without stirring or even

---

[1] Bitterne is now a suburb of Southampton, but before 1920 it was a village outside Southampton, surrounded by countryside. It sits less than ten miles east of the New Forest.

breathing, to stare in front of him without moving his lids.

"Like a snake," thought Falkland.

The features of Jessamy Dobree were flat and dull coloured, not ill shaped, but not agreeable, and he wore his dark grey hair straight and close like a monk's tonsure.

"I don't like the look of him," remarked Beale. "I never heard anything but good of him, but, damn it, I wish he would let me paint 'Mockways'—I'd do something with that."

"I'll find a chance to ask him," said Falkland confidently. "Who's the man with him anyway? I don't like him either."

"That's Harvey Manning—his secretary, I suppose. What's the matter with him?"

Falkland didn't quite know.

Manning sat opposite his immobile master, reading intently a book with a yellow cover; he was rather elegant, tall, lean and sallow, his slightly pointed features had just missed good looks; but even in his inaction he seemed servile; though he had an air of arrogance, it was the arrogance of a servant, a valued, pampered one, perhaps, but still a servant.

"Don't like the type," remarked Falkland decisively, finishing his coffee, "don't like either of them, but they both seem damned queer, perhaps, interesting."

He was still thinking of these two men, of this scrap of conversation when, an hour later, he was deep in the forest of Bitterne, walking away from the little town where he had left Beale in a room of the Headfort Arms, finishing the portrait of another American visitor.

Strangely enough as he lifted his eyes he saw Dobree riding towards him down the long shadowed forest path, riding very slowly with an air of indifference as to time or purpose.

The way was so narrow that Falkland stepped into the undergrowth to allow the horseman to pass, but could not avoid giving him an inquisitive glance.

Dobree looked down at him, one quick, sharp look, without a change of expression, and rode on; his heavy figure on the restive, spirited animal appeared imposing as he proceeded at a dignified pace down the cool dusk of the forest. Falkland gazed after him with interest, a near view of that flat, pale face had given him an impression of uncommon power and grandeur.

He felt fascinated by Jessamy Dobree, by that wealth of which he was the symbol, and he watched the lonely, massive and rigid figure until it had disappeared into the green gloom of the forest.

These words in a feminine voice and in good English over Falkland's shoulder startled him from his absorption:

"Excuse me, but could you tell me who that was, please?"

A girl was standing close behind him; she must have come up very quietly, or he have been very deep in reverie. She was almost breathless.

"I've surprised you," added the girl. "You didn't notice me?"

"No," smiled Falkland. "It's all right," as he recovered from the surprise. He answered her first question, "I think that is Mr. Jessamy Dobree, the American millionaire."

"I thought so," replied the young woman, and Falkland had an instant feeling that he had been imprudent to so candidly use this stranger's name.

The girl looked at him as if she could easily read his thoughts and a flush mounted to the young man's clear cheeks, for her eyes were singularly penetrating, cool and resolved; her expression was that uncommon one of purpose and decided energy so compelling and so impressive; for the rest, she had a long, smooth, well-bred face; her careless hat and light coat concealed her hair and her figure.

She said, with an ironic smile on her wide, well-shaped mouth, "He stays at the Headford Arms and rides every day in the woods. I generally pass him—but just now I only saw him in the distance."

She paused—too deliberately for it to be named a hesitation—then, thanking Falkland, turned into the undergrowth and made her way carefully and slowly through the trees that were here so dark and dense, that rose so high and intertwined their boughs so thickly that nothing of the sky was visible but distant sparkles of blue light.

Shortly after this interruption a sound that faintly disturbed the remote peace of the solitude made Falkland turn sharply. Surely the thud of a galloping horse; Falkland smiled, thinking of the legends of ghostly huntsmen who thundered in the twilight through the deserted glades.

But they were no phantom hoofs that came nearer, nearer, no phantom rider who plunged into the open space, but Jessamy Dobree struggling with a furious bolting horse that had thrown off all control; the rider's face was ashy and strained as he fought to restrain the rearing animal which was making every effort to throw him; despite his frantic drag on the bit the animal made a desperate swerve and turned, to dash into the thick trees.

Dobree gave a short, raucous shout, as Falkland had leaped across the path and contrived, by nerve and luck, to seize the bridle. There was a frenzied struggle; the animal dragged him a few paces; but Falkland was strong and used to horses; he hung on long enough to allow Dobree, who was quick for a man of his weight, to jump from the saddle with no more than a sprawling fall.

In a few moments the frightened beast, relieved of its rider, was quieted; Falkland led it, sweating, trembling and panting, to where Dobree stood under the trees, flicking the dirt from his clothes and wiping his forehead; his extreme pallor accentuated the peculiar flatness of his features, but he bore himself well for a man who had been so nearly dashed to death.

"I was mooning along like a fool, with a slack rein," he remarked dryly, "when a hare or something ran out—I believe there was some one in the undergrowth—I caught a glimpse of a flash of light stuff, I thought."

Falkland remembered the girl in the pale coat; he answered as he patted the trembling horse:

"Of course, sir, there are people in the woods, but one seldom meets them."

"Just so," said Dobree. "Well, something or some one frightened the beast, that's clear. Of course, I am very much obliged to you," he added, glancing directly at Falkland, "but that's a silly thing to say, isn't it? If we had hurtled into those trees I should have been pulp by now."

"Oh, any idiot would have done as much," said Falkland hurriedly; he hardly liked the other's manner, though he could not have said why.

Dobree brushed that aside with the air of a man used to dealing briefly and decisively with every situation.

"If I was to go off with a 'thank you,' " he remarked, "you'd be disgusted, wouldn't you?"

"Not at all."

"You would," Dobree smiled. "And there's my point of view. People don't care to owe their lives to any one without trying to square the obligation—come now, there's something I could do for you?"

Falkland resented this; there was something harsh and peremptory in the way this man wished to at once reward him for his service.

"Thank you, Mr. Dobree, there is no need to think of it like that."

"Oh, you know me, eh? I saw you outside the hôtel just now?"

"Yes." Then Falkland recalled the conversation by the little iron table, and Beale's remarks about "Mockways," and he, too, smiled.

"I was going to ask you a favour," he added. "My friend and I were talking of it——"

"That's odd," replied the millionaire ironically, "but then there are many people who want favours from me, as I dare say you know."

Falkland flushed and occupied himself with the horse to conceal his annoyance.

"This wasn't what you might think, Mr. Dobree; my friend is a painter and he wanted permission to paint something that belongs to you."

"Well, he can come along and talk about it," replied Dobree with a cold smile. "But what about yourself anyway?"

"Nothing at all about myself," said Falkland rather sharply. "If you could oblige my friend Beale, I should be grateful."

Dobree approached the horse which was quiet enough now.

"I must get back," he said. "You know where to find me, and I dare say you know a good deal about me."

A pellucid twilight had fallen; colour and light were slowly receding from the upper air and the forest surrounding them on all sides looked unutterably dark and lonely.

Falkland helped Dobree to mount; he tried to keep his good humour and to be amused, not vexed by the millionaire's grim, rather offensive manners.

"As for your friend," added Dobree, looking down from the saddle, "of course, if you ask for him, whatever it is, it's settled."

"Well, I'd like to ask that," said Falkland candidly, "he wants to paint a house of yours, he saw a photograph and it fascinated him——"

"A house of mine?"

"Yes—a place called 'Mockways.' "

Silence.

Dobree remained motionless, looking down; the queer half light made his face appear more ashy, almost distorted; Falkland, enthralled by his expression, at once blank and intense, returned that stony gaze almost against his will.

Dobree suddenly aroused himself.

"Why the devil does your friend want to paint 'Mockways?' "

"I don't know—he's got the idea into his head—it's an odd sort of house, I suppose, and suits some plan for a picture he's keen on——"

Dobree hardly seemed to hear this; he appeared absorbed in dark reflections; his large, pale hand was slowly caressing the horse's damp neck; his small, deep-set eyes, at once dull and alive, remained fixed on Falkland.

"That request is refused," he said in a flat, slow voice. "Tell your friend that I don't allow any of my places to be painted, or even photographed."

With no more than that he turned away, and moved off without looking back, along the darkling path that led to Bitterne.

Falkland was angry and amazed; he could hardly have imagined anything so churlish; and he thought cynically of Beale's talk of this man's reputation for kindness and benevolence.

"Oh, well!" The young man shrugged his shoulders.

After waiting and meditating a little, a sound like an echo came from behind him; he turned sharply to see the girl he had met earlier in the evening standing beneath the trees which now rose black and ghastly into the pallid, empty sky.

Her white coat was a blur in the dusk, her face he could hardly discern.

"I say, won't you get lost in the forest?" asked Falkland awkwardly. "It's getting dark."

"No, I am used to the woods," she replied. "What is he going to do for you for stopping his horse?"

"Oh, you saw that, did you?" and again the suspicion crossed his mind that she had startled the hare that had frightened Dobree's horse. "What should he do for me?" he added. "One doesn't put a value on that sort of thing; any one who had been here would have done as much——"

She came slightly nearer through the dusk; Falkland reflected, rather uneasily, that she must have been following Dobree, running after him, tracking him down through the forest labyrinth.

"Most people would want something from a man like that," she said. "However proud you are—there's something he could do for you."

"Well," smiled Falkland, "I did ask a favour and it was refused."

"Refused? He's usually generous—what did you ask?"

"Permission for a friend to paint a house of his."

The girl echoed as Dobree had himself echoed:

"A house of his?"

" 'Mockways.' "

"Oh," she seemed to peer at him through the gathering gloom, "don't ever go there."

"I don't want to—it's my friend's idea, he's keen on making a picture of the place, thinks it odd or something."

"For God's sake don't go to 'Mockways,' " said the girl, "at least, never go inside it—never, whatever inducement you have."

Falkland smiled more broadly at this.

"I'm not likely to ever get any inducement, seeing he has just refused to allow Beale to go near it."

"You might," she answered earnestly. "You never know how things will turn out——"

"I say, what do you know of all this? Mr. Dobree and 'Mockways?' " asked Falkland curiously. "And why are you bringing me into it? You are a stranger to me."

She replied hurriedly. "You're in it already—I'd like to help you, but I can't——"

"What the devil do you mean. I don't want help——"

"You may—I must go now, before it is quite dark." She paused, came close to Falkland and touched him on the hand. "If you want anything from Dobree, say these words to him——"

"I don't want anything——" protested Falkland.

"Sarah Lomax," whispered the girl unheeding. "Just say, 'Sarah Lomax,' and see what he does——"

She withdrew swiftly, with what seemed incredible lightness and speed, and as she disappeared, her last words were, "Don't go to 'Mockways'!"

Falkland discussed the extraordinary adventure with Beale that evening in their room above the inn porch in the main street of Bitterne, that artless yet artful "show village."

"Sounds to me uncommonly like blackmail," suggested Beale cheerfully, "but why doesn't she try it on herself? Why ask you—an utter stranger?"

Falkland thought of the whole of the happenings over again. He asked Beale for the photograph of "Mockways" and the artist searched for this in one of his portfolios; these, with a box of oils, were his sole stock in trade in the inn room.

"Ever heard of Sarah Lomax in connection with 'Mockways?' "

"Never—it belonged to some people called Powell but has been in Dobree's possession for years; that's all the guide book says. I've never been near it, myself, but I want to go."

He found the photograph, which had been cut out of a rather cheap local guide book and mounted.

Falkland, in this pleasant little room of the old house of the out-of-the-way village, looked eagerly at this picture of a mansion so far away, of which he had only just known the existence. "Mockways" was high and narrow, set on an open space of lawn with one enormous black cedar shadowing one side, the windows and door were flat, adorned only with stiff narrow pediments, the tympanums filled by masks.

"A God-forsaken hole," remarked Falkland.

But the artist with a grin, said:

"I could make a wonderful picture of it—look at that shadow—coffin shaped—on the grass——"

"So it is—but the tree and the house together make that shape, of course it's haunted——"

But, somehow, in staring at this printed photograph of "Mockways," Falkland seemed to see two faces, the face of Dobree with that glazed look of absorption on the flat, clay coloured features, the face of the girl, alert, determined, but also full of a strange abstraction, and a little chill, furtive but definite, for a second overlaid his cheerful spirits.

He tossed the photograph back to Beale.

"Well, it's nothing to do with me, and never will be, but it's all pretty queer, I think."

The artist took another view, he set his paints in order: Falkland idly noticed a broken tube of green.

"Why don't you try old Dobree with that name, just for fun? You don't know anything about it—and he's behaved atrociously, probably there's nothing in it, but just see how he takes it."

The result of a night of restless mental debate was that Falkland appeared early at the Headfort Arms and asked for Mr. Dobree.

He had come partly in a spirit of humorous bravado, and partly in one of curiosity mingled with a half conscious desire to teach manners to a man he disliked and who had behaved very badly—why shouldn't this old curmudgeon be forced to allow Beale to paint that hideous house?

Dobree received him at once in the elegant white panelled room behind the green shutters and the pink flowers.

"I thought you would come, Mr. Falkland," he remarked dryly, glancing at the young man's card. "I am still very mindful of your behaviour yesterday—and if there is anything you want——"

"Only what I asked yesterday," said Falkland easily. " 'Mockways'——"

The millionaire seemed to have been expecting this, for he at once interrupted:

"That is quite impossible, I hoped I had made so much clear."

Falkland was nettled; this curt refusal of a reasonable, modest request stung him considerably, and he said what he had scarcely meant to say as he entered the charming, sunny room so pleasant with Morland prints and dark oak furniture.

"There is something else, Mr. Dobree—do you know the name of Sarah Lomax?"

Dobree never stirred but he seemed to shrink and wither as he sat; Falkland had the impression that he was exercising the most remarkable self-control, and behind that blank, grey exterior the man's soul was like a rat in a trap; how he got such an impression Falkland did not know—it must have been the look in Dobree's eyes, for in no other way did he betray himself; indeed, it was with dull calm that he replied:

"The name is utterly unknown to me."

But Falkland, somehow convinced that he lied, was on the defensive.

"I'm sorry—I thought you might know——"

"Know what?" caught up Dobree.

"Something of Sarah Lomax," fenced Falkland.

"What do you know?" asked Dobree in a chill voice. "Why do you ask?"

"I know nothing—I just heard the name in connection with you—but, as you don't know it, of course," smiled Falkland, "it was a mistake."

"Where did you hear this?"

"I've forgotten," said Falkland. "Why bother, as there is nothing in it?"

The two men faced each other for a second; the glance of both was steady. Then Dobree suddenly rose and pressed a bell; an inner door opened at once and the tall sharp featured Harvey Manning appeared.

Dobree began to speak in quick, animated tones very different from his usual behaviour.

"This is Mr. Falkland, Manning, Mr. Edward Falkland, of whom I spoke to you yesterday, he stopped my mount—and we must do something for him, Manning, something worth while——"

Manning bowed and murmured some platitudes. Falkland sensed some understanding between the two men, and in a very subtle way, that they were both concerned in some hostility towards him; yet this seemed absurd for nothing could have been more genial than the suddenly lively manner of Dobree, who appeared, all at once, to be exerting himself to please.

Falkland was on the alert and guarding against surprise, yet what Dobree said astounded him utterly.

"Mr. Falkland, I require a new secretary and I offer you the post—and with it a great many opportunities. Your salary will be a thousand a year—the one condition is that you accompany me at once—I'm leaving Bitterne to-morrow."

"It's ridiculous, sir," said Falkland, "you know nothing of me."

"Nothing that Mr. Dobree does is ridiculous," smiled Manning. "Believe that, Mr. Falkland, and accept."

The young man's thoughts were racing—wasn't this a chance grotesque in its magnificence? He could easily get out of the modest little job waiting for him—why, no one but a fool——

"My ward, Isabel," said Dobree pleasantly, "will be joining us—and glad of young company. Come, it's settled?"

Falkland hesitated; with these two amiable men, in this pleasant room, he yet felt that something warned him—something whispered: "Don't accept."

But Falkland ignored this as nervous folly; he was dazzled; he forgot "Mockways," he forgot the woman in the wood; with a touch of bravado, of challenge, he said:

"I accept."

CHAPTER II

FALKLAND found himself in a state of reasonable excitement. He returned at once to the inn where he was staying with Beale, full of an eager desire to talk over this astonishing occurrence with his friend.

The artist was out, however, and Falkland hung about, waiting for him, standing at the door and glancing up and down the pleasant English scene, the wide village street, the cottages with the flower gardens, the rising hills and orchards beyond, the few people going about their quiet business, the cars of tourists passing through.

Meanwhile he was longing to talk over the whole thing with Beale and to tell him triumphantly:

"Well, it looks as if I could get you to 'Mockways' after all!"

But the painter did not appear; Falkland at last turned back into the inn and asked when he had gone out.

"He's left, sir," said the woman in the tiny office. "I thought you knew."

"Left! You mean left Bitterne?"

"Yes. As soon as you had gone out this morning a gentleman in a car came to see Mr. Beale—they left together. Mr. Beale put his things together and paid his bill, all in about ten minutes," she added curiously, impressed by the expression of amazement on Falkland's face.

"There's no message?" asked Falkland.

"No, sir. No message at all——"

"I'd just like to look round his room, if you don't mind—and what was the other man like?"

The woman was ready with her description:

"Tall, sharp featured he was, very polite, I believe I've seen him about—it was a beautiful car, too."

A name jumped at once into Falkland's mind—Harvey Manning—but no, surely that was a ridiculous guess.

It gave him, however, a hint to satisfy the curiosity of the staring woman; he replied, smoothly:

"Oh, I see, a friend of ours staying at the Headfort Arms, I dare say there was a sudden commission for Mr. Beale and he came to fetch him."

Standing in Beale's room, where he had chatted over the forest adventure yesterday and looked at the picture of "Mockways," he tried to cast over in his mind if it were possible for Harvey Manning to have fetched away Beale and yet returned to the Headfort Arms in time to meet him with Dobree.

He, Falkland, had walked to the hôtel, he had waited, there had been the interview; if Manning had come up immediately on his departure, there would have been time, in a swift car, for him to have picked up Beale, driven him to some destination not too far and come back to the Headfort Arms before Falkland left it—but what destination? And why should Manning want to get hold of Beale?

To this an unpleasant answer crept into Falkland's mind—*if* there was anything in the "Sarah Lomax" affair, why then, Dobree would naturally have his suspicions roused as to the other man, the man who had wanted to paint "Mockways," and might have sent Manning to get in touch with him, to find out all that he knew.

But what could have induced Beale to go and without leaving a message?

He looked eagerly round the room, opened drawers and cupboards, went through the litter of papers on the hearth—nothing.

The artist's few belongings had gone; there was no message, no clue as to his whereabouts.

"Well," thought Falkland uneasily, "I suppose he'll write or turn up."

And he reflected that he could not write to Beale for the artist seldom had a permanent address; he had intended to go abroad when he left Bitterne and had no London studio.

Falkland pulled himself together; he was due to lunch with Dobree soon; it had been a most cordial and charming invitation; there would be an opportunity to ask about Beale—about Harvey Manning.

He did not enter Dobree's sitting room with the same elation that he had left it a few hours ago; it was odd how the hasty disappearance of his friend had taken the bloom off his good luck, made him uneasy, even suspicious—and about what? and of what?

It was, after all, really absurd to associate the sudden departure of Beale with Dobree and Manning.

And yet, somehow, Falkland had come to the decision to try and put things on a clearer understanding with Dobree, to force him to explain himself and his offer, so unlikely, so curious.

"Of course," Falkland told himself, "I could get out of it, even now——"

Why should he want to "get out of it"—his great piece of good luck?

Harvey Manning entered the gracious little room so brightly filled with the late morning sunshine, and Falkland could not help giving him a quick look of curiosity; the man had certainly an odd personality, so still, so servile, and yet somehow, so insolent under those negative courteous manners.

"You must feel, Mr. Falkland, that this has been a very lucky day for you," he remarked with his quick smile.

"A puzzling day," replied Falkland, eagerly taking advantage of this opening. "I accepted Mr. Dobree's offer—rather impulsively—the more I think it over though——"

"Don't think it over," interrupted Manning smoothly. "You accepted—that's sufficient."

"Is it?" said Falkland slightly nettled, feeling somehow hostile and on the defensive. "I've not bound myself in any way, of course—Mr. Dobree was extremely generous, perhaps impulsively so——"

"No," said Manning, "no. Mr. Dobree never acts impulsively."

He gave his wide, meaningless smile.

"Then," remarked Falkland bluntly, "it is all rather mysterious."

Manning caught up the word.

"Mysterious, Mr. Falkland? Where is the mystery? I fail to see any mystery——"

"Well, then, not mysterious, but odd—why should I have been engaged for a post like this, at such a salary, at a minute's notice?"

With the slight movement of a thin upraised hand Manning checked Falkland and made him also feel rather foolish.

"My dear fellow," said Manning with a faint flavour of irony in his silky civility, "please don't bother your head about such details. Mr. Dobree was wanting a private secretary—he sees, suddenly, under romantic circumstances, a young man he thinks to be the very one for him——"

"That's all rather unconvincing," broke in Falkland.

"Do you know anything about Mr. Dobree?" inquired Manning casually.

"No—that's part of the—oddness—of the situation," smiled the young man frankly. "I'd hardly heard of him till yesterday, I only knew that he was very rich, and, I suppose, powerful."

"A man of many interests, of much influence," said Manning smoothly. "Not a man to make mistakes. You should be delighted at his interest in you."

"Yes, but I'd rather like to understand it—I wanted to talk over the whole thing with my friend, who has been staying with me—but he has gone—left suddenly while I was up here."

Manning showed the faintest of polite attention.

"Gone," repeated Falkland, walking up and down the room, "without a message—left suddenly in a car with a stranger."

"I'm afraid that I can't help," smiled Manning submissively.

"It was Beale who wanted to paint 'Mockways,' " added Falkland abruptly.

"Was it?" asked Manning. "But I don't see the connection."

At this point Jessamy Dobree entered the room with a sudden swiftness as if he had been waiting for some preconcerted signal outside.

Manning turned to him at once with deferential attention.

"Mr. Falkland, sir, seems troubled because his friend has left without a message."

"Well, I dare say you will get news of him soon," continued Dobree with the air of a man humouring a foolishness. "Meanwhile, let us get to our own affairs, Mr. Falkland. I hope you are prepared to leave Bitterne at once? I was only here for the shooting for a few days and really must be moving on——"

"*I* was only here for a holiday, idling," smiled Falkland. "I can leave any moment."

"Very good. I have to fetch my ward, Isabel Conway, from a place near here where she is staying, we will start immediately after luncheon—I'll send round for your things—nothing to detain you here, I suppose?"

No, there was nothing; yet Falkland hesitated—that same inner voice that yesterday had urged him "don't accept" now seemed to be saying "don't go."

Dobree led the way into the inner private room where luncheon was set out with expensive simplicity, and continued the conversation with indifferent ease as they took their seats.

"No letters to write, no relatives or friends to advise of change of plan, eh?"

"None," replied Falkland, but absently, for he was staring at Manning's arm, above the wrist that showed where the sleeve fell back as he stretched out for the wine; the thin dark flesh was stained with green, bright green oil paint that had been incompletely rubbed off and showed clearly in the grain of the coarse skin. Just such a bright green paint had oozed from a tube in Beale's untidy little sketching box last night.

Dobree's smooth, expressionless, powerful voice continued suavely:

"It's a very good thing for a young man to be quite free at the beginning of his career."

Falkland rallied himself—after all, a coincidence of a smear of paint!

"I wish you'd tell me, sir," he said earnestly, "something of what my duties are to be?—it's all been very quickly arranged and I'm quite in the dark——"

Dobree interrupted, rather impatiently:

"You know the duties of a private secretary, I suppose, since you were taking up such a post? Well, I shall ask nothing more of you than such duties. Only, Mr. Falkland, I shall expect you to be always there."

"Yes," repeated Manning softly, "you will have to be always there—day and night, Mr. Falkland."

"Day and night," smiled Mr. Dobree.

"The usual time to myself, I suppose," said Falkland more confidently than he felt.

"I pay very well, I offer big chances," remarked Dobree pleasantly, "and I shall expect you always—well, in sight, Mr. Falkland—I never know when I may want you."

"Seems uncommonly as if I was being watched," thought Falkland; despite an excellent luncheon, cheerful surroundings and the brilliant prospects of the immediate future, he felt troubled and depressed.

"I wish you'd let me know why you chose me for this post, sir," he broke out. "Why, you could have had thousands of men better qualified——"

"But I wanted," smiled Dobree, rising and smiling, "just you."

"You must not forget that you saved his life," added Manning with a fulsome intonation; but Falkland was thinking, "all this interest doesn't date from that—but from the moment I pronounced the name Sarah Lomax."

"I'll go and get my things together," he said with rather an effort; he was thinking: "if it *was* Manning who fetched Beale away, he went there openly, the people there would know him again," and he resolved, when he got back to the inn, to question closely about his friend's departure.

Dobree had gone into the inner room, silently, and the factotum approached Falkland.

"You were asking about your duties, perhaps I can tell you some of them, some of the habits and tastes of Mr. Dobree."

He sat down beside the young man and began to talk in a monotonous tone of the most trivial matters, urging punctuality, neatness, civility and so forth; impressing on Falkland the great opportunities placed before him. After half an hour of this Falkland suspected that he was being detained, that time was being purposely wasted for him; he sprang up, resolutely:

"I really must go and clear up my things——"

Manning touched the bell; Falkland again noted the green on his wrist.

"No need," he smiled. "Your things are already in the hôtel—we are, in fact, leaving immediately."

"They don't mean me to leave the place, to get out of their sight," flashed hurriedly through Falkland's mind. "I'll clear—I'll get out of this, I might have known that grotesque offer meant no good——"

In answer to the bell the waiter came with Falkland's hat and coat, the luggage from the inn was already in the car; he added that "Mr. Falkland was wanted on the telephone."

"Beale!" cried Falkland, relieved, and making for the door; but Manning took his arm.

"My dear fellow, there's a telephone here, I'll have you put through——"

There was no excuse with which to get out of this and Falkland found himself with Manning at his elbow while he spoke into the mouthpiece.

It was not Beale's voice that called him but that of a girl, surely the girl of last night.

"Are you Edward Falkland? Don't go with them. *Don't go.* You're in great danger—keep your wits about you."

Falkland saw Manning's steady dull eyes, that had a look of ashes, fixed on him.

"Who are you?" he asked boldly of the voice. "This doesn't help, you know, I'm quite in the dark——"

No answer; the person at the other end had rung off.

"That sounds mysterious," smiled Manning. "Been rung up already by strangers who've heard of your good luck?"

"I don't know," replied Falkland curtly, after waiting in vain for an answer, and hanging the receiver up. "And now I'll just run round to the inn, there are one or two things I must settle——"

"Everything has been settled," said Manning, "but if you wish we can stop at the inn when passing through the village——"

Falkland reflected that this would suit him very well, he could get out of the car and ask the cashier to identify Manning; he could, if he wished, get out of the car and never get in again; they couldn't force him, in a busy village street, in broad daylight; so he agreed, pleasantly; "I suppose," he thought, "we shan't be alone, there must be valets and a chauffeur."

There was neither; when he descended with Dobree to the front door the large handsome car was empty. Manning, it appeared, drove and the wealthy man travelled without servants; so luxurious were all the appointments of this car, so cringing the leave takings from the hôtel people, so bright and normal the scene that Falkland felt all his uneasiness ridiculous. How much more likely that the mysterious girl was working him for some criminal or vindictive ends of her own than that these two men were concerned in anything doubtful.

" 'The Plumes' is your place, where you want to stop?" asked Manning at the wheel.

Falkland was with Dobree behind; he said "Yes," feeling rather foolish.

Dobree brought out a bundle of papers and engaged his attention, asking him to look out a certain letter; Manning let the car out, and turned, not through the village, but straight towards the road that led through the forest; as the trees closed round them Falkland reminded his employer about "The Plumes."[2]

"I'm afraid Manning has forgotten," said Dobree coldly. "You'll have to write or telephone—will you find that letter, please?"

Falkland found it; all the documents that had been handed to him were of the most commonplace nature; he was thinking rapidly; his opinion of the two men swiftly reversed; they had never meant to stop at "The Plumes," they had never meant to give him a chance to escape; evidently they did believe that he knew a dangerous secret; he had bluffed too well, with that name "Sarah Lomax"; he would have to be careful, twice they had outmatched him already; he was at present in their power; he would have to be very careful.

The car sped swiftly and straight through the gloom of the trees between which so little of the autumn sunshine penetrated; it was a famous forest, beloved by picnickers, tourists and artists, one of the boasts of the west of England; but it was very lonely now; this avenue of beeches ran for ten miles without a house or cottage—with no one within call.

Dobree put away his papers, settled himself in his corner seat and appeared to be dozing; Manning in his great grey coat, at once gaunt and shapeless, sat huddled at the wheel; Falkland rapidly revolved many things in his mind, which was peculiarly alert and keen.

The speed of the car suddenly dropped; they passed over a bridge that spanned a ravine where a stream gurgled between rocks and ferns. Falkland glanced at this and a curious object flashed by his eye; on the wet stones of the ravine was surely a broken wooden box with tubes of paints scattered about it; an exclamation—

---

[2] Let the car out: increased the car's speed.

"Stop!" sprang from Falkland's lips, but he caught Dobree's glance, steady under half closed lids, and stifled it; the car picked up speed; after all, he might have been mistaken. Manning drove steadily for a few miles, the forest and the silence seemed unending, then he slowed again and stopped; Dobree roused himself.

"There is a wonderful view from here," he said. "Manning and I always stop to admire it."

Falkland looked out; there was no view; they were in the very depth of the forest; a stretch of pines spread to right and left, darkening the daylight; not far from the road the ground had been recently disturbed, turned over and shaped into a rough mound; Manning, turning from the wheel, was gazing at this; Dobree remained lax in his corner. Falkland tried the door of the car; it had automatically locked behind him; neither of the men said anything. Falkland stared at the mound so freshly made, perhaps that very morning, the length and shape of a grave.

"After all," murmured Dobree, "there is no view, Manning must have missed the place."

He touched the glass in front of him and Manning drove on; Falkland felt as cold as if the blood had ceased to circulate in his veins; he moistened his lips, he kept saying to himself, almost mechanically, "I mustn't funk, I mustn't show funk."[3] He was startled to hear his own voice, dry and jerky but cool, say:

"What is our destination, Mr. Dobree?"

The older man answered at once:

"I have some very important business on hand and am due at several places."

Falkland thought, with a deep shudder, "Surely I'm not such

[3] Funk: *v.* show cowardice, flinch, shrink in fear; *n.* fear, terror, cowardice.

a fool that I can't get away, that I can't get hold of the police, warn them about—that mound?"

And yet he wouldn't, couldn't believe that horror; no, his imagination was running riot; he must keep steady.

Out of the wood at last and on to the open high road.

Falkland wiped his forehead.

"We are going to fetch my ward first," added Dobree. "She has been staying near here."

Falkland's mind turned with wonder and pity on this girl; he had forgotten her though she had been mentioned twice before; supposing what he thought of them was true, was she their accomplice or their victim?

Dobree yawned, took out a map, appeared to be tracing a route; without raising his eyes from this he said:

"What is the most dangerous possession in the world, Mr. Falkland?"

"No use at riddles," replied the young man cautiously.

Dobree picked up the speaking-tube.

"Some one else's secret," he remarked, and in the same breath to Manning: "Let her out a bit, we'll be late for tea at 'The Elms.' "

This last sentence oddly consoled Falkland for the first; tea—and at a place with the common name of "The Elms."

They drove in silence along unfrequented roads until well on into the afternoon; Falkland, speeding along between those locked doors, was thinking of many devices which revolved in a tense confusion through his brain, when the car suddenly turned between two great gates that opened on to a long formal drive with a square stone house at the end. Falkland, with painful curiosity, put his head out of the window; there was only one person in sight, an elegantly dressed young girl carrying a valise, coming towards them.

With a grind and swerve the car was checked sharply beside this girl and Manning leaped from his seat and took her gently by the arm.

"Ah, Isabel!" exclaimed Dobree genially, unlocking the car door, "out for a walk—step in, my dear, and we will drive you back——"

Manning had taken her valise, he was drawing her towards the car; Falkland stared at her, fascinated, for she was unnaturally silent and her lovely blonde, childish face was distorted by some powerful emotion.

Surely that emotion he had been struggling to subdue in himself—fear—blind, panic fear.

Between them they drew and helped her into the car; Falkland rose to give her his seat. The door was open; possibly he might now have escaped. The men were both occupied by the mute, pallid girl, he might have raced away, back on to the road; but Falkland could not make this attempt to scape; precisely because he believed the girl had been trying to escape.

"How fortunate that we met you, Isabel!" smiled Dobree, as he drew her down beside him on the luxurious seat. "This is my new secretary, Mr. Falkland."

The young man, opposite now, saw the frozen features of the girl relax, and into the strained blue eyes spring an unmistakable glance of agonised appeal—the frantic appeal of utter helplessness; he could not escape now, even if he had the chance.

The car drove up to the blank, lonely house.

CHAPTER III

THEY entered the house, Dobree talking genially and Manning answering respectfully; there appeared to be no servants in this pretentious mansion which was in dreary disorder; a showy looking woman of about fifty had opened the door and assumed the air of mistress of the establishment; her withered painted face had expressed great dismay at the sight of Isabel.

"I met my ward on the drive," said Dobree coolly. "I thought it was understood that she was not to go out alone?"

"So it was," stammered the woman, "so it was—I don't understand——" Her bleared eyes shot hatred at Isabel.

"Well," interrupted Dobree, "it was very careless, but it doesn't matter, for we have come, Mrs. Milner, to take my ward away with us——"

At this point the girl spoke at last; she cried out:

"No! No! Oh, no!" in a tone that pinched Falkland's heart, and sitting down on one of the chairs in the wide dark hall, she put her face in her hands.

"There, there, dearie," smiled the woman with sudden unctuous sympathy, "don't you take on so, every one is looking after you, every one is being kind, you come with Mrs. Milner, dearie, and rest a bit——"

She bent over the silent girl, who, to Falkland's surprise, rose at once and followed her up the shadowed stairs.

"Very painful, eh?" remarked Dobree to Falkland. "The poor child is—not sane."

"Insane?" whispered Falkland, horrified to think of that

delightful, fragrant, childlike creature, so elegant and delicate, in connection with such a word.

"Disordered in her mind," continued Dobree, "subject to delusions, quite irresponsible, subject to fits of sheer madness. A dreadful case."

"Dreadful," echoed Manning.

"Every alienist in Europe has been tried;" the elder man appeared to speak with deep feeling.[4] "Hopeless. Every diversion—travel, gaiety, company. We've come to this. She's only twenty-three."

"How absolutely ghastly," said Falkland. "Who is she, Mr. Dobree?"

"My ward, no near relations. Bad family history, insanity both sides. But her father was my dearest friend."

"You would hardly believe," remarked Manning softly, "what Mr. Dobree has done for poor Miss Conway—the time and money that's been spent! The effort that has been made!"

They had now entered a large, ill-appointed room where everything was both showy and shabby and afternoon tea was carelessly and ostentatiously set out near the large window that looked on the park.

"What is this place?" asked Falkland; he heard a note of challenge in his own voice.

It was Manning who answered:

"A doctor's house, a private nursing home. Mr. Dobree had great confidence in them, but it was extraordinarily careless of them to allow Miss Conway to escape."

Escape! That word had been in Falkland's mind since he had first seen the frightened girl hurrying along the deserted drive; he

[4] Alienist: psychiatrist.

had been right, she had been trying to escape.

"Of course," said Dobree, "we should easily have found her again, poor child, she has no money and nowhere to go, but it was fortunate that we arrived in time."

"Very fortunate," murmured Manning, and Falkland shuddered where he sat; no fault was to be found with their words, but their tone, their look, this place, that flashy woman—was he losing his wits, or correct in thinking the whole affair more and more sinister?

He was not reassured by the appearance of a man addressed as "Dr. Milner"; a lean, slippered, shuffling, grey man who talked vaguely about occult powers and mediumistic communications in connection with the treatment of his patients.

"Patients?" repeated Falkland boldly, "have you, then, sir, any other patients beside Miss Conway?"

"Not at the moment, not at the moment, she has required all my time and care."

"But you have failed," said Manning as if he was making a suggestion. "You have failed badly, Miss Conway is not cured——"

"Not cured," agreed Dr. Milner hurriedly. "Oh, no, not cured!"

A raucous shriek rang through the house, followed by a gabble of screamed words; Milner and Falkland were at once on their feet; the other two supped their tea coolly.

"It's Mamie," said the doctor. "It's only Mamie——"

Falkland had turned sick; it had been a woman's voice, a woman wild with pain and terror; he had thought of Isabel Conway.

"I wonder that you keep Mamie," remarked Manning.

"Poor thing, poor thing," answered Milner hastily, nervously. "What can one do with her? Between these fits she's all right—a dear, good creature."

"I thought," said Falkland still on his feet, "you had only the one patient, Dr. Milner?"

"So I have," smiled the doctor. "Mamie is—a friend—a companion to my wife—a nurse——"

Falkland caught him up.

"And also insane?"

"Oh, dear, no! Mamie is very shrewd and capable, but she has a terrible temper, a most violent temper, dreadful fits of passion, Mr. Falkland."

"She is coming with us, isn't she?" asked Dobree. "To look after Isabel?"

"Certainly, certainly, she is very devoted to Miss Conway—of course, these fits——"

"We'll manage her," said Manning.

The dreadful sounds above had now died to a deep whimpering; Mrs. Milner entered the room; the blousy woman was flushed and panting, her lips twitching; she made a crude effort to be amiable, to cringe to Dobree as she took her place at the tea table.

"It was that tiresome Mamie," she remarked with a forced smile, "who allowed Miss Conway to escape, and when I chided her—well, I expect you gentlemen heard the row!"

"I heard," answered Falkland with meaning; he was convinced that it had taken more than a tongue thrashing to elicit those frantic screams; his whole soul went out in indignant championship towards those two wretched creatures upstairs, the girl who had tried to escape and the woman who had tried to help her—escape! How that word rang in the tension of his brain, but he must control himself.

"Not very encouraging for taking Mamie with you," said Dr. Milner with a wan smile.

"We shall have no trouble with Mamie," replied Dobree easily. "And Isabel is used to her—it would be tiresome to have a stranger with us, yes, we'll take Mamie——"

Falkland thought: "Perhaps Mamie knows too much, as I am supposed to know too much, as Beale was supposed, perhaps, to know too much—but of what?" If only he could find out, he was bewildered with fumbling in the dark.

The conversation flowed on indifferently between the other four people; Falkland contrived to put in a word now and then; he was struggling hard for an appearance of ease; he must be wary, alert and cautious till he could find out if they were villains or he was a fool; he became aware, that, under shelter of the commonplace talk, the Milners were observing hm very curiously, and he sensed that they were amazed to find him there and that the last thing they had expected to see at "The Elms" was a stranger.

At length Dobree looked at his watch and remarked pleasantly that "he hoped the ladies would soon be ready." Mrs. Milner at once rose and pulled the bell; within a few minutes Isabel Conway entered the room with another woman, the unfortunate Mamie.

The girl was silent, pale, expressionless; utterly terrorised, Falkland suspected; she wore a handsome travelling coat—no jewellery—no handbag; with a pang the young man recalled Dobree's sinister words—"No money, poor child, and nowhere to go."

Mamie was a plain, middle aged woman who appeared to be of the servant class, dressed simply in an imitation nurse's outfit; her face was blotched, her eyes red; she looked scared, defiant, and, Falkland was forced to admit to himself, half-witted; one of her hands was roughly bandaged.

"Mamie has burnt herself," said Mrs. Milner. "Mamie is very stupid."

And, dreadfully, Mamie winced and cringed before the speaker, muttering something thickly in her throat.

"They've frightened her all right," thought Falkland bitterly. "She'll be no use to any one."

He wished the girl would speak; her blank silence that had been only broken by that one violent protest, was ghastly; he was fidgeting to get away, to find out about these people, to get in touch with the outside world again, to trace Beale——

When they were all leaving he found a moment when he was beside the two women and Dobree and Manning were talking in the hall with the doctor and his wife; he had to risk Mamie's possible betrayal of him. He whispered swiftly, addressing Isabel:

"Can I help you? Tell me all you can."

She answered under her breath instantly:

"I want to escape. I shall be looking for a chance of that—or suicide. Who are you? What do you know of them?"

"A stranger. I know nothing—but they are afraid I do—make a chance to speak to me again——"

"Sh!" murmured Mamie, passing awkwardly between him and the girl. "They're coming—*I'm* with you——"

Under cover of opening the car door, Falkland whispered back:

"Trust me, be careful—I'll help."

Isabel got into the car; as she stepped past Falkland her fragrant face almost touched his and her lovely pallid lips framed again these appalling words:

"I'm looking for a chance of suicide."

Falkland almost recoiled; it must be true that her wits were unsettled, he could hardly conceive of the desperation that could drive a pretty young woman to such a confession; why didn't she get away?

And on this question came another, more startling——

"Why didn't he get away himself?"

They were settled in the car again, the doors locked on them; Mamie sat beside Manning in front; Isabel Conway, mute in her corner, was next to Dobree whose heavy bulk and saturnine face seemed to fill the car, and Falkland sat opposite.

As the great machine leaped along the road to he knew not what destination the young man made another attempt to challenge his fate.

"I've got letters to write, messages to send, Mr. Dobree," he remarked. "I've really had no time to put my affairs in order, I must ask you to allow me to stop somewhere to send off a wire or two—or telephone."

Dobree's sluggish, bilious eyes fixed him dully.

"Certainly, I'll tell Manning," but he did not move from his inert position; he spoke sleepily.

When they had been travelling for some distance on a lonely by-road he became aware of a motor cyclist persistently, for some miles, dogging the car; suddenly the cyclist shot past and threw a weighted package into the open window, then dashed ahead and far outdistanced Manning; Falkland had seen the face of this cyclist beneath the leather helmet and raised goggles; surely the face of the young woman who had taught him to say the fatal words—"Sarah Lomax."

With one accord he and Dobree clutched and struggled for the package.

CHAPTER IV

IT was extraordinary for Falkland to find himself struggling with Dobree in the swiftly moving car, a great relief to the long tension of the day to be able to come to grips with the man who had swept him so ruthlessly into his affairs—but there was a dangerous touch of fury in this sudden break of control. Falkland felt that in a moment he might be at his opponent's throat, breaking, smashing, shrieking—he pulled himself together with an effort and released the paper he had clutched, but not before he had seen the bold black drawing of a house with a coffin shaped shadow scrawled thereon.

"I was startled," he excused himself. "I was not sure if the message was meant for me, Mr. Dobree."

"For me," said Dobree, pushing the twisted letter into his pocket; he was flushed, but composed. "Did you see the man who threw it?—the man on the motor cycle?"

"It wasn't a man but a girl," replied Falkland abruptly, his nerves still on edge. "A girl I've met before, too, in the woods of Bitterne."

"Indeed?" murmured Dobree softly. "Then perhaps you know something of this persecution to which I am being subject?"

Now was the moment for Falkland to say—"I know nothing, that girl told me to use the name Sarah Lomax, beyond that I am ignorant of your affairs—they and you are utterly strange to me." But he did not say this; he thought that it was wiser to let this man believe that he did know something, to keep up a show of bluff; if he convinced Dobree that he was ignorant of his affairs he might dismiss him, but Falkland felt a spirit of dare-devilry, of curiosity that forbade him to give up the adventure so tamely; there was the disappearance of Beale to account for—there was the question of that silent girl in the corner seat.

So he replied evasively:

"What, sir, do you quite mean by persecution?"

Dobree assumed an air of condescending frankness.

"I am accounted a very charitable man, Mr. Falkland. I rose from poverty myself and have great sympathy with other strugglers—but I get imposed upon, very sorely. I helped certain people and they abused that help—when it was withdrawn they began a campaign of petty annoyances—like this——"

He touched his pocket and smiled; either he was a consummate actor or he spoke the truth; his manner was cordial; he appeared amused.

"I dare say you have thought it all rather mysterious," he added genially. "Perhaps that girl in Bitterne wood spoke to you—told some fantastic tale of me, eh?"

"No," said Falkland, "no fantastic tale."

"You must keep your head," advised Dobree, still amiable, "not listen to these people, not take any notice of these incidents—I have had a great many in my career."

Falkland glanced at Isabel Conway still immobile in her corner; dusk was filling the car now, he could not very distinctly see either his companions nor where he was going.

"Where are we stopping?" he asked. "Where are we putting up to-night? It must be getting late, sir. Shall I switch on the light?"

No answer.

Falkland could not endure this tension; he cautiously stole out his hand and switched on the light.

And as instantly switched it off again.

It had revealed a horrible face close to his own, leaning forward, a face like a mask of evil madness, white, snarling, fixed, silent, rabid, glittering eyes behind sagging pouches of flesh; with difficulty Falkland repressed a cry.

This loathsome countenance was Dobree's, who had silently bent across to him in the dark.

"I didn't see it," muttered Falkland, "I didn't see it—Oh, Heavens, I *couldn't* have seen it."

"I think we'll have the light now," came Dobree's suave voice from the corner; Falkland switched it on; the millionaire was placidly leaning back in his corner, half asleep.

"Steady," said Falkland to himself. "I must be careful. *I didn't see it.*"

With a swerve and a grind the car drew up.

"Well, here we are," remarked Dobree pleasantly. "It's been a long run——"

"Where are we?" asked Falkland.

It was now completely dark; a moonless night; the head-lamps only showed a long stretch of high wall above which grew a thick rampart of dense lofty trees; the place appeared very lonely. Falkland noted that there were no telephone or telegraph poles and that the road was unimportant, almost a lane; as he descended from the car after Dobree he saw they had stopped in front of tall, rusty, padlocked iron gates.

Manning had left the wheel; his dark, stooping figure went stiffly towards the gates, followed by Dobree; Falkland felt his arm clutched; the queer creature called Mamie was beside him, whispering in his ear:

"Don't leave us—don't believe what they tell you—*she* is as sane as I am, only they try to drive her mad——"

No time for more, the two men had unlocked the gate and turned back.

"Mamie," said Manning quietly, "you've got to behave yourself, you know,"—he wagged his gaunt forefinger—"got to be a good Mamie, eh? Not to talk nonsense, eh?"

The woman cowered away and busied herself with the wraps and hand luggage.

Falkland, standing by the car where Isabel Conway still sat, summoned desperately all his powers of reason and debated his next action; he did not want to go behind that high wall and padlocked gates with these two men, and he furiously cast over his chances of resistance; they were both powerful and armed for all he knew—for all he knew too the women might be indeed half-witted or their accomplices; one thing he might do—dash off in the darkness, but he did not think that he had much chance of eluding them if they wished to pursue him; and then, there was always the possibility that the women were victims—relying on him, in which case it was unthinkable that he should abandon them; each of them had asked for his help, he could not mistrust them.

Dobree and Manning were occupied in pushing back the iron gates which creaked and groaned; Isabel Conway was staring at them through the window of the car.

"I won't go in there," she whispered, "I wont, I won't——"

"Sh!" Falkland whispered back, "better be quiet—I'll look after you—we can't resist now."

And, then, as the gates reluctantly swung back on a grass grown drive hemmed in with dank, blackish laurel bushes, an extraordinary thing happened; a little man rushed out, gibbering with terror, stumbled on his knees and lay sprawling, grotesque and horrible in the acrid circle of light made by the headlights.

"She's come back," he gabbled. "She's come back! I've seen her—up in a tree!"

Manning thrust at him roughly with his foot.

"Get up, you fool," he said harshly. "Can't you see that Mr. Dobree is here?"

But the little man, who appeared to be wearing a disarrayed gamekeeper's clothes, continued to grovel on the ground in an extremity of fear, whimpering:

"I won't go back—I can't go back—she's here, I tell you *I've seen her*."

"Dear me," remarked Dobree mildly, "you seem to be suffering from nerves, Mathews. Will you please get up and explain yourself?"

"I can't stay, sir," whined the little man. "The things that have been happening, I've been trying to get out, waiting by the gate, trying to get out of the cursed place——"

Falkland set his lips grimly; he could foresee himself on the wrong side of those gates, trying to get out.

"Didn't I tell you we were coming?" demanded Manning, "bringing Miss Conway? Have you made everything ready?"

The servant, as Falkland took him to be, got to his feet and looked round the half circle of faces in a frenzy of terror, muttering incoherently and defiantly; Manning gave him a rough push between the gates.

"I must really find another caretaker," remarked Dobree coolly.

"You'll have to," retorted the little man, shivering. "Made things ready? I haven't been near the house, I can tell you. My cottage was bad enough. Who," he demanded hysterically, "is going to live like this—locked in?"

"Come," said Dobree ignoring him, "I'll take the ladies and Mr. Falkland in, Manning, you can follow with the car." He looked round, "Yes, we're all here—Mamie, Isabel, Mathews——" He broke off. "What is that?"

He was peering up the road, to the farthest limit of the headlights; Falkland looked too; he distinguished a drab object half in the ditch, half leaning against the wall.

A motor cycle.

He thought of the motor cycle that had pursued them, of the thrown letter, of the rider's face—had she abandoned her machine to enter this park or whatever it was?—was it she who had "come back" whom the gibbering servant had seen in a tree?

Out of the overwhelming silence of the lonely night rose a sudden wailing cry, suddenly checked.

"A night bird," remarked Dobree pleasantly. "Quite gruesome, isn't it?"

Falkland had seen the women's faces, blanched with panic; he felt that his own cheeks were pale, his own blood cold, his own lips stiff—well, he tried to tell himself that it might have been a night bird—though never had he heard one utter such a human note.

They reached the end of the avenue at last; an open space seemed to be in front of them—as Falkland's eyes became accustomed to the dark he discerned the square blackness of a house ponderous against the paler blackness of the sky; he instinctively recoiled, nearer the women.

"Where are we?" he asked.

Dobree replied with the name of the place Falkland had been twice warned not to enter.

"This is 'Mockways.' "

CHAPTER V

AS they proceeded across the lawn, guided by Dobree's torch, they were joined by Manning, who seemed to have been walking rapidly, for his breath came quickly as he said:

"Really, Mathews is becoming impossible—did you ever see such behaviour, Mr. Falkland? He has been the caretaker here for a number of years, but I'm afraid he will have to go now, after to-night."

"He seemed badly frightened," answered Falkland. "And who was it he said he had seen—in a tree? Someone who had come back?"

"The family ghost, I should think," said Dobree dryly.

Falkland tried to put on a bold resolute front.

"Where are we?" he asked firmly. "I mean, in what part of the world?—and why have we come to such a lonely place?"

"We are on the Welsh border," it was Manning's voice that replied; "and Mr. Dobree likes loneliness, sometimes."

"But I think," urged Falkland, "that it has been a long time since any one came to 'Mockways'——?"

There was no answer to this, and, despite his firm grip on himself, Falkland could not repress a shudder for they had now entered the house; Dobree had closed it behind them; a baying and howling of dogs had broken sharply on the silence, and this Manning explained.

"The hounds—we keep them about the place, loose every night."

"Well guarded," said Falkland with a wry smile. "And there doesn't seem much to guard——" He glanced about the hall and stairs that the light of the electric torch showed to be bare and decayed.

"No," replied Manning, "but as you've been told, this is supposed to be the worst haunted house in England, and that sort of thing is very fashionable just now, as you know; many people would give a great deal to pass the night here——"

He had come prepared for "Mockways" for he produced candles and matches from his pocket, and, leading the way into a large room, stuck the lit candles on the narrow dusty mantelshelf.

The room was gaunt, shabbily furnished and in considerable disrepair, cold, damp from being long shut away, the air close and musty.

Falkland made a considerable effort to shake off the horror that oppressed him, to master the situation. He faced Dobree squarely.

"This seems to me an extraordinary place to have brought these ladies to," he said grimly; "in fact, the whole thing is very extraordinary—I should like some sort of explanation—of a good many things—before I go any further——"

Dobree merely smiled, pulling off his gloves and taking off his coat slowly, and Manning cackled as if he had heard a joke.

"So you see," grinned Manning, "you've been drawn into investigating a haunted house—a rare chance. Mr. Dobree has got three months leisure which he means to devote to 'Mockways'—three months ought to be enough, don't you think, sir?" he cringed to his master.

"Quite enough."

And Falkland shivered inwardly.

"But I didn't bargain for this," he said stubbornly. "I wasn't engaged to hunt ghosts. I don't believe in that sort of thing. I don't like this place, Mr. Dobree, and I don't intend to stay here——"

Again Isabel Conway interposed.

"Oh, please, do stay, Mr. Falkland, we want a quite independent witness—like yourself——"

She spoke in the most commonplace tones, she turned to him eagerly and into her eyes flashed the look of frantic appeal he had seen before; she was bluffing then—trying to placate Dobree.

The other woman spoke.

"If you could see your way to stay, sir, I'm sure it would be much better for all of us; Miss Isabel has been wanting for a long time to explore 'Mockways.' "

Her look of warning and entreaty was surely unmistakable; the woman wanted him to stay, wanted him to placate the two men—either that or they were accomplices in some conspiracy, and that, looking at Isabel Conway's fragrant loveliness, he could not bring himself to believe.

"Well," he said, as genially as possible. "I dare say it will be very interesting. I wasn't prepared for anything of the kind, but since it's come my way——"

He was conscious that his words relieved the tension of the other four; Dobree's sagging yellowish face expressed an amused good humour.

I dare say you'll find it rather rough, we shall have to camp a bit. Mathews is a good servant when he shakes down—and Mamie can cook a bit."

"I'll do my best," said Mamie cheerfully. "Perhaps I could go upstairs, sir, and see our rooms?"

"Mathews and his wife were to have put everything in order," replied Manning, "but the silly woman, he tells me, has gone home to her mother——"

He had taken the torch and was going to the door when Falkland said:

"A moment, please. Are we alone in the house?"

All looked at him. Dobree answered crisply:

"Yes."

"Well," remarked Falkland, "if you listen a moment you'll hear footsteps overhead."

The women clutched each other, the men stood motionless, the flickering candles gave a dreary light in the neglected room; the low baying of the dogs sounded in the distance; then, as this sound died away, utter silence.

Then overhead, distinct creaking footsteps.

"Mathews," said Dobree unsteadily, "has thought better of it and come back to the house——"

No one answered, no one moved; and overhead went the creaking footsteps, to and fro.

"I'd like to go and see if it is Mathews," said Falkland.

"Oh, would you?" sneered Dobree. "Well, I'll go myself."

He took the torch from Manning and led the way out of the room and up the shallow, dusty stairs; the others followed. Falkland found himself beside Dobree on the dim-lit stairs; the others were ahead, Manning preceding the two women.

When they reached the landing Manning was searching in and out of the rooms that opened there, flashing his torch into every corner.

"No one," he remarked shortly. "Nothing."

"There was," answered Dobree. "They're hiding——"

He joined Manning in the search, nosing eagerly about the rooms, which were gloomy and half furnished; Falkland found himself alone with the two women on the landing. Isabel Conway instantly whispered to him:

"Play up to them, don't show that you're afraid, or suspect anything. *We are completely in their power.*"

"What are they up to?" breathed Falkland.

"I don't know, there's some secret. We'll think of a way to speak to you to-morrow."

"Watch me," whispered Mamie. "See if I don't manage it."

Falkland could hardly see them, for the flashes from Manning's torch were intermittent illuminations of the dark landing; but these agonised whispers could leave him in no doubt either of their sanity or their innocence; these women were desperately sincere, of that he felt sure, and desperately afraid; in that case he and they were in the toils of some colossal villainy which he must brace every nerve to meet.

Dobree and Manning returned from their search.

"Rats," said Manning with a grin. "We must really be on our guard against being deceived by the very odd noises that rats make."

But Falkland had lost his last vestige of trust for these men; he knew that it had not been rats overhead, any more than it had been an owl screaming in the park; rats, owls and ghosts were camouflage.

Two of these rooms, opening one from the other, had, it appeared, been prepared for the women; Falkland was thankful that they were at least together; he helped Manning carry up their few valises and had to watch Dobree lock the door on them and put the key in his pocket.

"I suppose," he said, with rather dry lips, "they've light and bells—in Miss Conway's state——"

"Mamie can manage her perfectly," smiled Dobree. "Now, I don't think we will do any ghost hunting to-night, Mr. Falkland. Your room will be upstairs——"

"And where do you two sleep?" asked Falkland, with an attempt at ease.

"We haven't decided," replied Dobree; the young man had expected this answer; they would not let him know where they lurked in the large empty house.

His own room was that above Isabel Conway's apartment and looked, he thought, on the front of the house; there was a comfortable looking bed, a little furniture, candles, matches, no bell, no electric light; in the first moment that he was alone Falkland rapidly ascertained that he also was locked in and that the window was barred.

A prisoner.

And why?

He tried to think the situation over clearly; the one conclusion to which his bewildered brain could come was that Dobree believed him to be in possession of some very dangerous secret, and was keeping him under observation; and this conclusion led to another, that his life was in danger. As to the case of the women—there he could make no guess; but he believed that they were in danger too; he had nothing but his wits with which to save all three of them.

As he paced up and down his room in deep agitation he heard peculiar sounds outside; he quenched the candle and tiptoed to the locked door and put his ear to the keyhole. The noises were those of heavy sighs, moans, scuffling and whispers; Falkland could distinguish words, whined bitter words—"after all these years—they aren't dead, then? or returned from the dead?" Another voice replied harshly: "Pull yourself together—*we must find it*, do you hear? He's after it too. Perhaps *he* knows where it is."

Falkland knew the tones now; Dobree and Manning, prowling the house, Dobree collapsing, Manning dragging him away. The shuffling died away, but in the distance he could hear the faint heavy groans of the elder man; then silence in the dark house.

"Find it?" thought Falkland with excitement. "Something I have got to find? Something hidden in 'Mockways.' Something *they* can't find!"

He tried to control and compose himself for he knew that he was to the last degree fatigued, bewildered and on edge; he forced himself to get into bed (after an exhaustive search in the room that revealed nothing) and to his own amazement, felt himself falling heavily asleep.

He woke suddenly, all his senses alert.

The room was utterly black about him; he could not even distinguish the square of the window; but he knew that he was not alone.

Some one was breathing, quite close to him, some was sitting on the bed.

As he moved, a hand was clapped swiftly over his mouth.

CHAPTER VI

FALKLAND lay still, his mind working with desperate swiftness; he noted that the hand over his mouth was not heavy nor resolute but light and fluttering, and he thought that perhaps one of the women had crept in to implore assistance—but how, with that locked door?

A trembling voice squeaked in his ear:

"Friend—keep quiet."

The shaking fingers were raised; Falkland sat up, trying to pierce the blackness; he could just make out the shape of some one seated on the bed, a man; the voice had been a man's voice; it repeated in the lowest of whispers:

"Keep quiet! I'm Mathews!"

"How on earth did you get in here?" breathed Falkland.

"I know the house pretty well, there's a secret way into this room, that's why you've got it——"

"Oh, is it?" answered Falkland, and again the shaking hand was clapped over his mouth.

"Don't talk so loud, sir. *They* may be outside, listening for all I know——"

"Well," urged Falkland, "say what you want to, then, quick. Who are you and why have you come here?"

"To warn you, sir. I've been looking after 'Mockways' for years, living in my cottage in the grounds. I don't say I wasn't in it, up to a point, and well paid, they wanted me to keep my mouth shut—but they've got scared and I don't like it——"

The frightened voice rambled on in husky whispers; Falkland

interrupted impatiently:

"Can you come to the point? I know nothing about any of it—"

"Oh, don't you, sir? But they think you do—and there is nothing they'll stop at——"

"Tell me the bottom of the whole matter——"

Falkland felt the little figure shudder.

"I can't, I daren't, not here. They think you know something or are looking for something—they'll watch you—I suppose it hasn't occurred to you," whispered the voice harshly, "how easily you could disappear in 'Mockways?' "

"It has," replied Falkland dryly.

"You'd better play up that you know something—for they'll want to find out what it is—how much—there's a secret here and they can't find it, and they'll trail you to see if you can—and when you've got it—*they'll get you*—Manning, he's the worst—to-day he——"

"Why," asked Falkland, with assumed boldness, "do you come here to warn me of all this?"

"Because I'm scared meself, sir," hissed the voice. "I want to get away, I thought we might get away together—us and them two women."

"Ah, the women," said Falkland. "What do you know of them?"

"Nothing—I've heard them talking, it's that villain Manning, he's got his eye on Miss Isabel as they call her——"

"Who is she? Is she sane?" whispered Falkland fiercely.

"Sane? As sane as any of us are likely to be if we stay here——"

Falkland thought with frantic rapidity; a possible link with the outside world flashed into his taut mind.

"There's your wife—couldn't you get in touch with her?"

"Wife? I ain't got a wife. A village woman used to come in

and help—she hasn't been here for days—don't you heed their lies——"

"How far are we from the village?"

"Miles," came the shuddering whisper. "We're shut in, there's acres of ground—sh! I can't stop——"

But Falkland clutched him.

"There's no one about—you're safe here——"

"Safe! You don't know what you're saying—that was a step—listen!"

Falkland felt the little man shake and heard his teeth chatter.

Both listened.

There was a faint creak that might have been a step; Mathews writhed with silent violence in Falkland's grip.

"I won't stay, sir, now—you pretend you don't suspect anything, that's my advice—listen to what I say, to-morrow, it will be an appointment, I'm going to tell you all I know——"

He writhed away; there was a faint "click"; the secret door, no doubt; then utter silence again.

Falkland sat up in bed, alert, rigid, all his senses acute; the advice of the frightened servant had been the same as that of the frightened woman; he was to bluff, to mark time, to pretend that he suspected nothing, to match his wits with the wits of these two men—to play a game where the stake appeared to be his life.

He could no more doubt the sincerity of the terrified Mathews than that of Isabel Conway, he could no longer hesitate to believe that he had stumbled into some black mystery and was completely in the power of two powerful, unscrupulous and desperate men.

Grimly he reckoned up his chances; he had been hurried away without money, without a chance to communicate with any one as to his movements, without, of course, any manner of weapon;

there was no one who would be likely to notice his disappearance, at least for some time, or be able to trace him if they did; Beale was the only person who would be concerned in this—and where was Beale?

Edward Falkland got no more sleep that night; as soon as it was light he searched feverishly for the secret entrance that Mathews had used, but could find nothing; he unpacked, put his things away, and slipped his razor into his breast pocket; it might, just possibly, be useful.

He found his door unlocked and went downstairs to the room he had been in last night; though bare and shabby, the warn autumn sunshine streaming in through the long windows brightened the dull room; there was a bright wood fire burning and a good breakfast on the table. Falkland felt his spirits rise; Mathews and Mamie seemed to be acting as servants and Isabel Conway was seated by the fire, warming her hands; the whole atmosphere seemed pleasant, genial, homely, and the events of yesterday and the night seemed a nightmare. If these three people were putting up a desperate bluff, well, they were doing it very well, and he, Falkland, must not be behind in the game; so he talked and joked about the ghosts which no one had seen, and which, he declared, he did not believe that any one would see.

Dobree and Manning joined them; they were both easy and agreeable, though the latter had, at best, a sombre and saturnine appearance and his amiability had far too servile a tinge to be pleasant.

Falkland ate a hearty breakfast with set purpose; he wanted to keep mind and body in health; he observed with rather a chilly sensation that the milk was tinned and that biscuit took the place of bread; did that mean that "Mockways" was provisioned like a ship for a long voyage and that Dobree was independent of the outside world as regarded food?

At the end of the meal Mathews said, in the most unconcerned way:

"Oh, Mr. Dobree, sir, could I show Mr. Falkland the Golden Labradors? I'm proud of those dogs, sir." He turned to Falkland. "I do a bit of dog breeding as a hobby, and I've got some lovely puppies now."

The young man's heart leapt; this was the appointment the man had spoken of.

"I'd like to see them," he answered carelessly, "though I can't say that I know much about dogs——"

"By all means go, Falkland," smiled Dobree in the most affable manner. "I have some little business to attend to with Manning, and then, when you have seen the dogs—and bought one, I dare say—I want to show you over the house."

Falkland felt a thrill of triumph, surely the first move in the game was his—Dobree was deceived.

"And you," continued that personage, smiling at Isabel, "will doubtless be occupied with Mamie in putting your room in order. If there is anything you want, ask for it and I will send for it at once——"

So the women were dismissed upstairs; Manning disappeared to see after the car, he said; the car was his hobby, no one else was allowed to touch it.

"Will eleven o'clock do for you to see the puppies, sir?" asked Mathews. "My cottage and kennels are straight down the avenue, and then to the left, by the pond——"

Dobree answered:

"Eleven will do very well, Mathews."

The servant cleared away the breakfast things, replenished the fire and left the room; Falkland yawned, carefully simulating bored indifference.

"There is a little work we might do to fill in the time," suggested Dobree and he led the way into an inner apartment, which was furnished in a plain, businesslike way; it seemed to be an office; there were two desks, files, a typewriter.

"Rather awkward without telephone, electric light or wireless, isn't it, sir?" remarked Falkland.

"On the contrary I enjoy seclusion—I like to get away from all possible interruption. And then, I am never here very long."

He settled his sprawling bulk in a worn arm-chair, drew a bundle of notes from his pocket and proceeded to dictate a series of wholly unimportant and dull letters to Falkland who took them down calmly enough; he could afford to be at ease for soon he would be talking with Mathews, hearing the explanation of the whole mystery, or at least, a great deal of it.

At about a quarter to eleven Dobree dismissed him, reminding him of his appointment to see the Labradors; Falkland could hardly believe in his good luck as he found himself on the steps of the house, with Dobree giving him pleasant directions as to how to find the cottage and the kennels.

"Evidently," he thought, "they think they've scared Matthews dumb—they're dead sure of him."

With considerable excitement he crossed the neglected grass patch which passed as a lawn, and plunged into the dank avenue which he had entered so unwillingly last night, and which, even now, in the full splendour of day, was dark and damp.

He felt relieved, elated; in half an hour's uninterrupted talk with Mathews he would surely be able to find out all the little man knew and to concert with him some plan of action; once he was in possession of Dobree's secret, it would not be so difficult to decide what to do—it was this moving in the dark which was so hideous, so terrifying.

He easily found the cottage which stood by a deep pond grown with willow trees; it was an ugly yellow one-storey cottage with a slate roof; either side were considerable kennels where hounds pressed to the bars and bayed at him; evidently the savage dogs that were loosed at night; he saw no Labradors.

He knocked at the small shut door; knocked again and got no answer. Stung with impatience he entered the cottage; the two rooms were empty. He called out: "Mathews!" and there was no reply.

The young man felt sick with a sense of rage and disappointment; had the man then been fooling or tricking him? Had he been afraid, after all, to keep the appointment?

Falkland searched in the small garden or yard at the back; the dogs howled and raged at the presence of a stranger; there was no other sound. Falkland could have wept with vexation; he pushed open the half ajar door of a shed with an iron roof—calling again: "Mathews!"

The word froze on his lips; there before him was Mathews, trussed with fine rope, bound hand and foot, hanging from a beam in the shed—dead.

CHAPTER VII

FALKLAND felt sick; he had to move into the outer air, to take great breaths of it; the sense of his great danger steadied him—what had he better do?

He remembered the advice of the wretched Mathews, bluff, play up—also the suggestion that, as long as they believed he knew something they would preserve his life to find out how much it was he did know and how far the ramifications of his knowledge went; his best chance, then, lay in the pretence of knowing this secret and in the hope of discovering it—*they* were looking for something in "Mockways," he must look too.

Falkland shuddered to his soul when he thought how he had sat fooling over those letters with Dobree, being purposely detained, of course, while Manning went down to the cottage where the miserable Mathews waited for his doom.

And there was another aspect of the case, the bitter disappointment he felt at not having heard what the servant had to say—why couldn't he have spoken last night?

Falkland braced himself to enter the cottage again in the frantic hope that there might be something left about that would be of use to him; not likely since Manning would have been carefully over the place.

Perhaps Manning was watching him now; this thought made the young man's heart leap, but he managed to retain his composure; it was essential that he should not show fear.

He went rapidly over the scanty effects in the two small rooms and found nothing of any interest but a small bunch of keys which he slipped into his pocket, but, as he returned to the outer apartment he observed a small note-book, half-burnt, lying on the hearth; there was no fire and the book had evidently had a match set to it, which had gone out before wholly consuming the pages.

Manning perhaps had tried to burn it—he had not had very long.

Falkland put the charred book in his pocket, he could discern some writing—perhaps it would be useful, perhaps not.

He searched round the room again, while he fought for composure and complete command of his faculties.

A slight cough behind him made him look round sharply.

Manning stood in the doorway; he must have been approaching quite silently.

"Dear me, Mr, Falkland," he remarked in his most servile manner, "this is very distressing indeed. I'm afraid that you must have had a great shock—you look quite white! How very, very unpleasant!"

"You mean about Mathews?" asked Falkland with dry lips. "Yes, I've seen him—in the shed."

"So have I," said Manning without moving from the doorway where he blotted out the light. "I came down to look at the dogs, too—I saw you go into the shed, I was really too overcome to prevent you, for I had just seen it myself! Dear, dear, Mr. Dobree will be upset!"

Falkland waited, taut, alert; Manning appeared most tall, nearly gigantic, to fill indeed the whole small room with his powerful stooping figure; his yellow face was expressionless, his leathery lids drooping; Falkland noted with horror the great size and massiveness of his hands. . . .

"Of course," he continued smoothly, "it isn't altogether unexpected—the poor fellow had been suffering from melancholia for years, imagining all sorts of things, you heard him last night, for instance! This was really the last place where he ought to have stayed——"

"Yes," said Falkland, "yes."

"——but nothing could get him away. Poor Mathews! Nothing could induce him to leave 'Mockways!' And now he has hanged himself!"

So that was the cue; it was to be glossed over as a case of suicide, a cunning device.

And yet it just flashed into Falkland's mind that *this might be true.*

"I don't know how he managed to tie himself up like that, Mr. Manning——"

"No—it's extraordinary what these wretched demented creatures will do! Extraordinary! We must go back to the house and tell Mr. Dobree. I'm afraid he will be distressed, he was quite fond of Mathews."

"You had better send for a doctor," said Falkland. "And at once—there'll have to be an inquest."

"Of course, of course," murmured Manning, "but don't trouble your head about those things, my dear fellow, I'll see to it all——"

"Yes," thought Falkland grimly, "with a mattock and spade."[5]

Aloud he remarked:

"I suppose I shall have to be called as a witness——"

"Not at all," replied Manning. "*I* found the unfortunate creature, I must have been here some moments before you arrived——"

Falkland could not forbear asking:

"Where were you?"

"Behind some trees," said Manning at once. "I had to sit down,

---

5 Mattock: an agricultural tool used for loosening and digging soil.

I was really quite exhausted—overcome, you know."

Exhausted; Falkland noted that word; used on purpose, no doubt; the whole object must be to intimidate him; that was why he had been allowed to see that mound in the wood, to find Mathews hanging from the beam.

They wanted to scare him into telling all he knew, perhaps scare him out of his wits, so that alive or dead he would be no menace to them; to terrorise him into a state of panic fear as they had already terrorised those unhappy women.

And he must not be terrorised; he must endeavour to show them that he could not be frightened, that he intended to hold his own in the atrocious game.

"We had better return to the house," he said dryly. "This is hardly an affair to hang about with, is it?"

Manning moved from the door.

"Certainly, certainly," he agreed. "Perhaps you would like a little brandy, Mr. Falkland. I always carry some with me, and I'm afraid you are very much shaken."

It might have been prudent to accept the flask proffered in the claw-like, powerful fingers, but Falkland could not bring himself to do so.

"I am all right, thanks," he answered abruptly.

As they walked up the dark, dank avenue together he was measuring his strength against that of the gaunt man stalking beside him—supposing that Manning should hurl himself on him—here and now?

He was thankful that he had brought that razor with him; but Manning ambled along in the most inoffensive manner, only remarking meekly:

"I shouldn't say anything of this sad business to the ladies."

"No," agreed Falkland dryly. "Indeed I should send them away from here as quickly as possible. It is really monstrous to keep Miss Conway in this isolation—in this atmosphere."

Manning shrugged his hunched shoulders.

"I obey Mr. Dobree," he remarked humbly. "He has his reasons, good ones no doubt."

Falkland could say no more; as they crossed the bleak patch of grass in front of "Mockways" he had for the first time a clear view of the house, which looked now exactly like the photograph that Beale had shown him—blank, plain, save for those masks in the tympanum, ugly, gaunt, with that great black cypress tree at one side.

When they entered the house Manning left him to enter the office-like room where Dobree appeared to be still closeted, and Falkland, who was quite sure that he would not have very long to himself, hastily took out the charred remnant of the note-book that he had found in Mathews' cottage; it was a little twopenny book with traces of ink writing in it—one or two sentences were still readable and were addressed to him:

"Mr. Falkland, dear sir, in case I don't have time to tell you, I've written down——"

Evidently then the servant had scribbled in this book the precious information he feared he might not have the chance to convey by word of mouth.

Falkland turned over the burnt pages desperately which crumbled into black flakes in his hands; all he could decipher was:

"His name's not Dobree . . ." then, on another fragment—"Manning is the one . . ." and last, most oddly: "*A knot of scarlet silk* . . ." underlined twice.

Falkland heard a step and cast the charred stump of paper

into the fire that, he recalled with horror, he had seen Mathews pile up with logs not so very long ago.

It was Mamie who entered the room; she had a tray and proceeded to lay the table; her glance flickered to Falkland.

"Where are they?" she whispered.

"Occupied, I think," he replied. "But, for Heaven's sake, be careful."

For he recalled last night and the consequences of the wretched servant's attempt at betrayal.

Mamie seemed quick and clever; she proceeded to lay the table for luncheon, clattering the knives and forks and whispering rapidly under cover of this noise.

"I don't know anything, not to say *know*; that Mrs. Milner's a devil, I went there from an Orphanage *not* so half-witted as you might think. *They* had some queer people there, funny business they did, the poor young lady was brought there to break her spirit, and I tried to help her to escape; fair got it, I did, held me arm down on the hot gas ring—well, we're in for it here, I'm sure, I don't like the looks of things; *you* keep your head screwed on, I'm pretending not to notice anything; *don't* believe she's crazy, she ain't."

This was delivered in a monotonous whisper which Falkland had to bend forward to catch as Mamie bustled about the table; at last she stopped before him, showing her bandaged arm, and added swiftly:

"They've got me here because they think I've seen a *leetle* bit too much; and because there ain't no one to ask after me if I disappears; convenient to them."

She returned to the table, her plain, drab face immobile but her little eyes as intelligent and faithful as those of a dog; from that moment Falkland trusted her absolutely.

"I'll stand by you," he breathed. "I'm on the alert—we're in danger, no doubt——"

Isabel Conway entered the room; she appeared so shaken and alarmed that Falkland feared that she had heard of the fate of Mathews; she appeared greatly relieved to see the young man and about to break into speech; but Mamie turned and gripped her by the wrist.

"Sh! miss—you keep quiet, this house is all ears, *listening*——"

"But I can't bear it," murmured Isabel, sinking into the chair beside the fire. "There is some one else in the house *besides them*. Oh, I'm not crazy—I won't go upstairs again, I won't, some one is moving about up there——"

"Who?" asked Falkland. "Who?"

Isabel twisted her hands together and muttered the very words Falkland had just read in Mathews' charred note-book——

"A knot of scarlet silk——"

CHAPTER VIII

"A KNOT of scarlet silk?" repeated Falkland utterly bewildered. "What do you mean? And how could that frighten you?"

Isabel Conway seemed too alarmed to answer this.

"They're listening all the time," she whispered. "And there is some one else hiding in the house——"

"I'll get you out of it," replied Falkland assuming a confidence that he was far indeed from feeling, "but you must tell me all you can—I'm quite in the dark, so terribly in the dark——"

Mamie made a great clutter by clumsily dropping a plate; Falkland looked up to see that Manning had stealthily entered the room. Isabel turned away from Falkland at once and bent over the fire as if warming her hands; but the young man stood his ground; he was resolute not to show fear; in a way he was not afraid for his blood was up and he was fully determined to face and overcome the monstrous and mysterious villainy that encompassed him and these two entrapped women.

"Ah, Mamie," smiled Manning, rubbing his powerful yellow hands together, "our useful Mamie! And now I am afraid that we shall have to rely entirely on you, Mamie—for that stupid Mathews has gone away—left, to join his wife——"

"I thought he didn't fancy the place," replied Mamie with surly solidity. "But I came here, sir, to look after Miss Isabel—I suppose I'm to have help with the house work?"

"There is so little to do," said Manning meekly, "that a good manager like yourself won't need any help, I'm sure."

"Indeed, sir!" she snorted. "And I'm to keep this great barn of a place in order?"

"No, oh, no, Mr. Dobree doesn't expect anything of that—only just the meals served, and Miss Isabel made comfortable." He bowed towards the girl who winced further forward against the side of the mantelpiece.

"I'd like help," Mamie protested stoutly. "There must be some woman who'd come in—and what are you going to do for a gardener?"

Manning playfully wagged a gaunt forefinger.

"Now, Mamie, now, you don't want to be sent back to Mrs. Milner, do you? Mrs. Milner wasn't very kind to you, was she, Mamie?"

The woman was silent.

"And Miss Isabel would miss you, I'm sure," added Manning with an odious smirk, "so behave yourself, Mamie, and do exactly as you are told. And now, Mr. Dobree and I have a little business together. We will have our lunch in his room—you see after Mr. Falkland and Miss Isabel."

With that he left them and they glanced at each other in incredulous astonishment. Were they actually to be left alone together?

They kept a cautious silence for a moment or so and then they saw, from the long window, the two men, whom they regarded as jailers, leave the house.

Falkland knew too well their destination—and their errand; he sighed with relief; their grim task could not be so easily or so quickly accomplished; he had some little time free.

"Now, quick, Miss Conway," he turned to the crouching girl who had not stirred; "we have a chance to talk—please tell me everything you know that will help me very much."

Mamie had arranged a cold meal and she suggested that they ate some of it.

Miss Isabel is frightened," she said. "Food would put a bit of courage into her——"

But the girl shook her head.

"I can't eat, I can't eat," she whispered, and huddle closer to the fire.

Falkland besought her to speak, besought her desperately.

"I want to help you, I'm sure I can help you," he urged. "There must be a way out—this state of affairs is too monstrous. What hold have these two men got over you, and why do they hold you against your will? Haven't you any relative, and friends?"

She replied in a low, quivering voice:

"My father worked for Mr. Dobree, he was very good to us; when father fell ill, I worked in one of Mr. Dobree's offices, I was very young. Mr. Dobree helped us a great deal. When father died he left me as ward to Mr. Dobree and I felt quite safe and content—we travelled about with a French lady and there was a great deal of money spent on me. I was happy; Mr. Manning was always there. And then, after about two years of this pleasant life I heard that Mr. Manning wanted to marry me, and Mr. Dobree said I was to say, 'yes' "

She paused, turned her great eyes on to Falkland, and added:

"I said no, no, no—and they began to shut me away—we kept moving about, Madame Saint Quentin left—hotels and hotels—and maids who were spies, my letters intercepted—then doctors and nursing homes. They said I was mad, they told every one I was mad—they sent me at last to Mr. Milner's—oh, I believe they want to make me mad!"

Falkland stifled a frantic exclamation.

"Mr. Dobree seemed sorry for me—I kept on begging him to let me go, to earn my own living—anywhere, and I think he held Mr. Manning off, but at last he tuned on me, too—he said I was to consent or I should find myself in an asylum——"

"He knows Mr. Dobree's secret," repeated Mamie grimly.

"But what," cried Falkland desperately, "*is* this secret? What hold can Manning have over Dobree? What could it be so tremendous as to cause him to go these lengths—these ghastly lengths?"

"I don't know," said Isabel wearily.

"I don't know," repeated Mamie, "but I'm going to have a jolly good try to find out."

Falkland glanced at her with gratitude and admiration; she was an ally worth having, brave, resolute, loyal and shrewd, he was sure—an ignorant, ill-treated drudge from a nefarious bogus private asylum perhaps, but a creature of courage and character once her affections had been roused—as they had been by the helpless Isabel.

"Let us have a meal," he said, "we mustn't get run down—I suppose all this stuff was in the house?"

"Lord bless you," answered Mamie, "there's provisions for months downstairs, *they* don't mean to have no tradesmen calling."

They seated themselves at the table, Falkland facing the window, which, high and uncurtained, commanded such a clear view; there he would be able to see the return of Manning and Dobree—unless they returned, uncomfortable thought, by some other way.

On this reflection he uttered a warning.

"We had better be careful now what we say—they might creep into the house and listen."

Mamie nodded and Isabel looked piteously at Falkland as if trying to gain some confidence from his resolution.

And then a most bewildering thing happened; they were all

silent, seated round the table in the bare, large, high shabby room with the two tall windows, when a hoarse voice said, right in the midst of them:

"*Every word you've spoken has been overheard.*"

Even Falkland could not repress an exclamation; all three sprang to their feet, nearly upsetting the table

"I told you," sobbed Isabel, "there was some one else in the house!"

"But where?" cried Falkland, staring frantically round, "where?"

"The place is full of secret passages and hiding places," shuddered Mamie, and Falkland thought of his own room to which Mathews had been able to gain admission.

"Overheard," repeated the raucous voice, "overheard!"

It seemed to come from the ceiling; with surprising courage Mamie glanced up.

"All right, you old fool!" she shouted, "I hope you heard some good of yourself! We knew you was listening all right!"

"It's upstairs," said Falkland. "I think there is a hole by that chandelier——"

For there was a large ornament in the centre of the ceiling from which depended a disused chandelier.

A low, hoarse, chuckling laugh followed and then an odd flapping or shuffling noise.

"I'm going upstairs," announced Falkland. "Perhaps Manning has returned secretly and is playing these tricks on us. Heaven help us," he added bitterly, "I believe we are in the hands of maniacs!"

"Maniacs!" echoed the voice now on a screaming note. "Maniacs!"

Falkland dashed to the door; the handle turned purposely in his hand.

Locked—they were locked in.

The young man felt his whole body chill with horror. The invisibility of the enemy was ghastly.

"I can't get out," he muttered, struggling with the door, vain as he knew that struggle to be, but unable to control himself.

"There's the windows, ain't there?" said Mamie. "What's the matter with them?"

"Of course," answered Falkland with deep relief—long French windows they were, even if locked, the glass was easily broken, but as he turned, Isabel Conway clutched his arm.

"You don't know what may be outside," she murmured frantically.

"I'll risk that," he answered. "We can't stay locked in here—make for that window on the left, behind me—I know it was open this morning——"

But for reply the girl, uttering a shriek, sagged against him, pointing to the window.

Against the glass dangled a knot of scarlet silk suspended from a fine thread that was jerked up and down.

CHAPTER IX

"IT'S a signal," said Falkland. "Is it for us?"

He thought of the line in the charred note-book, of what Isabel had said in her terror when she had first entered the room.

"Have you seen it before?" he asked of the shrinking girl as they gazed at the knot of red silk dangling in front of the long clear pane.

"Yes," she breathed, "just now—in front of my window above."

"There is some one else in the house, that's clear," said Falkland briefly, and he advanced towards the window though the two women endeavoured to hold him back with an instinctive clutch at his coat—"some one fooling about," he nearly added, but, remembering what he had just seen in the shed at Mathews' cottage, he could hardly use the word "fooling."

He was at the window and had opened it and was out in the clear autumn sunshine in a moment.

A fine thread was hanging from the upper window and being moved up and down; it was obvious that some one was holding it. Falkland suspected Manning; the fellow wanted to frighten them and had probably crept into the house at the back.

"What is this?" he shouted boldly, "trying to scare a couple of women with this child's play!"

The thread was loosened, the knot dropped at Falkland's feet and at the same instant a form appeared at the black dark square of the window—form scarcely described it for it was shapeless, neither man, woman nor beast, but something grey and cloaked, with a linen white face in which features were scarcely distinguishable and which yet had an expression of loathsome horror.

Falkland thought it was Manning, masked and disguised, and called out strongly; with a chattering cry the appearance vanished from the window, and Falkland, turning, saw both Manning and Dobree coming across the bleak expanse of neglected grass.

His heart gave a sick swerve; there was then a third person in the house, some one who could lock doors, speak through the ceiling, dangle strings from windows—an ally or a spy?

The most likely supposition was that it was an accomplice of the two men; Falkland put his foot on the silk knot and tried to maintain a composed demeanour.

The incident was the uglier and the more disturbing as he believed that the room where he had seen the hideous thing was that occupied by Isabel Conway.

He reflected with a shiver that Dobree and Manning had been very quick over their gruesome labour, why, hardly half an hour——

"Have you finished your luncheon?" asked Dobree genially, "for I should like to take you and Isabel round the grounds, they have some curious features, have they not, Manning?"

And Manning agreed with a servile smile, that they had, oh, yes, indeed!

Falkland had instantly decided to say nothing of the strange occurrences; he hoped the women would be equally discreet. As the two men entered the house by the open French window he hastily picked up the knot of scarlet silk; as he thrust it into his pocket he felt that it contained something hard, he dare not look to see what; as he followed Dobree into the dining-room he saw at once that he need not have worried about either Isabel or Mamie; with admirable presence of mind they had assumed a perfect composure; the girl was even seated at the table, eating a biscuit and drinking a glass of wine, while Mamie was bustling about the fire.

Dobree repeated his invitation to explore the grounds of "Mockways" and Isabel calmly accepted, asking Mamie "to run up stairs and fetch her coat and hat."

Falkland's heart swelled with admiration for her courage in circumstances so deadly and swore to himself that things should go hard indeed for him if he did not rescue her from the extraordinary circumstances in which she was caught.

Mamie opened the door without difficulty; it had then been unlocked as silently as it had been locked and by the same person no doubt—the creature of the white mask and raucous voice.

So he found himself with the two men and the girl walking in the autumn park which would have been pleasant enough with the great yellowing trees and wide glades in the mellow afternoon sunshine if it had not been for the sinister atmosphere overhanging Falkland's mind which dulled the natural beauty of the scene; he observed, as no doubt he reminded himself bitterly he was intended to observe, the great extent of the grounds, and presently, when they reached there, the great height of the walls which were, in many places, crowned by the sharp points of broken glass.

"The late owner," remarked Manning blandly, "was a very eccentric sort of man. A recluse. He took, as you will observe, Mr. Falkland, every precaution not to be disturbed."

"I observe," replied Falkland dryly. "The late owner, you say? I thought that the house had always been in the family of Mr. Dobree."

He said this just to hear what lie they would concoct for he remembered what Beale had told him about "Mockways"—that it had once belonged to some people named Powell.

"No," said Dobree with an air of frankness, " 'Mockways' was left to me—a great many years ago, by my first friend, an old man,

Jabez Powell. It was in a way the foundations of my fortune, Mr. Falkland, and therefore I have always felt an affection for the place though it is long since I have lived here——"

He had then spoken the truth—Powell had certainly been the name; Falkland thought this a good chance to put in some show of knowledge of their affairs—he remembered that he had got to bluff, that had been the wretched Mathews' advice, the advice of the women.

"I know something about him," he said, drawing a bow wildly at a venture, but speaking calmly. "He was connected with that Sarah Lomax of whom I spoke——"

Dobree gave a short cry and recoiled in his path.

"I nearly," he remarked, "trod on a snake—a little snake in the undergrowth——"

"That," said Manning, "is the best thing to do with snakes—tread on them——"

Falkland raised his voice:

"I think you said you had never heard the name of Sarah Lomax, Mr. Dobree?"

"Did I?" replied that personage, still searching among the undergrowth and dead leaves with his stick. "I don't remember the incident, I don't remember ever hearing the name before."

"I'm afraid," smiled Manning, "that Mr. Dobree is too busy to keep trivialities in his head. I also knew Mr. Powell, and he certainly had no connection with that name—he was a recluse, as I have said—unmarried with no women at all in his life."

"Perhaps," thought Falkland, "I drew a blank there, but Dobree was plainly shocked—there was no snake."

They had now turned down a narrow path that led to a most neglected part of the grounds, a tangle of dry fern, twisting brambles, bushes and weeds; but Falkland noted that the path through this wilderness though overgrown, showed signs of recent use, as if some one had forced their way through not long before.

The path led to a cluster of trees and in the midst of the trees was a very peculiar looking building of old, purplish brick.

This was oval in shape, a tower in height, with a plain sloping roof like a cap; there were no windows nor doors, but in the top a small, round, unglazed aperture.

"Have you ever seen one of these before?" asked Manning genially. "We regard it as a great curiosity—an old mausoleum."

Isabel drew nearer Falkland.

"The old burial place of the family who had 'Mockways' before Powell," explained Dobree. "I dare say there are some secrets in there, if that was opened!"

They walked round the sinister building; on the other side was a wooden door with a railing in front, both padlocked, both recently disturbed—the rust and damp were rubbed away—the padlocks were new; he felt the girl for a second lean against him as if she also had noticed the significance of these horrid details.

He felt too his own forehead grow damp; with every hour he was realising more and more the ghastly peril and the ghastly hopelessness of his position.

Trapped!

And through his own folly.

They had all stood silent, looking at the door of the mausoleum with those bright new padlocks.

It was Isabel who spoke first.

"We don't want to stay here, do we?" she said. "It is rather a gloomy place."

"Oh, yes," answered Manning stroking his chin, "but interesting, don't you think? The door and railing seemed broken down so I had new locks put on, as you observe."

Falkland felt so desperate that it was almost recklessly that he answered, with an assumed air of menacing boldness.

"I observe a great deal, Mr. Manning, and I understand a great deal—he who laughs last, you know!"

He slipped his hand into his pocket and the feel of Mathews' keys and that something hard in the knot of scarlet silk, gave him a certain sensation of confidence. Who knew what these might not be the clue to?

Isabel prevented either of the other two men replying to this challenge by seizing Falkland's arm and exclaiming:

"Who's that? Running away in the bushes! A large dark man—he's been watching us!"

Dobree and Manning leaped forward in the direction she had indicated; in the second that they turned away from immediate observation of her, Isabel leant forward and whispered to Falkland:

"*Don't trust Mamie——*"

CHAPTER X

"NOT trust Mamie!" repeated Falkland, dismayed beyond expression.

"But she helped you to escape from Mrs. Milner——"

"I know, but may that not have been to gain my confidence because she knew that just at that moment Dobree would arrive?"

Falkland was bewildered.

"But she was punished—we heard her screams."

"Was that pretence?" whispered Isabel. "I have never seen under the bandage on her arm——"

Dobree and Manning now came plunging back through the undergrowth.

"No one," snapped Manning.

For answer Isabel called sharply:

"Look out! There he is, just behind you!"

Falkland, who was standing beside Dobree, turned instantly; there, a few yards away, crouching on all fours in the high, harsh, dry bracken was a man as Isabel had described, in a brown suit, with a coarse, dark face, gazing at them intently. When he saw that he was observed, he turned rapidly and hurried through the tangle of dead undergrowth.

Manning and Dobree were instantly after him, but he proceeded with horrible swiftness and, in those coloured clothes, was soon lost to sight.

"Isn't this a chance?" whispered Isabel frantically. "Couldn't we escape?"

"Yes, it might be a chance. But I don't know where to go,"

he said bitterly, "nor even where I am——"

"Let us try," pleaded the girl. "I can't go back to the house—there is *something* in my room——"

There was; Falkland had seen it—the masked figure (if mask it was) that had dropped the red silk thread, and if she couldn't trust Mamie——

"Very well," he said grimly, "we'll make a try—these people are certainly lunatics or criminals—it doesn't seem fair to abandon Mamie, but if you say she is one of them——"

"I don't know!" sobbed Isabel, whose courage seemed near the breaking point. "I don't trust her—oh, if I have to go back to that house, I would rather die; please, if you cannot help me to escape, help me to die——"

"We'll escape," said Falkland, "never fear." He was deeply moved by the desperate plight of this young girl, so tender and charming, who turned to him for protection; in her service he meant to strain every sinew, every wit he possessed.

Taking her arm he moved off rapidly in the opposite direction to that taken by Manning and Dobree.

His first object must be to get out of the park; once on the high road, surely he could soon get help; once in touch with the normal world there would be no difficulty in getting on the track of these two villains; he had something definite against them now, at best the concealment of the suicide of Mathews, at worst—murder.

And there was the question of Beale, he was wild to find out if Beale was safe—or if there again was—murder.

But before anything he must get out of Mockways Park; at present they were hurrying aimlessly away from the mausoleum.

"Do you know," he asked Isabel, "anything of this place?"

"No," she answered, "I was never here before—I could find my way back to the house—by the path we came along—should we not go in the opposite direction to reach the gates?"

"Yes, but there are so many little side paths and the gates are certain to be locked—we had better try to find the wall, and get over that somehow——"

At least they did not come in sight of the house, nor of Mathews' cottage, nor of the kennels, and all Falkland could conclude was that they were going away from all these and towards the walls.

Nor were they pursued; silence, broken only by the scamper of a rabbit across their lonely path, encompassed them; the air was pure, the sunshine mellow, the scene beautiful in autumn grandeur, the free sky overhead; Falkland felt his spirits rise; he reflected that it would be very difficult for Dobree and Manning, once they had lost sight of them to track them again; they were lost in the confusion of the walk, glades and trees of the immense grounds, and if they searched long enough they must, finally, discover the limits of the park; Falkland considered it most unlikely that an estate so huge was walled all round; somewhere there must be fencing, or railings.

At the end of a wide glade they came upon a tower or pagoda that stood, solitary and neglected, beside a small pool, full of broken reeds.

It occurred to Falkland that if he went to the top of this he would gain a good view of the park and possibly of the way out of the park; at least he must be able to see the house, and, by placing that, locate himself.

But the door of the tower was locked and he pushed his shoulder against it in vain.

Isabel sat down on the side of the knoll on which the tower stood; they had been walking long and rapidly and she was exhausted; she was also more at ease than she had been for months; "Mockways" and its inhabitants seemed already far away; she felt a warm confidence in the stalwart young man who had taken her destiny into his hands; reassured and almost light hearted with the elastic spirit of youth, she took some chocolate from her pocket and nibbled it as Falkland tried the door; he had suddenly remembered the bunch of keys that he had taken from Mathews' cottage—the keys that Manning, disturbed by his coming, must have overlooked; one of them did fit and open the door into the pagoda.

"Here's luck!" he cried. "We'll run up and have a look round—"

Isabel jumped up, scattering her chocolate.

"There is someone coming!" she cried hoarsely.

Instantly Falkland drew her inside the tower and shut and locked the door, asking:

"Who? Where?"

"Coming along the avenue—towards the tower," she answered. "I think it was Manning——"

"Well, we are safe here," said Falkland with forced calm, but he knew that the word should have been "trapped." If Manning had seen them go in—well, he had nothing to do but force the door, or even wait outside.

The interior of the tower was bare and dusty and Falkland's hope of a view from the top was crudely disappointed, for there were neither stories nor stairs; the building was hollow as a pipe, and the only light was a livid glow from the high placed slits that served as windows.

"We must wait here," he told the dismayed girl, "till he has gone—very likely he didn't notice us, and when he has gone we can come out—perhaps, too, it wasn't Manning——"

Even as he spoke there were three loud knocks on the door; loud, distinct blows.

Isabel shrieked in her gloomy prison and Falkland felt his blood chill—better to have been caught in the open than here; he wondered how long the door would hold, if Manning had another key; the knocks were repeated.

Falkland, looking round at the last pitch of desperation, saw a ring in the floor of the dusty chamber; he told Isabel to help, and between them they tugged at the iron loop.

A trap door opened, beneath a flight of steps into darkness.

"That must lead somewhere," said Falkland. "Will you risk it?"

"Yes, yes, make haste," she implored.

They descended the steps; he struck a match, pulled the stone into place above their heads, and catching hold of Isabel hurried along the black corridor ahead of them, striking matches at intervals until the box he carried was almost exhausted.

The passage was fairly wide and airy and in good repair; one of the last matches saw them brought up sharp by a door; another of the keys from Mathews' bunch unlocked this; as the creaking hinges swung back they were greeted by a burst of daylight that caused Isabel to give a cry of joy; they had come out on a hillside that was masked by a barn, so that the secret door of the passage appeared like an ordinary door in the barn.

Before them lay a field and beyond the field the road; they looked at each other with inexpressible delight; they were free!

Setting off briskly along the road, they discussed their plans; Isabel knew of several friends with whom she could get in touch, people who believed that she was enjoying herself abroad—but she had no money. Falkland, searching in his pocket to see the extent of his resources, discovered what he had forgotten, the knot of scarlet silk; he paused to examine this; there was a paper inside, wrapped round a wooden reel; on this paper was written:

"A Papier Mâché box, hidden somewhere in 'Mockways' contains what they want to find. The red silk knot is a signal for you."

Neither of them could understand the meaning of this, nor if it was even meant for them; there did not seem any need to trouble now, since they were free; Falkland meant to ask for assistance at the first house they came to—but they walked the lonely road, which appeared to twist round the side of the mountain, for hours and saw no one; with the fall of the dusk, Isabel's strength deserted her; she sank down by the side of the road, unable to walk another step, faint, giddy and incapable of urging her courage further. Falkland gazed at her in despair; he was exhausted and hungry himself—and there was something sinister in this intolerable, continuous loneliness.

At last, as they sat helpless by the wayside, he saw to his unutterable relief a car approaching; he jumped up and signalled for it to stop; it pulled up and in the dusk Falkland saw it was empty save for the driver in helmet and goggles and scarf. Falkland briefly asked for a lift to the next village and helped Isabel into the car.

As he did so, the driver took off his goggles; the light of the motor lamps showed that it was Manning.

CHAPTER XI

FALKLAND was astounded by the extent of this misfortune; he was as awed as a man face to face with the supernatural, there seemed indeed something diabolical about Manning, about this deadly pursuit and quiet capture.

Isabel was half swooning, she dropped into a corner of the car like a dead creature.

"Well met," smiled Manning. "I'm afraid that you have been over walking Miss Conway, she seems quite tired! Such a pity; now, if you had let me know, I could have motored you anywhere you wanted to go——"

This fiendish jeering was too much for Falkland; exhausted as he was, he could not give in without a struggle; they were at least on the open road, he could not so easily be thrust into that car and swept back to the horror of "Mockways," nor so easily allow the girl—the girl who had relied on him to be so swept back, either.

"Look here," he said, turning defiantly on Manning, "I've had enough of this foolery—neither Miss Conway nor I wish to stay in 'Mockways'—we were trying to escape and you know it——"

"Trying to escape from what?" asked Manning softly.

"From you," said Falkland.

"Dear me, how very unpleasant you are, Mr. Falkland, and I really don't know what you mean——"

For answer Falkland hurled himself on him; if he could only knock Manning down, jump into the car and ride off—he could drive most cars; he had Manning by the throat——

But those great powerful hands that Falkland had noted before with dread now held him off.

"Quietly, quietly," said Manning, undisturbed. "Rather losing your head, aren't you?"

But Falkland was desperate, he would no longer be put off with these suave sneers; he disengaged himself from Manning and glared at him across the darkling road; he wished that he could signal to the girl crouching in the car to take this opportunity to escape, why, if she darted off on to the hillside she must surely come to some manner of help, and if she did not, it would be better for her to perish of exposure than return to "Mockways," thought Falkland in his desperation.

But Isobel did not stir, utterly exhausted, she remained inert, with no effort to save herself from impending fate.

"Look here," said Falkland, hoarsely, "I'm not going to get into that car, and I am not going to allow you to drive away Miss Conway. I've been playing up to you long enough—you've gone too far, altogether too far."

Falkland hardly knew what words he was choosing to voice his fury, his hate and his despair, for though he put up this valiant defiance, he had little hope of eluding Manning who seemed to have, as he stood, gaunt, dark and threatening in the twilight, the omnipotence of evil.

"Don't be foolish," answered Manning, softly. "You're rather overwrought, aren't you? Tired, perhaps, with your long walk—please get into the car and allow me to drive you *home*."

There was a horrid emphasis on this last word—when "Mockways" was home.

"I won't go," said Falkland through his teeth, "I won't go——"

But Manning took him by the arm and forced him towards

the car; Falkland began to struggle.

"Ah," he whispered, "you want to dispose of me as you disposed of Beale—and Mathews——"

"That's ugly talk," replied Manning. "You will frighten Miss Conway——"

"Better frighten her than allow her to go back to 'Mockways'—"

But Manning had whipped out a revolver from the heavy folds of his coat; Falkland saw the dark blue gleam in the last light——

He might have known that—the man was armed.

The game was up, it had been folly to try to use force, Falkland would not have done so if he had not been exhausted and taken by surprise with the bitterness of his disappointment—folly, though, folly, and doubtless one for which he would have to pay—guile had been the only possible weapon.

"On to the seat beside me," commanded Manning, and Falkland, sick with fury, obeyed; the car was not lit inside and he could only see Isabel as a blur—her pale coat and dress a dim shape in the corner.

Manning swung the car round and took the long road twisting along the mountain at high speed; Falkland tried to keep calm, to set his vexed and horrified mind in some sort of order, ah, he had reached the end of all his wits, all his courage!

How had Manning found them?

Falkland thrust his hand into his pocket—there were the keys and the message in the knot of red silk——

What had the message been, the message in the knot of scarlet silk?

"They are looking for something in a *papier mâché* box——"

Was the secret in that?—well, he must look, too, if he could keep his wits.

He lurched on to Manning and said in a tone of despair:

"Look here, what is all this about? A joke? *I* don't know what you are all playing at—if you'll let us go I'll take it all as a joke——"

"You don't fool me," Manning replied impassively.

"I'm not trying to fool you," said Falkland desperately. "I want you to understand that I know nothing of you or your affairs—and if you'll let us go——"

"Us?" interrupted Manning with a sneer. "Are you, then, intending to elope with Miss Conway?"

"Leave that," said Falkland, roughly. "I'm trying to tell you that I know nothing about you."

"That's an easy, cheap trick, isn't it?" jeered Manning crouching over the wheel. "You know too much, I can tell you—*you've seen too much.*"

That was true—Beale and Mathews, nor could Falkland, even at this desperate moment swear that he would not speak of these things, nor, he reflected bitterly, would it be of much use if he did swear.

He tried, however, to take a high hand.

"I've seen nothing—what do you mean?"

"You know very well what I mean," replied Manning. "Don't try to play the innocent, you should not have interfered in this game." He thrust his detestable face towards Falkland. "Why did you?"

"I didn't interfere," protested Falkland. "I saved Mr. Dobree's life—he offered me a job——"

"And you," finished Manning, "asked him if he had ever heard of Sarah Lomax, didn't you?"

Falkland, in his frantic plight, thought that he had better continue to put up some manner of bluff—perhaps if Manning thought he knew nothing he would murder him out of hand and send him to join Mathews in the mausoleum; he was, as his captor had sarcastically reminded him, too deeply involved to be allowed to go free—even if he had known nothing when he had joined Dobree, he had now seen *too much.*

Therefore, perhaps it was wiser to pretend that he did know something so that they might keep him alive to find out how much that knowledge was.

"Well, I happen to know of the connection between you, your master, and Sarah Lomax," he said, plunging wildly. "Also of a certain *papier mâché* box——"

The car lurched and swerved under Manning's grip; the chance shot had told.

"You're rash!" he snarled.

Falkland thought of the girl behind, crouching helplessly in the dark; not rash, but desperate.

"Am I?" he said, putting up as cool a show of bluff as possible. "I don't know. I've friends outside, people who also know about Sarah Lomax."

Manning did not answer—this shot must have told too—nothing would scare these two more than the thought that Falkland's knowledge of their secret was shared by others, people who were free of them.

"Friends who will be making inquiries after Beale," added Falkland.

"Friends who won't be able to find out where you are, anyhow," sneered Manning.

"Oh, I don't know," Falkland ventured frantically, though with outward calm. "What about that man you were chasing, eh?"

"He," said Manning, grimly, "was soon disposed of——"

Falkland shuddered—he could scarcely, remembering Beale and Mathews, affect to despise this sinister comment; he did not know who the stranger had been, friend or foe; and he was silent, in a sick despair.

They swept into the gateway of "Mockways," the iron gates stood open now, and up the long, dank, dark drive, and round the neglected, bleak patch of grass in front of the house, now so hatefully familiar.

There were lights in some of the windows of the atrocious mansion which baulked sombre dark against the darkening sky.

Dobree was on the step when the car drew up; Manning got down from the wheel and seized Falkland's arm, Dobree gripped him the other side; they forced him into the house—he had no chance of a word or a signal to Isabel, even of a glance in her direction; no doubt she was locked into the car and therefore they did not trouble about her yet.

"Well, well," smiled Dobree, "quite a little adventure, eh? You seem very tired, Mr. Falkland, allow me to help you upstairs."

Falkland set his teeth and controlled himself as best he could; to resist would be not only futile but absurd—to appeal to them would be equally grotesque.

They guided him along the gloomy ill-lit corridor, up the drab ugly stairs; higher up this time than where he had been lodged before.

"We thought you would be more comfortable here," said Dobree, opening a small door, "less likely to be disturbed at night."

He referred, of course, to the visit of the wretched Mathews. Falkland did not trouble to answer; the room was unfurnished save for a bed, a chair, a table on which was placed a meal.

"Good-night," said Dobree, and, followed by Manning, left the room and turned the key; Falkland tried to keep his mind off

Isabel and forced himself to eat the food before him, though his hunger had long passed, leaving a faint nausea.

As he ate he was disturbed by a tap at the window, and looking round, saw pressed against the pane the face of the man in the brown suit who had been chased by Dobree from the mausoleum.

CHAPTER XII

THE man looking through the window grinned in the most normal and pleasant manner, and Falkland felt his spirits rise incredibly—here surely was help—an ally!

He went to the window and opened it—the stranger was standing, perilously enough, on the deep cut pilasters and ornaments beneath the window, but seemed composed and even amused.

"Help me into the room," he whispered. "I'm getting stiff."

And Falkland helped him in.

"I say," he added, "this is a bit if an adventure, isn't it? Something exciting at last."

"I don't know about exciting," said Falkland, dryly. "I don't know who you are and I'm really past caring——"

"Bit of a hole?" asked the stranger.

"Considerably in a hole," admitted Falkland.

"Well, I've broken in," said the other, "been hanging round the place all day—those two lunatics gave me a fine chase. But I beat them—easy."

"Take care," whispered Falkland. "I'm locked in here and probably there's some one listening at the door—the place is a network of secret passages and traps——"

"Jolly old place," smiled the stranger. "I made up my mind I'd get inside it, somehow."

"Who are you?" asked Falkland.

"I'm John Compton—this is my stunt, investigating these places—haunted houses, you know—and when that sour old eccentric, Dobree, refused, I made up my mind to have a look for myself. Pretty good fun," he added shrewdly, "for it seems to me that if there are not ghosts here there's something else."

"There is," said Falkland. "The ghost part is trumped up nonsense—these two men are up to no good——"

He hesitated, wondering if this candid looking young man was, after all, only a spy, an accomplice of Dobree's; since he had been at "Mockways" he had come to be distrustful of every one; but he found it hard to disbelieve in the sincerity of John Compton.

That young man now spoke more earnestly, leaning across the supper table with the candle light full on his fair face.

"You're Edward Falkland, aren't you?"

"Yes."

"Supposed to be this old boy's secretary?"

"Yes—but——"

"Well, it was partly because of you I came here."

"How on earth did you know that I was here?"

"Beale told me."

Falkland nearly shouted in his surprise.

"Beale told you! I thought Beale——"

His voice trailed away; he was thinking of that mound in Bitterne wood, of the green smear on Manning's wrist, of the scattered painting apparatus in the ravine——

"Beale felt uneasy about you," continued Compton. "He was swept off so quickly and when he came back you and Dobree and Manning had all gone he didn't know where——"

"Oh," said Falkland with the deepest relief, "he did come back?"

"Oh, yes, looking for you—meaning to give you a warning——"

"Ah, a warning?"

"Not to trust these fellows too much. He didn't like Manning's behaviour—very odd."

"Lower your voice," said Falkland eagerly, "and tell me what happened——"

"Well, Manning came to the inn in a hurry, and said he had come to fetch Beale to join the party for 'Mockways'—an invitation from Dobree to paint the place, all formal and civil, a message from you, too. Well, Beale threw his things together and got into the car and Manning shot off through the woods; he said they were to meet at the cross roads, but he kept driving in and out of bye lanes, right into the heart of the forest. At last when they had been driving about half an hour he said something was the matter with the car and asked Beale to get out; as soon as he had done so, Manning drove off and was out of sight in a twinkling!"

So it had been as simple as all that—the whole thing staged to frighten him; how easy for Manning to smear his wrist with green—to build up that mound in the wood!

"Well, Beale wandered about for hours, lost of course; he found his valises left under a tree and his painting things thrown down a ravine, and when he did get back, found you'd gone. Of course, he was pretty mad. A very silly joke, if it was a joke."

"It wasn't," said Falkland, "there was a design behind it, I think."

"Well, he thought there might be, though he couldn't say what, and he guessed you might be at 'Mockways' and thought it jolly odd he hadn't heard from you—he couldn't come to look you up himself as he's got a commission up north he can't afford to lose, so he asked me to take it on, knowing I'm keen on these kind of things."

"I'm very grateful," said Falkland fervently. "I hope you won't regret your interference——"

"I'm enjoying it immensely—I couldn't get in though I rang and knocked, so I broke in—that great wall doesn't go all round, as you may imagine—and then I came on the lot of you by that old burial place——"

"And you gave them a good run!" smiled Falkland.

"Yes, and doubled back to the house and got up that great tree at the side; I've been there, all day, cosy enough—I saw them run you in and guessed you were here—what's up?" he added quickly.

"I don't know. There's some mystery, some secret——"

"Not with a man like Dobree!"

"There is. Or else every one is crazy."

And Falkland told Compton all he knew of "Mockways" and the affairs of Dobree and Manning—and that other person in the house who had so queerly sent the message, "Look for the '*Papier Mâché*' box."

"And I'm a prisoner," he finished. "They're afraid that I know something—which I don't—I would to Heaven that I had never heard of the name of Sarah Lomax!"

Compton turned the affair over in the calm light of common sense.

"It's either a lot of foolery," he said at last, "or there is something serious behind it—all their explanations *might* be correct, if you allow for atmosphere and worked up effects, this creature here might be a practical joker—even the girl, this Miss Conway, she *might* be really off her head—there is really, you see, nothing against them—meanwhile I've broken into Dobree's house, and I suppose he could make it awkward for me——"

"You'd better go," advised Falkland, "the way you came and before you are caught——"

"And you'd better come with me," said his visitor. "It's easy to get down by the tree and I know the way out now, there'll be a moon presently——"

"I can't go," replied Falkland, "and leave Miss Conway—she's relying on me——"

But Compton objected that he didn't see what possible use Falkland was to any one, besides the fact that the girl might be really "off her head."

But Falkland was obstinate.

"Whatever the truth," he declared, "it is obvious that the girl is frightened out of her life—she's frantic to escape and I must see that she does escape—besides I do feel I'd rather like to see the adventure to an end and have a look for that box——"

"Nonsense," said Compton. "They're playing you up—come with me and clear out of it all."

Falkland shook his head but urged the other young man to beat a quick retreat.

"Get in touch with Beale," he said, "and try to get us both out of this——"

Compton looked puzzled.

"I don't see how I am to," he confessed. "There is nothing against them, is there? Nothing, I mean, to go to the police with—all you've said would seem a string of nonsense and I've got nothing to say because I had no right to break in——"

It was with a pang that he saw the bright faced Compton, like a schoolboy on an adventure, cautiously step out of the window; he felt that his last link with the normal, pleasant outside world was leaving him; it was hard not to be able to follow Compton, to clutch at the stout boughs of the gigantic tree, to lower himself into freedom, but not for a moment could he contemplate an escape that left Isabel Conway behind.

The moon was now up and riding through sombre hanks of cloud above the heavy masses of the still, close foliage; Falkland put out his guttering candle and watched the descent of the young man until he was lost to sight in the thick shadows.

A shot sounded.

Falkland started as if the bullet had touched him, so desperate was his surprise and dismay; he leant forward peering frantically into the bewilderment of shadows.

Nothing more; again the utter silence of the night. Falkland, shivering, went back into the dark room and sat down heavily by the table; he did not know how long he had sat before the door opened and Manning entered, holding a candle.

"Good-night, Mr. Falkland, I hope that shot didn't alarm you—a burglar or a tramp—he's been wounded and we're keeping him in 'Mockways.' Good-night."

Falkland felt his heart like lead—Compton, too, was then a prisoner.

CHAPTER XIII

BUT young Compton had escaped; when, from the darkness of the trees and the shadows of the trees he had crossed a patch of moonlight and been in full view of the house he had heard the shot ring out as if some one had been watching him; but he was unhurt, the bullet missed its mark and Compton dodged instantly into the blackness of the shrubbery and ran swiftly away from the house.

He felt that his escapade was becoming something more than the joke with which it began, but his lighthearted spirit was not long depressed and it was with a grin that he slackened his pace and made his way through the park in the strong moonlight.

Vast as the grounds were he pretty well knew them by heart; there were not many paths or alleys that he had not doubled up or down when Manning and Dobree had been chasing him, a chase that, for his part, he had enjoyed, for it had been easy to outdistance the two much older men, one of whom, Dobree, was heavy and stout; they had not been, luckily for him, armed, or he had no doubt they would have checked his flight with a shot as they had just endeavoured to check his escape from the house; but now it was clear that he was no longer pursued, and, having found the path that led to the railings where he had entered, John Compton sat down under a beech tree in full moonlight an ate the rest of the sandwiches he had brought with him while he reflected on the jolly good adventure he had to relate to Beale who had seemed so oddly anxious about the safety of his friend.

Compton did not know what to make of Falkland—whether

he was a joker and the whole thing a hoax, or whether that young man was in serious difficulty.

Certainly, going over all Falkland had said, he could find nothing criminal so far, save in detaining Falkland against his will, and he had only the young man's word for that, though from his vantage in the tree he had certainly seen him bustled into the house.

A horrid, ugly house, too, but Compton was delighted that he had seen it and even been able to make a rough sketch of it; he would be the only person amongst his acquaintances who had ever seen the famous, haunted "Mockways," and that alone had been worth the day's adventure.

As for the pursuit and the shot, Compton had not felt and did not feel now the slightest ill will about that; he had been a trespasser and they had had every right to try to make him give an account of himself.

The young man finished, with relish, his rather stale meal, and rose to make for the railings that divided the park from the hillside round which a tolerable path ran; Compton had taken his bearings perfectly and knew exactly where, by a heap of white stones, he had left his motor cycle; save for the unlikely chance of this having been found or stolen, he would be soon on the high road and soon at the nearest town on the direct route to London.

He was leaving his comfortable seat and struggling against a sense of drowsiness, when he heard a movement in the bushes behind him. He thought this was a rabbit, but he listened acutely.

The movement was repeated, surely a step—and with rather a quickening of his pulses Compton wondered if, after all, he had been pursued from the house.

"Hullo!" he said looking in the direction where the shadowed bushes seemed to bend and break. "Who is there?"

A thin thread of a voice answered:

"Sh! Don't speak so loud, sir, please!"

And a little man in a long coat and soft hat emerged into the moonlight, looking apprehensively about him.

"I've been following you ever since you passed the avenue," whispered this person. "I saw you this morning when they were chasing you—but I couldn't get out, sir. Are you a friend of Mr. Falkland?"

"Well, yes," said Compton. "Friend of a friend, anyway, and who are you?"

"My name is Mathews, sir, and I've been here for years, looking after the place——"

"The very person I want to get hold of," said Compton cheerfully. "I dare say you can clear up all this mystery——"

"Well, I can and I can't, sir," whispered Mathews. "They're up to some tricks—there's years they've never been here, and then they comes, sudden like."

"To investigate ghosts," said Compton, rising.

"Ghosts, sir, is rubbish," replied Mathews. "There's some one in 'Mockways' besides Mr. Dobree and company, but it ain't a ghost." He leant forward and whispered eagerly: "It's an easy house to hide in, any number of secret passages and trap doors; old Mr. Powell loved them——"

"Who was old Mr. Powell?"

"The old gent who had 'Mockways'; Mr. Dobree was his secretary, but he wasn't Mr. Dobree then. I was only a lad then, but I saw something——" He paused, as if frightened, looked round and gripped Compton's strong arm. "I tried to warn Mr. Falkland, sir, got him to come to my cottage to see the dogs—but Mr. Manning was too sharp for that, he overheard somehow and he comes down and locks me up—and what else does he do, sir? Dresses up a waxwork in my clothes and hangs it from the beam in the shed—so poor Mr. Falkland, he takes one look and hurries away, thinking, with the bad light and his own fear, it's me. Now, what do you think of that, sir?"

"It's a *farrago* to me," said Compton. "I don't understand what you're talking about——"

"Old Mr. Powell," mumbles Mathews, "had a room of waxworks, broken up now, but none the less horrid for that—why, it gave me the horrors, seeing meself hanging like that——"

"Where were you all the time?"

"Shut in the cupboard, not daring to move, I can tell you—Mr. Manning he carries a revolver."

"Look here," said Compton brusquely, "all this seems to me a lot of tomfoolery—you're in a bad state of nerves and this idiot Manning seems to be a practical joker of the silliest sort——"

But Mathews interrupted, shivering and meandering in the moonlight.

"There's more in it than that, I assure you, sir, and if I was a friend of Mr. Falkland I'd get him out of it, quick——"

"He won't come, there is some young woman to consider——"

"Ah, Miss Isabel—ah, yes" replied the little man vaguely.

"Who is she?"

"A ward of Mr. Dobree's and they say she is off her head, but I don't know, sir, I don't know."

"Well, look here, you seem a bit long winded, and I can't hang about here for ever—supposing you come with me—I'm going back to London."

"I wouldn't dare," muttered Mathews, "I wouldn't dare—they'd find me out."

Compton saw that the little man was scared almost out of his senses and that it was hopeless to expect anything coherent from him.

"I'd better get back home," added Mathews, "they might come and look for me—and it isn't only *them*," he added hoarsely, "it's *her*, the night they arrived I saw her—up in a tree——"

"Well," said Compton, "I've just been up in a tree myself——"

"Oh, don't joke about it, sir, don't joke—it was——" He checked himself and put his trembling hand over his mouth as if to hold back a name, and then added, "You get Mr. Falkland away, and the young lady too, that's my advice——"

"You might give me some clue to the whole thing," said Compton.

The little man came even nearer and said in a low voice, reedy and shaken:

"They're looking for something. They think it's hidden in 'Mockways,' something like a *papier mâché* box—they think Mr. Falkland is looking for it, too——"

"Well, is he?"

"Oh, I don't know, sir, he said he knew nothing about it—but how did he get here, that's what I'd like to know. He shouldn't have interfered, he shouldn't."

"Look here," said Compton, "you'd better come with me—I can take you on my carrier—we'd be in London to-morrow——"

Mathews looked at him wistfully.

"I've lived here so long, I'd hardly dare get away, sir—I know a bit too much——"

"You don't seem very anxious to tell it," interrupted Compton. "I can't help if you keep me in the dark, can I? Now, what is at the bottom of all this?"

Mathews peered about him in the moonlight, then whispered the name that had been the beginning of all the trouble for Falkland, the name that the strange girl had whispered in Bitterne woods:

"Sarah Lomax."

Compton could hardly hear these two words so low were they spoken; but he had no chance to repeat them, for no sooner had Mathews breathed the name, than, in what seemed an excess of fear, he turned and shuffled away into the undergrowth, soon utterly lost in the shadows.

CHAPTER XIV

COMPTON arrived in London without further incident, and the distance between his home and "Mockways" seemed just the distance between reality and unreality; and, looking back on his adventures in the so-called haunted house, he could not recall one which did not now appear wholly fantastic, as a remembered dream must seem fantastic in the sane light of normal day. Being a very practical young man, he believed that he had been the victim of a sinister joke, or the antics of very eccentric people. He even began to question the good faith of Falkland, and possibly the good faith of Beale. Being also a young man of some leisure, and a very enterprising turn of mind, and seeing in all this considerable material for his work—for he was a journalist and an artist of some reputation—he decided not to let the matter drop, but to take it at least a stage further.

He had a certain amount of money, and that same day he went up north to the small village where Beale had a commission to paint a couple of pictures. It was evening before Compton found Beale, working away, pleasantly and cheerfully, in a barn which had been arranged as a temporary studio, and where he was busily engaged on the two portraits, which turned out to be, not those of human beings, but of dogs. Compton was reminded of the kennels at "Mockways," and Mathews' story of Falkland's visit to see the Golden Labradors.

Beale seemed surprised to see him, and very eager to know the outcome of his visit to "Mockways"; and Compton told him all that had occurred—and told it with a humorous and even mocking intonation. But Beale listened very seriously. He frowned, and said at once:

"I don't care for that at all; no, Compton, I don't like the sound of it."

And Compton laughed.

"Certainly," he admitted, "it appears very romantic; but what can there be in it? Somebody is fooling—that is certain; but I don't think there's more than fooling in it."

But Beale said it was rather like a jigsaw puzzle, each little bit seemed incoherent nonsense, taken by itself but, all taken together, they made a perfectly coherent and even commonplace picture.

"And I think that is where we stand now," he said. "We are stumbling about with little odd bits, each meaning nothing in itself, very important as part of a whole. I think we ought to get Falkland out of 'Mockways.' "

"I don't see how we can," remarked Compton. "He had the chance to come with me. He might have made a fair get-away, but he wouldn't. There was the question of this girl: he could not leave her. Of course, I don't know anything about it—whether she was sane or not; but that was his attitude; that he could not leave her in the hands of Manning and Dobree."

"I quite understand that," agreed Beale. "I don't suppose you or I would have left her, Compton, if it had come to it. Of course, everything else you say may be part of a joke, or a series of coincidences; or it may not. And I think our obvious course is to get hold of Falkland—to write to him or go and see him, to try to get things on a more commonplace plane. They can't keep him shut up there a prisoner.

Compton smiled.

"Well, I don't know so much about that. It's an extraordinarily lonely place, standing in the middle of very large grounds, and I should say that, if they wanted to, they *could* keep him a prisoner for a considerable time."

"Well, we can try," said Beale; "there is certainly something up, and even if it's only lunacy or practical jokes, it ought to be stopped. There is the question, too, of the girl; supposing there *is* something in that, and she is being kept in 'Mockways' by force; it's not a pleasant thought, you must admit."

"Well," said Compton, "it seems to me that when you have finished your work here, we had better see what we can find out about Dobree and Manning, and, if possible, about this mysterious Sarah Lomax, whose name seems to be at the bottom of all the trouble. It should not be difficult to find out about a man like Dobree—a public character, and more or less living in the open, as it were."

"I can't get away at once," replied Beale. But he suggested that Compton should return immediately to London and find out what he could about Dobree and Manning.

That energetic young man was nothing loth to undertake this task, and the next day found him in London, doing his best to get the information that Beale had asked him to procure.

It was, of course, not at all difficult to find out the known facts about Dobree, although there appeared to be no one who knew very much about his early life. His public career went back about twenty or twenty-five years, when he had appeared on the scene as a promising financier; and since then he had never looked back, but gone on making money in several directions. Never had he mixed in any kind of society, nor shown any manner of activity beyond that of making money. He had never married, nor seemed to have had any intimate friends or relations; and Compton discovered without much effort that his name was not really Dobree at all, but Vane; the name "Dobree" had been assumed some years ago by letters patent; and he appeared to be of very obscure and humble origin, as, indeed, on several occasions, he had made a boast of himself.

It was more difficult to discover anything about Manning. He appeared to have come from abroad about twenty years or more ago, and had attached himself at once to Dobree, from whom he had been inseparable ever since. There was nothing for him or against him; his personality and his career seemed alike isolated; but Compton gathered that it was more than likely that his name also was assumed, and that with his old name he had left an old life behind him.

As for Isabel Conway, her story, as she had whispered it to Falkland at the agitated interview at "Mockways," was perfectly true. She had been working in Dobree's office—a post she had gained through her since dead father; and there she had attracted the kindness and attention of Dobree—and the attention, without the kindness, of Manning.

So far, the story was clear. But it also appeared clear, unfortunately, that the girl had "gone off her head," as Compton put it, and had had to be confined. But, so far as Compton could find out, she had always been treated with the greatest consideration and kindness, and considerable sums of money had been expended on her attempted cure. There had been nothing whatever sinister or mysterious in all this; nor could several days of close acute and clever investigations on the part of Compton discover anything to the discredit either of Manning or of Dobree.

As for the ill-reputed house of "Mockways," it had belonged to an old man named Powell, whose secretary Dobree had been in the days of his early career, and who had treated him with a good deal of affection; finally leaving him the house and a smallish sum of money.

Dobree had visited the house now and then during his life, but had very seldom been there for long and this continued desertion of the lonely building had no doubt gone to swell the reports as to its sinister reputation.

There were several famous ghost stories attached to "Mockways," but they all went back beyond the lifetime of Dobree, and even beyond that of Powell. "Mockways" seemed to Compton to have nothing to do with the present state of affairs.

Compton, who felt rather disappointed that he had discovered nothing whatever sensational, sent an account of these meagre results to Beale, and also sent off a wire to Falkland at "Mockways," asking him if he could come to London on important business. He did this as a test, to see if Falkland would answer, and to give him a chance, if he got the wire, to leave "Mockways." He still felt rather uneasy at the thought that the young man whom he had seen in that gloomy little room, and the young girl whom he had not seen, were prisoners in "Mockways."

When Beale returned to London, Compton gave him an even fuller account of all he had done.

"But there is one person," said Beale, "of whom you say nothing; and that person is the most important of all."

"Who is that?" asked Compton.

"Sarah Lomax, of course," smiled Beale. "She seems the key to the whole thing. Didn't you find out anything of a Sarah Lomax in Dobree's career?"

Compton was forced to admit that she was indeed the mystery of the case; and that he had found out nothing whatever about her.

"I think the whole thing is a hoax or a fraud," he declared. "I don't believe there *is* such a person as Sarah Lomax."

And Beale said:

"Well, there was certainly a girl following Dobree about—the girl who spoke to Falkland in the Bitterne woods; and that was the whole trouble. And according to what that fellow Mathews said, there was a girl, or somebody or other, hidden in 'Mockways'; and there was something they were looking for—something to do with Sarah Lomax. It's all very well, but I still believe there is something behind all this, and it's up to you and me to find out what it is. I've got a bit of leisure now, and a bit of money, and I don't mean to rest till I've got to the bottom of it all. I can't forgive that hoax of Manning's; I mean to get even with him on that score, if on no other."

While they, still hopefully, in the dark, were discussing their future plans, a letter arrived, addressed to Beale at the hotel where he was now staying. It was directed in an unknown hand, and when he came to open it it bore no address. There was merely one line, and that said: "Please use all your best endeavours to rescue Falkland and Isabel Conway. This is not a joke, but a matter of life and death." It was signed "Sarah Lomax."

CHAPTER XV

BEALE and Compton both found this letter maddening. There was no clue whatever as to the writer, and, discuss the matter as long and as wearisomely as they would, they could, of course, discover none.

Compton was more inclined than ever to treat the whole thing as a joke; but Beale was convinced that there was something serious behind it all.

"Even if it is a joke," he insisted, "we must investigate."

An answer had come to the telegram which they had sent to Falkland. It said:

"All well, but impossible to get away. Writing. Edward Falkland."

Of course, as Beale at once suggested, Manning could easily have forged this wire. He might have intercepted the telegram and sent this answer without having even let Falkland know anything of either.

"There's nothing for it," the artist insisted, "but to go to 'Mockways' ourselves, and try to force an entrance."

But Compton knew, from his own experience, that this was almost an impossibility.

"The man Mathews is scared to death," he said, "and there is no one else who could possibly let you in. And as for breaking in; I've done it once, and should not care to try again. I nearly got a bullet in me as it was."

Falkland must be given help, but neither of the young men could decide what form this help should take.

Compton had, however, made a note of the name of the

nursing home to which Miss Conway had been sent, and without very great trouble they found out that "The Elms," kept by a Dr. Milner, was situated in a very remote part of the Welsh Border not too far from "Mockways"; though, no doubt, Manning had made it appear a long way off by driving round and round roads unknown either to Miss Conway or to Falkland.

Beale and Compton then set off to visit this place, and find out what they could there of Isabel Conway.

On the afternoon, therefore, of a dankish autumn day, Beale and Compton, leaving their modest two-seater outside the big iron gates of "The Elms," walked up on foot along the straight and bleak drive towards the dull grey façade of the dingy-looking house.

"It seems ordinary enough," remarked Beale, "not the sort of place you would associate with any mystery."

"I don't suppose there's any mystery here," said Compton; "but it is just possible that these people were bribed to keep the girl more or less a prisoner, although they knew perfectly well that she was not insane; and then there is that rather dreadful Mamie, of whom Falkland spoke. We ought to be able to discover something about her. I don't suppose the Milners will be very easy people to handle, but at the same time I dare say we could find out something—not from the truth they tell, but from the truth they conceal. Very often you can discover a great deal," the shrewd young man added, "by the way people lie."

The house looked very blank, but there were curtains at the windows. No smoke came up from any of the chimneys, but a dog barked from a kennel round the corner.

With the last rusty leaves clinging to the boughs of the large, gaunt, dark trees, and a wintry, iron-coloured sky overhead, the place seemed dreary enough, and the young men agreed that it was the last sort of residence to which to send any one weak-minded, fanciful or sick.

"Enough," said Beale, "to give one melancholia, even if one were quite right when one came here. I must confess the look of this place makes me very much doubt the good faith of Dobree, taking the girl first here and then to 'Mockways' is not exactly the sort of thing any one would do with honest intentions."

He rang the old-fashioned iron bell which hung down by the pilasters at the door, which were now flaking plaster in the dampness of the wintry weather.

The bell clanged, giving a curious sense of emptiness inside the house. The two men listened to the echoes. They were unaccompanied by any footsteps. No one answered either the first, second or third ring, though Beale and Compton clanged louder and louder, and a dog barked fiercely at the jangling sound.

"They're all out," remarked Compton, "or they won't come" was Beale's comment. "I don't like the look of it at all. The place seems to have been uninhabited for some time."

"But what about the dog?" asked Compton. "Some one must be here to feed him. He's on a chain and his kennel is fairly clean. There's water, too, and bones."

They walked round the house, examining every possible entrance. There was a door at the side and a door at the back, but both were securely fastened. No knocking or rattling produced any answer whatever from the interior of the house.

They went back and surveyed the windows. Some of those had the blinds down, and some the curtains were drawn. At none was there any sign of life.

"A curious sort of nursing-home," scoffed Compton, ironically. "I suppose the patients are all dead."

But Beale could not take it all so easily; he felt a growing sense of uneasiness which was increased by the loneliness of the wintry landscape.

After having examined the house thoroughly, and having made all the noise they could to attract the attention of any possible inmate, the young men gave up the attempt in despair, and turned away down the long drive, decided to go direct to "Mockways" and try to get hold of Falkland by some means or other—either honestly to gain an entrance, or to climb in through the break in the railings that Compton remembered.

Before, however, they left "The Elms," they saw, to their delight, and old gardener, raking up the leaves under the trees. They asked him where Dr. Milner was, and if any one was in charge of the house.

The old man replied that Dr. Milner and his wife had left several days ago, and he did not know when, if ever, they were returning. In fact, he knew nothing at all, and repeated cross-questioning elicited no further information from him. He was either stupid, or had been told to be silent. There was just this much to be gathered from him; that the Milners were away, and for ever, he believed. As for patients, he did not know of any, nor could he remember Miss Isabel Conway. There had been a good many patients at one time, he said, but very few lately.

Nor could he tell them of any one who would be likely to give them any further information. The house was lonely, he declared—in fact, the only big house round about. The next large establishment of any kind was that of Mr. Dobree, at "Mockways."

"Well," said Beale, "I'm going on there. Perhaps I can find out there what I wanted to find out here." And he asked the old man to show them the way, bringing out his pocket-map and asking him to indicate the route.

The old fellow was incapable of doing this, but he was able to give them pretty fair directions as to how they might reach the sinister house. He was also full of ghost stories, confused horrors, signs and wonders connected with "Mockways," and advised them not to go near the place.

"Well," remarked Beale, grimly, "Mr. Dobree himself is in residence there, and a friend of mine is his secretary. I intend to pay him a visit."

They soon found themselves on the road which Compton remembered as that which he had taken when he had gone to "Mockways," and after a not so very long drive, they found themselves at the iron gates where Compton had looked through on his former visit.

There was the long, damp, dark avenue; there were the gaunt trees, now further stripped of leaves; indeed, almost bare against the darkening sky; and there was the long, high stone wall with the broken pieces of glass at the top.

The house they could not see; but that effect of the long, dreary, high wall and the long row of bare trees was gloomy enough, and Beale did not feel his spirits improved by the prospect.

He had not quite realised the utter loneliness of the place. "Well," he said, "we'd better try and get hold of that man Mathews. Perhaps when he sees two of us, he will try and pluck up courage to let us in."

And so he pealed the bell at the gate, which he had noticed was securely locked, barred and chained.

"I wonder," grinned Compton, "how our telegram got there. Somebody got it, even if it wasn't Falkland."

They had to ring several times before there was any response whatever, and their hopes were dying when Mathews appeared, shuffling through the greenery on the other side of the gate.

He greeted them as if he had never seen them before. Either he did not remember Compton, or was pretending that he had never seen him.

"What are you doing here, sir?" he asked, at once timidly and roughly. "No good any one coming here; that's been said again and again. This is 'Mockways,' and no one is allowed in."

"Don't you remember me?" asked Compton, "and all the stuff you told me?"

"No, I don't, sir," said Mathews, peevishly, making no effort whatever to open the gate. "I don't remember anybody; and you ain't going to get in; I can tell yer that. Them's my orders, and I sticks to 'em."

"But *I* think I *am* going to get in," said Beale, with more assurance than he really felt. "I want to see Mr. Falkland, Mr. Dobree's secretary."

"You can't," said Mathews. "They're all away; they've all gone to France."

CHAPTER XVI

THE two young men stood and gazed at Mathews gazing back at them between the stout bars of the large heavy gates; they felt quite helpless and hopeless.

No prospect could have been more dreary and depressing, the long sweep of the lonely road to right and left, the high wall with the jagged points of glass, the barricade of bare trees rising into the darkening sky, and in front this dank, sombre avenue cluttered with dead leaves, and the obstinate, scared looking little man clinging to the gate and refusing them admission.

Compton tried to take the high handed tone.

"Look here, my man," he said vigorously, "this won't do—we know perfectly well that Mr. Dobree *is* in 'Mockways,' and Mr. Falkland too—we had a telegram the other day——"

"I don't care what you had, sir," answered Mathews peevishly. "Mr. Dobree left for France this morning with Mr. Manning *and* Mr. Falkland, and Miss Conway and the nurse they call Mamie."

"You mean to say that you are staying here alone, then?" asked Beale.

"Yes, I've got my dogs, sir, and there's company enough. I've been caretaker here for years, sir, and I don't mind being alone——"

"You seemed frightened enough the other night," Compton reminded him. "What was that you were saying about Mr. Manning?"

At mention of that name Mathews interrupted with weak fury:

"I couldn't never have mentioned Mr. Manning to you, sir, for I've never seen you before."

"Come now," said Compton angrily, "don't you remember the other evening, in the avenue—and all the fine tales you told me? Warning me to get Mr. Falkland out of 'Mockways'? Well, it's partly because of that we're here now——"

But Mathews' wizened face hardened into a look of angry obstinacy.

"Then, sir," he replied sullenly, "you're a fool for your pains. How many times am I to tell you that I ain't seen you before?"

"But you're alone," remarked Beale pleasantly, "and therefore you might as well speak out—what have you to be frightened of, if every one is away?"

"I'm not frightened," retorted Mathews. "I'm telling you the truth—every one left for France this morning."

Thereupon, as a last resource, Beale drew from his pocket the letter signed "Sarah Lomax" which he had received in London and which contained a warning about the safety of Falkland in "Mockways"; leaning close to the gate Beale read it out to Mathews, adding:

"Here is another reason for our visit."

Mathews moved away from the gate, whimpering; there could be no possible doubt that the letter, or the name attached to the letter, had scared him badly though he persisted in his blank denials of everything.

"I don't know what you two gentlemen are getting at," he whined. "And my orders is strict no one is to come into 'Mockways'—and don't you try it," he added with meaning, "any other way—slipping in the back, or climbing over the railings—the dogs are loose now, every night——"

"Ah," said Compton, "you do remember how I got in before, then?"

"I remember nothing, sir," muttered Mathews. "And don't you remember nothing either, that's the wisest plan."

"You wouldn't lose by answering frankly," suggested Beale, putting his hand in his pocket, but at this hint of a bribe Mathews sneered bitterly.

"I've no more time to waste," he remarked sourly. "I'm not going to stay here all night, even if you like to."

And he turned away into the shadowed darkness of the avenue, for the twilight was descending, obscuring the sombre prospect.

"He is terrorised," said Beale, "that's clear—nothing to be got out of him. Are you, though, sure that is the same man who spoke to you before? Moonlight is very deceptive."

But Compton was quite sure; he had, he said, observed the fellow very closely, and could not have been mistaken.

"But now," he added, "what are you going to do? Would you like to try to get in my way and see for yourself if the house is empty or not?"

"I don't suppose it is as easy now as you found it," smiled Beale. "No doubt they are on the look out for trespassers——"

"They may really be all away," suggested Compton. "Dobree may have swept them all off to France. We ought to have asked that old fool their address!"

"Of course he would only have lied."

But Compton again pealed the great iron bell; this time there was no response; Mathews had evidently decided not to appear again.

After a brief consultation the young men drove off to the spot where Compton, after an exhaustive search, had found his entrance into "Mockways." Leaving the car where the road wound into a footpath round the side of the mountain, they proceeded by the light of electric torches to where the ditch and railings marked the boundary of Mockways Park from the open, wild countryside.

Compton was able to find the place where he had forced

himself in—there was the broken bracken and trodden earth where he had scrambled through the ditch, and there should have been the gap in the railings, mended by fencing that he had been able to struggle over—but there it was no longer; the railings had been repaired; tall, spear headed rails rose up six feet or so and behind them a large wolf hound was running up and down, baying savagely; he was answered by distant howls.

It was clear that the park was full of loose, fierce dogs.

"Well, they're up to our little game," said Compton ruefully. "I don't see much sense in trying to force in there even if we could—"

As he spoke the dog hurled himself at the railings, furious at the lights and the strangers, and the two young men put out their torches and beat a hasty retreat into the bracken.

"If there is any one there," remarked Beale dryly, "they'll soon find out where we are by the way that beast's behaving——"

"It's obvious they are ready for us," Compton agreed, and as if by a common instinct they hurried down the rough slope of bracken—each with the same thought, that if any one had taken or tampered with the car, they were in a fairly unpleasant position. It was, however, where they had left it, and it was with some relief that they jumped in and drove off.

The whole incident had made a deep impression even on Compton, practical and hard headed as he was; there seemed to him something very sinister about the flat denial with which Mathews had met him, the mended railing and the prowling dogs—and the fact that it was all so intangible added to the vague horror with which Compton was beginning to regard the episode of Falkland and "Mockways."

As for Beale, he was quite convinced that there was something very odd at the bottom of the mystery, but he had not the slightest clue as to what this might be; he felt both puzzled and uneasy, and, what was worse than either sensation, helpless.

The young men decided not to return to London but to put up at the nearest town to "Mockways," a fair sized ancient cathedral city about twenty-five miles from the hateful house; they both thought that it would be odd if they could not discover something of Dobree's movements and reputation and something of the history of the former owner of "Mockways," old Mr. Powell who appeared to have founded the fortunes of Vane as Dobree was then called.

But they soon discovered that a wealthy man may very easily cover up his tracks; telephone calls and prepaid wires to all the various addresses in London associated with Dobree produced no results—the one formula was the reply to all inquiries: "Mr. Dobree is out of town, letters will be forwarded."

Nor was a day spent in cautious investigation in the old city more fruitful; no one seemed to know anything of Dobree nor of "Mockways" beyond that the first was very wealthy and the second haunted. Dobree did not appear to ever come to the old country town nor to deal with any of the people there, and neither Compton not Beale were lucky enough to find any one who had known Mr. Powell, who had died thirty years before in "Mockways" an eccentric recluse.

On the second day of their search, Compton pointed out a paragraph in one of the morning papers:

"*Mr. Jessamy Dobree has left 'Mockways' for his villa in Mentone; Miss Isabel Conway, his niece, accompanies Mr. Dobree.*"

"Niece, eh?" said Beale. "We know that's a lie; the girl is no relation whatever."

"Still, his ward, and I suppose he might call her that," objected the practical Compton. "The question is—is it true? Have they all gone to Mentone? If so, we'll have to give it up. I don't see how we can go racing over the continent after them—with really nothing to go on."

Beale felt baffled too, but by no means reassured; the fact that nothing whatever was to be discovered about these two men seemed the reverse of satisfactory, as if money and influence had been used to keep their careers profoundly quiet; of course, as Compton kept continually saying, there was "nothing to go upon" save the queer behaviour of Manning towards himself and the wild tale told by Falkland to Compton when he had adventured into "Mockways."

But these things were, to Beale, sufficient.

Yet he was held up, at a loose end—completely baffled and he had begun to think that he must return to London and for the moment abandon the chase of Falkland.

Swift on this resolution an incident occurred that gave him a little hope, even a possible clue.

He had seen in a small old fashioned print shop outside the cathedral close an ancient water colour drawing of "Mockways," done perhaps a hundred years ago when the house was neat and trim and the gardens well kept and before the great gloomy cedar tree had been planted at the side.

Beale at once went into the shop and made inquiries about the drawing, and incidentally, about the house, excusing himself by saying that he was a painter himself and would like to paint "Mockways"—which was true enough, he reflected grimly, since his wish to paint the haunted house had been the beginning of all the trouble for poor Falkland.

"Well, sir," smiled the shopkeeper, "you won't ever get permission to paint 'Mockways"—there's a heap of people would like to get inside that place, it's got such a name for being haunted, but he won't have any one near it——"

"I know—is he there now?" asked Beale casually.

"I'm sure I don't know, sir."

Beale made a few fruitless inquiries about Powell, bought the drawing, and left the shop; thinking no more of the matter than as another hopeless attempt to elucidate the mystery of "Mockways."

But that evening the boy who brought the drawing (which was so large and heavily framed that Beale had asked for it to be sent round to the inn) sent a message in to say that if the gentleman was interested in "Mockways" his grandfather could tell him "all about it, and about Mr. Powell too."

Beale at once set off with the boy to find this valuable old man.

CHAPTER XVII

THE old man, whose name was Clement, lived in a charming little house in a tiny, paved alley on the outskirts of the town towards the river, which flowed so gracefully through the meadows by the cathedral. Beale discovered him sitting up in an easy-chair beside the fire, wrapped in a great shawl and looking forward very eagerly to the appearance of his visitor.

He excused himself from rising, declaring that he was too feeble to do so, but he seemed, for all that, a very lively and intelligent old man, with slight sign of age or decrepitude about him. His senses had not yet failed him—nor, it appeared, his memory, for no sooner was Beale sitting on the other side of the bright, leaping fire than he began at once a whole string of reminiscences about "Mockways" and old Mr. Powell.

But Beale cut him short; he did not want to hear a whole lot of legends of hundreds of years ago, which could have very little bearing on Dobree and Falkland—to say nothing of Manning. He wanted to know something of the immediate history of "Mockways," and not legends and tales that old Clement had heard when he was a child, related to him by his grandfather.

"Can't you tell me," he said, gently interrupting the old man's eager flow of memories, "something definite about old Mr. Powell? He is the person I am interested in and Mr. Vane—who is now Mr. Dobree, the present owner of 'Mockways.' I should rather like to hear something about him; but perhaps you never knew him, or do not remember anything of him."

But the old man declared that this was not so. He had, he

said, been employed at "Mockways" when he was young, had stayed there almost to old age and could remember perfectly old Mr. Powell and young Mr. Vane, as he had then been.

"Mr. Vane," he said, with a certain pride in imparting the knowledge, "was nothing, sir; no more than I was myself; only he took the fancy of old Mr. Powell, and got into his favours."

"What do you mean," asked Beale, "by saying 'he was nothing'? I always understood that he came from humble beginnings: do you quite know what these were?"

And old Clement declared, with some vigour and indignation, that he had been nothing but a ragged street boy, running about this very town, and had gone up to "Mockways" as odd boy in the kitchen and garden—to help him, the very old man who sat there now.

It seemed to Beale extremely unlikely, but he was not able to refute the statement. He knew very well how reports about well-known people became exaggerated; and, not wishing to check the old man, bade him say what else he knew.

"Well, sir, I remember them two gentlemen you were talking about. Young Vane, as I say, was just an odd boy when I was there, working in the garden; and Mr, Powell, he was that eccentric that he took a great liking to him, and young Vane being sharp, was able to make his advantage out of it, and soon got to do Mr. Powell's work for him—helping him with old books and papers. He seemed to pick up a bit of education as he went along, and got right into old Mr. Powell's favour, so that he could do almost everything with him."

"Yes," said Beale; "so I've always understood; in fact, Mr. Powell left him all his property, didn't he—'Mockways,' and a little bit of money?"

"More than a little bit," smiled old Clement. "He left him a very good bit; Mr. Powell was a miser, sir, and had a great deal of money hoarded away. I don't think that Vane would ever have made the big fortune he did without old Mr. Powell's money to start with."

This, in truth, was rather a revelation to Beale, who had always understood that the sum of money left to Vane and Dobree had been almost insignificant.

"I don't say," added the old man, "that young Vane didn't work for his money; for years he lived in that lonely place, shut up with the old man—who wasn't an easy customer, I can tell you! Putting up with him and all his whims, and quite cut off from every one. But as he was one of those homeless orphans, that mattered less; for there was no one to miss him. Anyhow, he feathered his nest pretty well, and wasn't liked for the doing of it, I can tell you. Then, when Mr. Powell died, he went away from the neighbourhood, and we never saw much more of him. I am talking of thirty years ago, sir, though it do seem like yesterday to me. I got sent off when Mr. Powell died and came here to live with my son."

Beale could not see much assistance for his own particular matters in all this, and, though he sat there and let the old man talk for another half-hour or so, he got nothing more out of him than these rather rambling and incomplete reminiscences; and all it seemed to amount to was that Vane, a sharp and, no doubt, unscrupulous youth, had used every means to acquire influence over the eccentric and perhaps weak-minded miser, and had in the end done so and inherited all his means.

"But," he remarked aloud, stopping the flow of the old man's narrative, "there is really no harm in that, you know; especially as I suppose old Mr. Powell had no one else to whom to leave his fortune."

"Ah, hadn't he, though?" said old Clement, with a cunning look. "That was just where all the trouble came in, and where all the nasty things began to be said."

"Oh!" exclaimed Beale, pricking up his ears. "Nasty things were said, were they, and there was trouble? . . . It's just what I want to find out."

"Oh, I see!" said the old man, with more sense than Beale would have credited him with. "You want to find out something of Mr. Dobree's past, do you, sir? That isn't what I understood: I thought you was going to write a book about the legends of 'Mockways.' "

Beale could not help smiling, for this was indeed the excuse that he had given the child.

"I dare say," continued the old man, without giving him time to answer, "that when a man has got on like Mr. Dobree has got on, and makes the money he has made, there are a lot of people would like to find out something funny in his past."

"I am not out for that sort of information," Beale hastened to say.

But the old man interrupted querulously, with the peevishness of old age not being allowed full play for talk.

"I don't care if you are, sir," he said. "I don't care if any harm happens to Mr. Dobree; he was never a friend of mine, and very shabbily he treated all of us who were working at 'Mockways' when he came into his money: he and that fellow Manning."

"Ah!" cried Beale. "So then you also know something of Mr. Manning?"

"Yes," smiled Clement, nodding his head, delighted to be able to give the information required and to feel himself, after years of neglect, as of some importance. "Yes; I know something about Mr.

Manning—and not to his credit, either, I may tell you. It was he who got hold of Mr. Vane—or Mr. Dobree, as I suppose I ought to call him."

"Got hold of him?" Beale could not keep the eagerness from his voice. "What do you mean by saying 'Got hold of him?' "

"Well, I think he rather frightened Mr. Dobree: he managed to find out a thing or two—I don't know what, and I shouldn't care to commit meself; but, you see, sir, there was a question of the wife."

"The wife!" exclaimed Beale. "This is the first I've heard of her. Who was she? Whose wife do you mean?"

"I mean Mr. Powell's wife; he married, you see, sir, late in life, and there was a quarrel, and she ran away—and he never would have her back. We used to say that Mr. Dobree took good care he *didn't* have her back, or in any way help her."

"Ah!" said Beale. "Were there any children?"

"No," replied Clement. "I don't think there were any children, sir; but it was all a bit before my time. I remember," he added, "that when Mr. Powell died there was a great hunting for something in 'Mockways'—something in a '*papier mâché* box.' "

CHAPTER XVIII

AT the words "*papier mâché* box," Beale became all animation. "Have you," he asked, eagerly, "any idea what was in the box?"

No, Clement had no idea at all. He could only remember the incident after all these years because it had been impressed on his mind by the fact that a large reward had been offered. It was soon after old Mr. Powell's death, he said.

"Mr. Manning and Mr. Dobree were both there, and when they were winding up Mr. Powell's affairs they offered us—that's the servant's I mean, sir—a big reward if we could find a certain *papier mâché* box. Vane said that old Mr. Powell had probably hidden it somewhere, and that it might have in it some jewels which were missing; for the old man used to collect jewels, sir, and it seems there was a box of them which they could not find. There were three of us employed there; the other two are long since dead, sir, and you may be sure we hunted high and low, in the house and out of the house. I never saw such a place for passages and secret doors and traps. A lot of them was made when the house was built, and a great many more had been put in by old Mr. Powell when he bought it: for he was as queer as you please, and always liked to think there was plenty of places he could hide in. He had a kind of terror, as you may say, sir, of being found, and got to live, as he became older, more and more hidden away."

"And you never knew any more as to the contents of this same box?" urged Beale. "Beyond the rumour that there were some precious stones in it?"

And Clement repeated that he had never heard anything beside that.

"What could there be?" he added, ingenuously, "except the precious stones, sir, that could have been worth that sum?"

Beale was silent, but he did not think it likely that men like Dobree and Manning would come back to "Mockways" after thirty years to look for jewels: a search which had been given up as hopeless so long before. Dobree had now sufficient money to buy all the jewels he needed, and he need not go to these lengths to discover the treasure of old Mr. Powell. Beale felt convinced that, if the *papoer mâché* box had ever existed, it had contained something more valuable and important than mere jewels. He did not, however, confide this suspicion to the old man, but led him on to relate further anecdotes of his service with Mr. Powell, when Dobree—or Vane—had been his secretary and attendant.

He gathered from Clement's rambling relation that Powell had been eccentric indeed—almost to the point of craziness; and the story that Mathews had told Falkland was curiously confirmed by Clement's chuckling narration of a room full of waxworks that Mr. Powell had made for his amusement and kept locked away in a remote room of "Mockways."

"I dare say, sir," smiled the old man, "that it was them waxworks gave 'Mockways' a bad name. They were very queer figures, some of them, I can tell you, and seeing them suddenly, sitting about at the windows—as Mr. Powell used to put them—was enough to make any one think of ghosts. Not," he added, "that there may not have been some ghosts as well: there's one or two queer stories told about 'Mockways,' long before Mr. Powell bought the place."

"I don't want to hear those," interrupted Beale. "Only all

you can tell me of what you saw and heard yourself, when you were in service there."

But the old man now declared that there was nothing more, except a good deal of trivial information about the daily life and habits of the miser, who had made his money abroad in youth and middle age, and then chosen to retire from the world in this peculiar manner, taking no joy in anything but the hoarding up of his money.

"That's why he bought 'Mockways,' sir: it was the loneliest house he could find, and a bad reputation kept people away. But, you see, he wasn't safe, even there: young Vane took hold of him right enough, and had all the money in the end."

"I suppose," asked Beale, "you never heard the name of Sarah Lomax?"

He watched the old man's face closely as he spoke, but Clement showed no change in his countenance as he answered glibly that he had never heard that name.

"No one seems to have heard it," said Beale, rather bitterly; "but it is the name, or the assumed name, of some one who has a great deal to do with 'Mockways' and Dobree; and I would give a lot to find out who she is. And then Manning," he added. "There is something curious there. If Vane got hold of Powell, how did Manning get hold of Vane?"

Clement shook his head. He could remember Manning coming to "Mockways," but did not know where he came from or the object of his visit.

"Mr. Vane went away to stay for a while, and when he came back he brought Mr. Manning with him; both young they were, but Mr. Manning's a bit older, I think. He would have been then about five-and-twenty. I always understood, sir, that he was a medical student—a kind of doctor. He used to look after Mr. Powell in his illness, and the old man swore by him, saying he and his medicine did him a power of good."

"Oh, a doctor, eh?" said Beale, thinking of the Milners' nursing home, and a possible connection there.

"Well, I don't know about a doctor, sir, but one learning to be one. I think he gave up the doctoring when he got in with Mr. Vane."

This was about all the information that Beale could extract from the ancient gardener of "Mockways." Better than nothing, no doubt, but it did not lead him very far.

When he returned to his inn and related to Compton what he had discovered, that hard-headed young man was more inclined than ever to say there was nothing in the "Mockways" affair. Of course, he admitted the hunt for the *papier mâché* box was a curious coincidence, but one that, like most coincidences, might be explained away. Anyhow, he could not see what it had to do with the supposed detention of Falkland in "Mockways."

"Unless," answered Beale, "they think he knows where it is, or intends to look for it."

And there they had to leave the matter, since this discussion only took them over and over the same ground.

The next morning, as Beale was putting his things together preparatory to leaving, the maid came up and said a young lady wanted to speak with him.

"A young lady?" repeated Beale, amazed.

"Yes, sir, and she says it's important."

"Does she not give a name?" asked Beale eagerly.

"Yes, sir—Miss Sarah Lomax!"

CHAPTER XIX

NEVER had Beale felt so delighted and surprised; it seemed to him as if he had been long fumbling in the dark and then come suddenly into the light.

Compton was out and Beale could therefore not confide his good luck to any one; he hastened downstairs to the stuffy little parlour with cases of birds and fishes and dark furniture which was the only public room in the inn, and opened the door with the greatest possible expectancy; here at last would surely be a complete "clear up" of the mystery, if mystery it was.

A small fire had been lit in the old fashioned grate and near this stood a young woman of an ordinary appearance, carelessly dressed, but with an air of considerable resolution and strength; her face was pallid but not unhealthy, her eyes, dark and serene, conveyed remarkable power.

Beale was as impressed by her personality, the moment he entered the room, as if he had been speaking to her, standing close to her and holding her hand.

"You are Sarah Lomax?" he asked eagerly.

"Yes," she replied, "and you are Henry Beale, the painter? I know a little about you, you see."

Beale asked her to sit down, and if he might smoke? She nodded without replying and seated herself on one of the worn horse-hair chairs; the young man would have given a good deal to know if this was the girl who had spoken to Falkland in Bitterne woods—he was, in that respect, at her mercy, he had no means of testing the truth of what she said.

"I wrote to you," she began, "at the hotel where you were staying in London—you got that letter?"

"Yes."

"And acted upon it, I hope, Mr. Beale?" the girl asked in a business like manner.

"Well, there's a good deal in the answer to that," he replied cautiously. "It would help things awfully if you would explain yourself, Miss Lomax, I'm a god deal in the dark——"

The girl replied with a kind of subdued passion:

"I can't explain myself, I'm tied hand and foot, I'm a good deal in the dark myself."

"But you can tell me what you know and how you are involved in this affair," he uttered.

"What affair?" she demanded with a darkening of her peculiar eyes. "What affair do you mean, Mr. Beale?"

"The business of Mr. Dobree—are you the lady who spoke to Edward Falkland in Bitterne woods?" he added abruptly.

"I am," she replied, "and what I said to him has involved him in trouble—I want to make amends for that."

"You gave him your name, if it is your name, Miss Lomax, and told him to mention it to Mr. Dobree——"

"Yes," she admitted sharply. "That was wrong of me—I saw him save Mr. Dobree's life and heard Mr. Dobree repulse his request—about 'Mockways.' I was quite close to them in the twilight," she added with an odd smile, "though they were too excited to notice me—and I could not resist giving my name to Mr. Falkland to see what effect it might have on Mr. Dobree. I was moved to that," she continued quietly, "by the mention of 'Mockways.' An odd coincidence that they should speak of 'Mockways,' Mr. Beale."

"What effect did you think it might have on Mr. Dobree?" asked the young man.

"I thought," she replied with every appearance of candour, "that he would at once give Mr. Falkland what he wanted—it never occurred to me,"—her level voice was very bitter—"that he would dare to kidnap him——"

"Kidnap?" exclaimed Beale. "You call it that, do you? He offered Falkland a secretaryship——"

"A mere blind," she interrupted impatiently. "He kidnapped him, Mr. Beale, getting you safely out of the way first by an audacious trick, and he took him straight to 'Mockways' and kept him a prisoner."

"Why?"

"That is what I would like to know," said the energetic young woman grimly. "I believe I do know, but cannot be sure of it yet; what was only a deep suspicion has become almost a certainty through the behaviour of Mr. Dobree—he must," she added passionately, "have been very frightened to have acted like that—to have dared to act like that."

"Why should he be frightened?"

"That I cannot, I must not say," she replied. "I have watched—but I have not been able to act. Edward Falkland knows nothing," she continued quickly, "but he will not be able, now, to convince Dobree *or* Manning of that——"

"Is Falkland still in 'Mockways?' " asked Beale. "It has been given out that they have all gone to France——"

"A lie. He is still there. They are all there. Dobree has money and influence—there is nothing he cannot carry off in that way. I have nothing but my own resolution."

And that was sufficient, Beale thought, looking at her, to combat even money and influence.

"Mr. Falkland is nothing to me," she continued steadily, "but I involved him in this and should not like evil to happen to him——"

"Do you think it could?"

"I do."

"And you won't tell me why?"

"I can't. Not yet. There is a secret, no foolery, nor ghost, nor insanity," she declared vigorously, "but what I know I can speak of. I want no help. But I would like you to get your friend out of this. Only you must be very careful."

"I should think so," replied Beale grimly, remembering his unsuccessful attempt to enter "Mockways." "You seem to be setting me a very difficult task, Miss Lomax. Is it something that you could go to the police about?"

"It is not," she replied scornfully. "If it had been it would have been settled long ago."

"Tell me," asked Beale, "is this matter personal to you and Mr. Dobree?"

"I have never," said the girl, "spoken to Mr. Dobree in my life."

Beale was as baffled and bewildered as he had been when, so full of hope, he had entered the room; it was clear to him that he could not make this resolute and formidable young woman say a word more than she wished to say.

She now rose, as if the interview was over, and Beale asked rather desperately:

"Will you assure me that all this is not a trick or a joke on your part?"

"I can," she answered seriously, "assure you of that."

"And can you tell me anything of the lady also in 'Mockways'—Miss Conway?"

"I know very little of her—she was in Mr. Dobree's employment and then adopted by him—Mr. Manning wishes to marry her, I believe, and seems to be forcing Dobree to bring pressure on Miss Conway——"

"Who is, then, in a ghastly position shut up in that horrible house," exclaimed Beale. "I suppose it is not true that she is insane or partially insane?"

"I do not believe it," replied the girl grimly, "but I have no doubt they will succeed in making her so if she is not got away from 'Mockways'——"

"That's very ugly!" cried Beale furiously, "worse than kidnapping Falkland! And I don't know what to do, I feel so helpless!"

"I, too, am helpless," she replied calmly. "I would save Miss Conway if I could though she is no concern of mine. There is a certain *papier mâché* box," she sighed. "I believe they are looking for that——"

Beale recalled the tale he had heard from the ancient gardener, old Clement, and exclaimed:

"After all these years! It seems incredible!"

"How do you know," she asked sharply, "that they were looking for it years ago?"

He told her briefly of his visit of the day before to the old man.

"That is interesting," she said thoughtfully. "I dare say it is true. The old man would remember that—the big reward offered for such a trivial thing."

"There were supposed to be valuable jewels in it."

"I don't think there were," she replied coldly. "Perhaps there never was such a box—I don't know, but I believe they are looking for it and that they think that Mr. Falkland is looking for it too. I can't say any more."

"I wish you would," pleaded Beale. "I feel so helpless——"

"So do I," she interrupted dryly. "I cannot tell you anything more, but I will swear to my good faith in what I have said."

"And can't you tell me where I can find you? Where to write you?"

She shook her head.

"I have no address. I dare say we shall not meet again. If I could do more I would. I am devoted to one task and nothing must interfere with that."

She picked up her gloves and handbag, and, saying "good-bye," left the room abruptly. Beale went after her, but she passed swiftly down the dark passage and into the busy High Street; Beale followed her to the door; she was soon lost to sight in the crowds of mid-morning shoppers.

Beale knew it would be useless to pursue her; he went back into the inn and told the whole interview to Compton who had now returned and was getting the car ready for their departure.

That young man was both very interested and very disappointed and inclined to blame Beale for not getting "more out of her" as he put it; but Beale knew well enough that no one would be able to get out of the girl who called herself "Sarah Lomax" more than she wished to tell.

The sum of their rapid consultation was a long letter which they despatched to Edward Falkland at "Mockways"; and a departure for London where that at once set to work on the trail of Mr. Powell, the very wealthy, crazy old man, with his collection of jewels and waxworks who had died in "Mockways" thirty years ago leaving all his money to young Vane, his secretary, now Mr. Jessamy Dobree.

"There's the beginning of it all," declared Compton, "as far as I can put two and two together—Vane, helped by Manning, who sprang from goodness knows where, did Powell's wife out of the money, securing it for himself—he must have been a very shrewd, patient young man to put up with that life at 'Mockways' for years and you may be sure he had his reward for for it—I expect he and Manning practically forced the old fellow to make a will in their favour—of course, it doesn't all fit in, yet, but I expect you'll find old Powell's money at the bottom of it——"

Beale was inclined to agree, and to think that the *papier mâché* box, if such had ever existed, had contained a perhaps later will leaving the hoarded Powell fortune to the wife.

But this theory soon fell to the ground, for the first investigations proved that the Powell fortune was non-existent; a perusal of the old man's will at Somerset House proved that he had nothing to leave; tales of wealth and jewels had been tales indeed; the old man was no miser, but a recluse living on a small annuity that died with him, and all he had left to his secretary and attendant, young Vane, was the dilapidated house of "Mockways" and the contents thereof "for long, faithful and unpaid services."

CHAPTER XX

COMPTON was inclined to think that this discovery of the contents of old Mr. Powell's will took away all suspicion from the conduct of Dobree. He seemed, on the face of it, to have behaved, far from disgracefully, very well indeed. For years—probably out of gratitude—he had served "faithfully," as the will said, "and unpaid," this difficult, sickly and tiresome old man (for such Mr. Powell had been, by all accounts) and served him with no prospect of any reward.

Beale thought regretfully of the tale of the *papier mâché* box and the jewels; it had now to be dismissed as a fable. Either the old gardener, Clement, was in his dotage, or had been romancing and exaggerating, as very old people often like to romance and exaggerate when relating what they consider the wonders of their youth.

At the same time, neither of the young men could wholly dismiss the visit of the girl calling herself "Sarah Lomax," nor what she had said.

Beale, in particular, who had seen and spoken to her, was convinced of her sincerity.

"She may be mistaken," he declared, "but I am sure she is not lying or fooling. She believes there is *something* there."

"But why," asked Compton, impatiently, "could she not say what that *something* was? It seems absurd to expect us to work in the dark."

That evening they found, at Compton's rooms in Bloomsbury (the address which they had given Falkland in the letter which they had sent to him at "Mockways") an answer to their previous communication. It was typewritten, but signed in what seemed, to their keenest scrutiny, to be the handwriting of Edward Falkland.

The note was brief, and couched in the liveliest strain. It rebuked them for their fears as to his safety, and treated all the preceding incidents as a joke. It declared that he (Falkland) was quite happy in "Mockways," and most interested in the investigations which were being made in the haunted house. Dobree, he declared, was the most considerate and amiable of employers, and there was nothing against Manning except his appearance, and a rather odd fancy for crude practical jokes. Miss Conway was also quite well and happy in the care of an experienced nurse. Some servants had now joined the establishment, which was fairly comfortable. Dobree wished it to be believed that he had gone to France, for the reputation of "Mockways" was such that there was always some one trying to gain admission in the hope of seeing or hearing some ghostly phenomena.

The letter concluded with a cheery invitation to both the young men to come and spend the following week-end at "Mockways," and see for themselves how baseless was all the mystery that had somehow been worked up round Dobree and Manning.

"A trap," suggested Compton, as he finished the letter. "What do you think, eh?"

They decided to reply to it by a wire, in which they said: "Impossible get down to 'Mockways,' can't you run up to town for the day and talk things over?" If Falkland is really free there was no reason why he should not come! Compton argued.

"And if it is all a trap, well, then, it will show Manning that we are not really so easily deceived."

The wire was not answered, and their suspicions were confirmed. All the same, Beale was for a second attempt on "Mockways." He could not, he said, endure to remain inactive any longer.

Having taken what he considered due precautions, Compton was quite ready for another visit to "Mockways." They arrived at that ill-reputed house in the late afternoon of a dark day. The place looked exactly as it had looked before—just as gaunt and lonely and desolate—but to their surprise, Mathews came at the first ring and instantly admitted them.

CHAPTER XXI

BOTH the young men were very much taken aback by this ready response to their ring. There was something more sinister in it, somehow, than there had been on the other occasion, when Mathews, with his white, wizened face pressed to the bars, had so long and obstinately refused them admittance; and even Compton, hard-headed as he was, could not wholly suppress a shudder as he stepped into that dank avenue into which he had before peered so long and so vainly.

"You're Mr. Compton and Mr. Beale, aren't you?" asked Mathews, with a servile air. "Mr. Dobree is expecting you. He told me I was to look out for you, and admit you immediately."

"Very kind of you, I'm sure," said Beale, sarcastically. "A pity you couldn't have acted like this before, Mathews, when you told us that they had all gone to France."

"I told you what I was bid to say," replied Mathews, sullenly. "Mr. Dobree has a fair job to keep curiosity-mongers away from 'Mockways,' and that was his excuse. I wasn't to know you was friends of his."

"Come, come," said Compton, briskly. "Don't go on with this nonsense, Mathews. You remember me, and what happened when we last met."

"I don't remember you at all, sir," returned the man, obstinately, "and if I was you I should have a short memory too, sir, now you have got inside 'Mockways.' "

He spoke these last words in a lower tone, and the young men exchanged glances in the twilight of the avenue. Was it possible that the man was trying to warn them of something or somebody?

He was walking a little in front of them under dank-looking laurels, which retained their coarse leaves even though all the other boughs were bare. But Beale stepped forward and shook him by the shoulder.

"Look here," said the young man, in a low voice, "You'd better let us know if there is any mischief afoot; we've got friends outside."

"That's no matter of mine," replied the old man, in a terrified whisper, "and I don't know what you mean, sir. You've come to stay the week-end at 'Mockways,' ain't you—the 'ouse as you always wanted to paint. Well, that's all there is to it, sir. Mr. Falkland will tell you all the rest there *is* to tell—about the ghosts and things," he added, with a shrill, quavering laugh. "About all them funny goings-on in 'Mockways,' sir, which so many like to investigate."

They had now come out on to the blank space of grass that served as a lawn, and Beale saw for the first time, full in front of him, the house of which he had heard so much.

It still looked very like the old water-colour he had bought in the ancient cathedral town. It stood up square, dark and blank against the gloomy, late afternoon sky. The big cedar tree in which Compton had hidden during his daring visit was gloomy, hard, of bitter blackness at one's side, casting a gloomy shadow on the neglected ground, which was still cumbered with a sad litter of dead and decaying leaves and rubbish.

The house was ugly enough, and there was also certainly something very unpleasant in its cold, hard aspect. There was also an air very grim and impressive in the neglected grounds, the masses of bare trees and the tangled undergrowth that flanked the house on either side. It seemed as if many, many years had elapsed since any one made their dwelling here. Surely it had not been touched since old Mr. Powell led his secluded life here with young Vane as his attendant!

The light was too poor for Beale to be able to distinguish the masks and pilasters that had fascinated him in the photograph in the guide book. He could only see the blank squares of the house and the darker blot of the tree at the side.

There were no lights in any of the windows save that on the left of the door, which was uncurtained, and illuminated by the reddish glow of what Beale took to be an oil lamp.

"A rough king of a place, sir," said Mathews, peering up at him as they crossed the space of neglected grass. "No electric light here, sir; no telephone; no anything, as you might say. Just yerself and the ghosts."

"Ghosts don't trouble me," said Beale.

"Nor me!" added Compton. "We haven't come here to bother about ghosts."

They thought it as well to let Mathews know from the first that they were not easily to be frightened by any tricks or pretended apparitions.

"I suppose you haven't seen any ghosts yourself?" added Compton, as they approached the house. "No result to all the investigations that have been going on, eh?"

"I don't know," said Mathews, in a voice that seemed to sink to a whisper, "what I have seen and what I ain't seen, sir. It ain't my business to tell no tales. Ghosts there is at 'Mockways,' and them as looks for 'em will no doubt find 'em."

They had now reached the narrow front door, which Mathews opened at once, and ushered them into the gloomy hall with the drab-coloured paper and one feeble light, a low-turned lamp on a bracket. He then preceded them into the room which had shown the illuminated window across the lawn.

It was the sitting or dining-room—the main room of the house, it seemed: the one that had been most frequently used in the old days when Mr. Powell had closed up most of the rest of the house. But it was a gloomy enough apartment, high, with dreary long curtains at the long windows, now looped back on the darkening prospect of the deserted park.

There were one or two prints on the discoloured walls, and in the middle of the room an old-fashioned mahogany table, set out with a simple cold supper and a white glass oil lamp.

A big fire burned in the old-fashioned grate. The furniture was horsehair, and shabby. Compton and Beale took in all these details at a rapid glance.

Four people sat round the fire: Falkland, a girl, whom they at once took to be Isabel Conway, and two men whom they both knew by sight as Dobree and Manning. In the most ordinary, cheerful way, these were grouped together: the girl and Falkland were playing chess, the board being placed on a small table between them. The other two were watching the game and making jovial comments.

The same thought flashed through the minds of both the young men. It had been, after all, a fuss about nothing, and Falkland's letter was perfectly genuine.

Dobree rose and greeted them cordially.

"This is Mr. Beale, I believe," he said addressing the elder of the two young men, "the artist who wanted to paint 'Mockways.' Well, I'm glad to see you here at last. We have been carrying out a very interesting series of experiments. This is Mr. Manning, and this Miss Conway—and here's your friend Falkland."

The most usual and pleasant salutations were exchanged. Beale could discover nothing extraordinary in the appearance either of Falkland or his very pretty, nicely dressed companion. Manning was most civil, and Dobree more than pleasant. But Falkland knocked over a chessman near to Beale.

Beale stooped to pick it up.

Falkland stooped too, and Beale heard him whisper:

"*For Heaven's sake, get out of it! Get out of it, quick!*"

CHAPTER XXII

BEALE replaced the chessman on the board; he smiled as calmly as he could to conceal the sudden excitement that the flashing whisper had roused in him.

There was then "something up" and he and Compton had walked into a trap; he was thankful that they were both armed.

Evidently Falkland and the girl were terrorised, in the power of these two men and whatever allies they might have in the background. Beale reflected grimly—either under compulsion Falkland had written that letter or Manning had forged it.

Beale joined the group by the fire, looking out for an early opportunity to pass the warning on to Compton.

"Get out of it—get out of it—*quick!*" Falkland had said, and Beale was quickly revolving in his acute mind what this meant—were they then to escape and leave him to his fate?—leave him and the girl?

Had their appearance only added to Falkland's troubles?

Beale could not understand his advice; after all they were three to two now, the younger men, to say nothing of the help the girl might give.

The talk flowed on pleasantly from one to another, "making conversation" no doubt, but making it very agreeably; Manning had even the effrontery to refer to the trick he had played on Beale in Bitterne woods.

"Where ever did you go to?" he asked with his peculiar cringing smile. "Mr. Falkland was so disappointed when you did not turn up—I suppose you saw a view that pleased you and forgot about me! The absent-mindedness of genius, Mr. Beale!"

"Manning says he stopped to do something to the car," smiled Dobree, "and that you wandered away into the woods and he couldn't find you again——"

"Did I?" replied Beale, casually. "I missed Mr. Manning, anyhow—a pity, wasn't it?"

He was looking at the girl of whom he had heard so much; very delicate and pretty she was, with a fair, fragrant childish beauty more often described than seen; and, if half of what he had heard was true, she must be as brave as she was charming, for her position was atrocious.

She smiled and talked with Falkland, carefully moving her ivory pieces on the old-fashioned board, but Beale, scrutinising her closely under cover of the light conversation, saw that her eyes were shadowed underneath and her fine features strained; and, as he looked at her, she, conscious of his gaze, suddenly flashed at him a look of sheer terror.

That glance from Isabel Conway convinced Beale as it had convinced Falkland—both that she was absolutely sane and in deep distress.

"We live very simply here," Dobree was saying, "a perpetual picnic as you see!"

He smiled towards the supper on the table.

"We can't," he continued, "be troubled with servants, we content ourselves with Mamie and old Mathews who is a little eccentric himself," and Dobree laughed sourly. "What sort of a trick do you think he played the other day, Mr. Beale? Dressed up a dummy to look like himself and hung it from a beam in a dark corner of the shed. I'm afraid that it gave Mr. Falkland quite a fright."

"I shouldn't keep such a chap about," struck in Compton's resolute young voice, "especially in a place like this—he might go right off his head."

"Quite," agreed Manning, "quite. But 'Mockways' is so popular, Mr. Compton, so many people want to see or investigate the place that any ordinary servant might accept bribes to let them in. Poor old Mathews wouldn't do that—he is faithful."

"Yes," added Dobree smoothly, fixing his eyes, at once dull and heavy, on Compton, "we have a lot of bother with impertinent strangers here—one young rascal actually broke in through some damaged railings and gave me and Manning a fine chase—got up the cedar tree at the side of the house."

"A thief, I suppose," grinned Compton, by no means out of countenance.

"I dare say—though it must be well known that there is nothing valuable here," replied Dobree. "More likely an enterprising journalist, eh, Manning?"

Manning smiled towards Compton in a way that made even that bold young man feel faintly uncomfortable; he had rather forgotten that he would be instantly recognised as the intruder pursued through "Mockways" a few days ago.

Mamie came in with a tray; both Beale and Compton scrutinised her keenly enough; they saw an ordinary homely middle-aged woman of the lower classes, with rather hurried movements and quick eyes.

Beale suddenly asked after the car, which had been left at the gates. Manning replied that Mathews would see to it—there was a garage at his cottage though nothing but stables at the house itself.

Silence followed; the dull beams of the old opal glass lamp and the flickering light of the fire in the gloomy iron grate emphasised the sombre aspect of the room which was tall, gaunt and dismally furnished with old, faded and miserable looking furniture; the walls were covered with dingy discoloured paper and the ceiling was discoloured both by smoke and near the tall windows, damp.

Falkland and Isabel Conway played chess in silence; Mamie shuffled about with trays, setting out pickles, cold meat, cheese, biscuits and dried fruit.

Manning rose but with an effort as if he had grown drowsy; he would, he said, show the visitors their rooms.

"Funny old place, isn't it?" remarked Compton as they mounted the narrow, dreary stairs. "Full of trapdoors and secret passages and all that sort of thing, I suppose. You generally find," he added cheerfully, "that these houses which are supposed to be haunted have plenty of odd holes and corners for rats to run about in and the wind to whistle through."

"Yes, it is a rambling old place," replied Manning in an expressionless voice, "and only half-furnished—I'm afraid we shall have to put you right at the top—there are no free beds anywhere else——"

They followed him up the gloomy stairs which were only lit by little hand lamps on brackets here and there which just served to show the general neglect, the dusty walls, the uncarpeted treads, the broken banisters.

Manning opened two doors on the top landing and showed them into two smallish, almost attic rooms that looked, evidently, on the back of the house; the windows were small and barred.

"This used to be a nursery," smiled Manning, "in Mr. Powell's time——"

"A nursery?" questioned Compton sharply, "but Mr. Powell had no children——"

"Ah, you seem well informed! Perhaps it was before his time, then, but, as you see, the windows are barred. I think your valises are here and when you wish you can come down to supper. We shall wait for you——"

He left them and Compton pounced on his valise which presumably Mathews had brought up from the car; it had been tampered with—the lock forced and several useful little things that Compton had had the precaution to bring with him had gone, including cartridges, a file, electric torches, a camera, and a coil of stout wire rope. Beale's valise had been rifled in the same way, nothing was left in either but their clothes.

The two young men looked at each other rather ruefully; Beale told Compton of Falkland's warning.

"We're not sharp enough for these chaps," said Compton grimly. "No use making a noise, I suppose?"

"None whatever. You heard how he turned off his treatment of me? And Dobree's account of the mock suicide. No, keep quiet—and *look out.*"

They carefully examined the two rooms which were bare save for a set of cheap bedroom furniture, and discovered nothing.

"Better go down now," suggested Beale, but Compton wanted to see what was at the end of the corridor; each of them had a small lamp standing lit on the table and Compton took his and went down the short corridor.

There were two similar rooms standing empty, dirty and dismal enough, and at the end a third room that ran across the side of the house and appeared to have been altered from the original design.

Holding the lamp aloft Compton peered in, Beale gazing over his shoulder; and here the gloomy, feeble illumination did reveal something unusual, even extraordinary.

For the attic was fitted up like a blacksmith's forge—furnace, anvil, hammer and several fragments of iron work, fire backs, grates and horse-shoes, all filthy, rusty, smothered and dusty and scattered about in utter neglect as if they had not been touched for years.

There was another curious feature about this attic room.

It had been papered, walls and ceiling with a stout cheap wall paper of a crude design, and this had been stripped off and left, so that the shreds lay on the floor or still hung in mouldering tatters; in some places two or three layers of paper seemed to have been torn off; all over the room the plaster was laid bare; the effect of this, overlaid by the dirt, cobwebs and dust of years was most grotesquely dismal and hideous.

"Odd," remarked Compton, "but it doesn't help at all. I suppose some one was an amateur blacksmith—though why they should go to the trouble of first papering such a place and then stripping it off——"

"Better come down," urged Beale. "They wouldn't have left us alone up here if there was anything we could possibly discover."

And with a last look at the odd room the two young men returned to their own attics and set out their things, "such as were left," as Compton grimly remarked, then went downstairs.

Every one was now gathered round the table; Mamie was waiting on them; an odd picture it made, this table and the company about it in the high, dark shabby room.

Dobree and Manning kept up a light conversation of commonplaces, and both Falkland and Miss Conway betrayed no agitation whatever; if it had not been for that whispered warning and the rifled valises Beale would have been inclined to believe that there was nothing out of the way in the house at all.

Towards the end of the meal, Dobree said:

"I suppose you two young men will sit up with me to-night to watch for the ghost?"

CHAPTER XXIII

AT these words a little space of silence fell on the company gathered round the table. Even Compton's bold self-assurance could not find an immediate reply to Dobree's question. Not that there was anything particularly sinister in the question, but there was something undoubtedly sinister in the man's looks, in Manning's looks—in, indeed, the whole atmosphere.

It was Falkland who at length spoke.

"We've been doing that," he remarked; "sitting up to watch for ghosts. And I have quite a budget of notes."

"Seen anything?" asked Compton. And Beale looked at Miss Conway, who, however, kept her glance on the plate before her on the table.

"It's rather difficult," said Falkland, carefully, "to tell what we've seen and what we haven't seen."

Beale thought of Mathews' remark in the avenue, which had been to the same effect.

Dobree rose briskly, and Manning rose with him.

"You run upstairs with Mamie, Isabel," he commanded, "and you, Falkland, go and get your notes from my study. I want to have a word or two with these young friends of yours, who seem to take such an interest in 'Mockways.' "

At these words, Isabel at once followed Mamie from the room, without as much as a backward glance at the men, though Beale was looking at her intently in the hope of some signal or some expression on her face, from which he might possibly gather a clue as to her feelings or apprehensions.

Falkland also left the room, and he also gave no sign or glance; and Beale and Compton were left facing Manning and Dobree.

"Leave the supper things," said Manning, as Mamie came back with her inevitable tray; "leave all that, Mamie, and let us be alone for a moment or two."

The woman crept out. She had, Beale thought, a hunted, beaten look.

Dobree seated himself in the easy-chair by the fire which he had occupied before supper, and Manning stood behind him, looking very tall, dark and grim and sombre, with his great, dancing shadow thrown by the firelight on the dingy wall behind him.

Beale and Compton remained standing the other side of the meagre hearth. Manning had handed cigarettes, but no one was smoking.

Beale put his hand into his pocket where his small revolver lay. It seemed an absurd thing to feel there, and yet he was glad that he did feel it. At the same time, he felt fairly sure that provision had been made against anything as crude as firearms, and he thought, with rather a shiver, of the rifled valises. Manning and Dobree knew, of course, why they had come: that was obvious.

There was just a second's silence, during which Dobree's sunken eyes glanced from one to another of the young men. Then he leant forward, a hand on either knee, and said, in a low but vibrant voice:

"You two young men have taken the liberty to make a great many inquiries about me and my past life. I think you have spent all the last few days in making such inquiries. Investigations perhaps is a better word. You have spent the last few days in making investigations about me, and about old Mr. Powell, who used to own this house, and about Manning, my friend here. Now, I should like to know why. What is the reason for you two young men giving up time and trouble, and spending your money on such an employment as that?"

Neither of the young men was altogether surprised by this. They had not troubled to think very much about it, but all the same it had been, of course, fairly obvious that Dobree could quite easily have been acquainted with all their recent movements and inquiries; especially as they had taken no great trouble to disguise these, but had called, written, and telephoned to his various houses and offices in pursuit of him, besides coming to "Mockways" in person.

Compton, putting a bold face on it, replied bluntly:

"Well, sir, you're rather a mysterious person, you know, and our curiosity was roused by the disappearance of Falkland."

"Disappearance?" Dobree caught heavily at that word. "Where has the disappearance been? Edward Falkland was engaged as my secretary, and came here to 'Mockways' to help me make some investigations about the reputed hauntings."

"So you say, sir," replied Compton, undauntedly; "so, of course, we must accept; but I was inclined to think it all a little odd: what you might call a romantic story. And I suppose there's no harm in trying to find out what one can about a public character like yourself, sir?"

Beale glanced at him in admiration for his impudence: successful impudence, it seemed, for Dobree made no answer, and Manning cast down his eyes.

"We couldn't get any answer out of Falkland, you see," resumed Compton, cheerfully; "and so, sir, we tried to find out things for ourselves."

"And found out nothing," said Manning curtly; "nothing whatever; because, Mr. Compton, there was nothing to find out."

Dobree now looked up sharply.

"And there was no occasion for you to come here armed," he remarked. "Please, gentlemen, put your revolvers on the table."

Compton calmly refused. If he had to sit up all night looking for ghosts, he would be armed, he stated.

"In case there's any trick, sir; it's always best. I've been in haunted houses, before, and believe me a revolver's a very useful thing."

At this, Beale saw a look leap into Manning's eyes that he believed meant trouble, immediate and certain violence. But he was mistaken. Manning moved away towards the window, and Dobree merely shrugged his heavy shoulders, saying:

"Very well; as you please. But firearms are of no use in 'Mockways.' "

No one answered this, and Edward Falkland entered the room, with a portfolio of papers, which he placed on the table.

"This room is supposed to be the haunted room," announced Dobree, as coolly as if the preceding conversation had not taken place, and he was the best of friends with all the young men. "That is why we live here—why there is always some one here; so that if any appearance is made we cannot fail to see it."

"But you don't, I suppose," asked Beale, copying his careless tone, "sit up every night?"

"No," agreed Dobree; "not, of course, every night. We take it turn and turn about. To-night, however, I think"—he added—"we will *all* sit up. Something very curious occurred last night, and we are very anxious to see if it will be repeated. First of all, I have something to see about in my office, and Mr. Falkland will entertain you till my return."

Beale thought at once:

"So we are to be given a chance to talk together, and no doubt some one will be listening to what we say!"

Outwardly, he smiled, and made some trivial remark.

Compton asked if Miss Conway ever joined this grim party of watchers.

“Sometimes,” replied Dobree, “but not, I think, to-night.”

“What’s the story associated with the ghost?” asked Compton, easily, lighting a cigarette.

“A story of crime, of course!” replied Falkland, at once.

All three of them looked at Manning and Dobree.

“A story of crime?” repeated Beale.

“A story of murder,” replied Falkland.

CHAPTER XXIV

THE word "murder" rang gloomily round the tall, sombre room, and for a little space no one spoke.

Then Dobree rose clumsily, and with what seemed a sigh, and bade Manning follow him.

When they had gone, Falkland spoke at once.

"Of course, there is a purpose in leaving us alone here; they will be listening to hear what we say. But it doesn't really matter. They know quite well why you've come."

"Are you a prisoner here?" asked Beale, eagerly. "Tell us all you can, no matter whether we are overheard or not. We must know where we stand."

Falkland putting his hand to his head with a weary gesture, replied:

"I don't know myself where I stand. There's nothing to go on, nothing whatever. Of course, I and Miss Conway are both prisoners here—watched and spied on at every turn; our letters intercepted, and no possible chance given us to escape, or communicate with the outside world. They found out through your letters to me what you were up to, and I fear they mean to hold you prisoners too. That's why I tried to warn you to clear out: you can't help us, and you'd better save yourselves."

He spoke like a man whose nerve was broken, or breaking, and the other two looked at him with some alarm.

"Can't you tell us what happened?" they both asked, together.

"No, I can't; that's the really horrible part of it. Nothing has happened; here I've been and here she's been—just shut up in our separate rooms, and meeting here at meal times and in the evenings; and all having to pretend that we're looking for ghosts. And, of course, ghosts don't enter into it at all. But we have to pretend; we daren't show outwardly that we really understand there's something else on foot."

"But I can't see where I am," protested Beale. "What *is* this other thing that's on foot?"

"That's what I don't know," said Falkland, desperately; "but I can't persuade them I don't know. They think I'm looking for what *they're* looking for, and I'm not. I don't even know what it is."

And he raised his voice frantically, hoping that the two men spying outside would hear, and believe what he said. But he also, at the same time, laughed at himself for this hope.

"No good!" he said, sinking in an exhausted fashion into the arm-chair by the fireplace; "they won't believe, ever since I said that name 'Sarah Lomax,' they won't believe that I know nothing about it."

Falkland sighed with an air of bitter strain.

"Well, here we all are," he said; "and here we're likely to remain, I think. They don't intend to let any of us go until they discover just how much we know or how much we can find out. This ghost-stalking is all nonsense, just to test and rack our nerves for us. I believe they're playing tricks all along the line, like that trick they played on you, Beale, in Bitterne woods, and the trick on me about Mathews."

Beale was at this point going to tell Falkland about the interview with the girl who had called herself Sarah Lomax, and also his talk with the old man in the backwaters of the cathedral town nearby; but he quickly stopped himself, for he felt that Dobree, or Manning, or both would be sure to be listening, and he did not wish to give them this information, such as it was.

He turned away, therefore, and said as casually as possible, not for the benefit of Falkland but for the benefit of those unseen listeners:

"Well, it all seems to me a lot of trouble and bother for nothing. I'm sick of 'Mockways' and the ghost of 'Mockways'; I'll clear off early in the morning, quite satisfied to have seen the place. You seem to have got a very dreary job, Falkland, and if I were you I should throw it up. Personally, I don't like these eccentric millionaires."

Falkland took the cue, and yawned as if he were tired and bored.

"We found out nothing about either Dobree or Manning," Beale declared. "They are both, I should think, perfectly straight. Probably a little bit crazy, but nothing more than that."

And he tried to signal Falkland that he spoke merely to deceive the spies, who undoubtedly were, of course, listening.

For the same reason, all three young men now turned the talk on commonplaces, and after they had been talking in this strain for a moment or two Dobree and Manning returned, as if they had either seen through the ruse or were weary listening when there was nothing interesting to be heard.

The vigil began with the wearisome preparations by now so well-known to Falkland. Several nights since he had come to "Mockways" had been spent in this manner, at once so futile and so sinister—and contrived for what purpose he knew not. But to-night he was particularly on his guard, since he felt convinced that both Dobree and Manning meant to do something to dispose either of the suspicion or the company of the two newcomers.

The two windows were set wide on the winter night; the lamp was put out, and two candles were placed on the table, round which the men grouped themselves.

"The ghost, or whatever it is," smiled Dobree, "comes in from the garden, and here we sit and watch its passage across the room. I think it has something to say—a message to give us; and for that we wait. Every night Falkland takes notes of the time and manner of its appearance."

"I take notes," added Falkland, "of what you and Mr. Manning say, you see, Mr. Dobree. For myself"—and he glanced at his two friends—"I have never seen anything whatever."

"But you will," murmured Manning, in a sort of purr; "you *will* see something, Mr. Falkland, without a doubt; and perhaps to-night!"

"They have prepared a trick, no doubt," thought Falkland, wearily; "some faked apparition."

So far he had, indeed, seen nothing. All the hours he had spent, seated at this table between Manning and Dobree, sometimes with the valiant but terrified Isabel Conway in the company, he had certainly seen nothing, though it had been horrible enough to observe Dobree and Manning rise up, turn, stare and mouth, as though they were held and fascinated by some appearance which came in through the window, crossed the floor and disappeared through the closed door.

This was what they declared they saw, and what Falkland had to make copious notes about.

He now prepared his paper and pencil, and seated himself beside Compton and Beale, who brought out a pocket-book and asked if he could make a sketch of anything he chanced to see.

"I might," he suggested, "behold an apparition that would make a very good foreground to my picture of 'Mockways,' if I am ever allowed to paint it, Mr. Dobree."

And Dobree gave a rather sharp ghastly grin, and said he would be only too pleased if Mr. Beale would make such a drawing of any appearance he chanced to see.

"For," he added, "to me it alters. Some nights it takes some form, some nights another. We want," he said in a peculiar tone, "to identify it, Mr. Beale; to identify it."

"And now," said Manning, "we must be quiet. Nothing comes whilst we talk, you know. Silence please, all of you; and keep awake and alert—and watch the window."

Beale thought, as Falkland had thought before him, that the only person available to play any trick was Mathews; and he reminded himself that Mathews was short and wizened, so that he could identify him under any guise he might assume.

Silence fell, and for a while there was nothing but this silence. A long while it seemed to the three young men in this sinister atmosphere of the gloomy room, lit with the two dim candles, and those two tall windows open on the dark, while Manning and Dobree, sat heavily and solemnly at the table, staring out at the night. If they were doing all this for effect, they were doing it pretty well, for there was no doubt that the atmosphere was very horrible. Even Compton felt uneasy. As time went on the tension became greater and more pronounced. The clock struck several times, and no one did more than stir slightly in his chair.

Compton would have spoken, but Manning raised one of his powerful hands, and breathed "Hush! hush!" and again there was a long, dragging silence.

Dobree sat as if in a stupor, with his heavy eyes closed; and Manning, too, appeared to be half asleep or drowsy, with his gaunt shoulders hunched up to his ears, and his large, ugly hands folded on the table in front of him.

"They're both armed, I suppose," thought Compton, wondering if it would be wise to make a dash for it out through the open window. "But," he thought, "that is perhaps just what they are hoping we shall do, so that they may have a chance of shooting."

At last, out of the unbearable stillness, there did come a faint noise—a rustling or shuffling—outside the window in the intense darkness of the night; the moon was overcast with heavy clouds and there was no light whatever beyond the window.

"Look out!" whispered Beale. "I think there is something coming."

Manning and Dobree did not move, but Compton and Beale crowded eagerly forward in front of the table, and fixed straining eyes on the window.

"What do you see?" breathed Falkland; and he himself, for the first time in these vigils, thought he saw something himself: the dim, quavering figure of an old man outlined in the window.

At this moment the door behind them was flung open violently, and Mamie rushed in, shouting:

"Quick, sir, quick! Miss Isabel has found the *papier mâché* box."

CHAPTER XXV

MANNING got silently to his feet, while Dobree, still with drowsy air, gazed over his shoulder at the newcomer as if stupefied by her words.

Mamie advanced into the room; she was in an obvious state of considerable agitation.

"It's all a funny business, isn't it, sir?" she quavered. "Miss Isabel thought she heard some one outside the door—the ghost perhaps, just a light shuffling and tapping on the stairs, as you might say—and we both crept to the door, and there's a faint light travelling up the stairs, brighter than the lamps what's there, sir—and we follows it up—and—and—" her eyes grew round with terror, "there was footsteps in the rooms you've given the two young gentlemen—and then in that funny place got up like a forge——"

She paused, with every aspect of a quivering terror, and her pallid face and dark figure in the light of the one candle looked ghastly enough.

"Go on," said Manning, who was watching her keenly and seemed absorbed by her relation, while Dobree regarded her with dull heaviness.

"Well, sir, we crept in there—and there was a light in the room, like moonlight, but I couldn't say where it was coming from, and there, on that rusty old anvil was the *papier mâché* box—one of them old things like you said you was looking for——"

Dobree's great head sank on his breast; he heaved a sigh; Manning shot a dark glance at Falkland.

"And what did you do with it?" he asked softly. "What did you do with it, eh?"

"Bless you, sir!" cried Mamie with an air of stupid candour. "We left it there, *I* can tell you! Perhaps you'd like to go and see it for yourself!"

"Yes," said Manning in an absorbed manner, "yes. There are some valuable jewels in that box, Mamie, if it is the right box—old Mr. Powell hid them, he was very eccentric, you know——"

"But it's odd how it got on the anvil, isn't it?" whispered Dobree in a husky voice. "Are you sure you haven't been hunting about yourself, Mamie, and found it, eh?"

He rose and caught hold of Manning's arm as if he was stiff from long sitting; his bulky body cast a deeper shadow into the murk of the room; his face looked the colour of tallow in the candle light—the second candle of the vigil, now burning to the socket; he and Manning both appeared to have forgotten the three young men, to be wholly held by Mamie's story.

"I wish I had," she answered. "I'd have held it up for a bit of a reward, sir, but we was that scared by the *funniness* of it that I never thought of that! Miss Isabel's so frightened she's shut herself in her room——"

"Come up and look," said Manning to Dobree as if they were alone in the room. "Perhaps we have found it at last——"

They left the room with a certain heavy quickness and Mamie remained staring at the three young men across the solitary candle.

"Hush!" she breathed and held up her hand.

The footsteps of Manning and Dobree died away on the stairs; Mamie leant forward and whispered:

"Got them!"

"A trick?" breathed Falkland, who, like Isabel Conway, was

always in cruel uncertainty as to the good faith of Mamie.

"Yes," she answered swiftly. "Of course, there was no box—I made all that up—pretty good, eh?"

"Bravo!" said Compton, but Mamie cut short even this one word.

"Clear!" she whispered, "clear out! You've only a moment—quick——"

"Where?" asked Beale.

"Through the windows!" she breathed impatiently. "They're open, ain't they?"

"And Miss Isabel?" asked Falkland.

"She's coming—as soon as she hears them pass her door she's slipping down here——"

This convinced Falkland at least of Mamie's faith, but Compton still feared a trap, and said:

"Where are we going—like this—out into the dark, in this lonely place?"

Mamie turned on him:

"Anywhere—you'd better clear, they mean to shut you up—if not worse—they're getting *desperate*."

The door opened softly and Isabel Conway crept into the room, dressed in coat and hat and carrying a small bag; she went at once to Falkland, saying with pale lips:

"Take me away, please—this is just a chance—Mamie planned it——"

Falkland needed no more; he took the girl's arm and hurried out into the night.

The whole transaction had only taken a moment or so; Mamie put out the candle; from the dark, only faintly scattered by the dying fire embers, she whispered:

"You'd better clear out, I tell you, they are getting desperate—they've gone so far they've got to go a bit farther."

Despite this Compton wanted to stay and see the thing out; he hated leaving the adventure in the middle, as it were; but Beale, more prudent, seized him by the arm.

"We ought to help Falkland and that unfortunate girl, I don't like the look of things at all—they're lunatics at best."

"Come on—come on," urged Mamie with rear terror now in her voice. "They'll kill me for this—I've done me best for you——"

Compton could resist no longer; he stepped out of the long window on the lawn, after the other two; the vigil had been longer than he had believed it to have been; a dismal pallor of dawn was overspreading the wintry sky.

"Do you know your way?" whispered Beale.

Compton replied that he did and smiled to think that this was the second time that he had left "Mockways" under these circumstances; they hastened round the lawn in the shrubbery and soon overtook Falkland and Isabel; none of them could forebear looking back at the black square of the house against the ghastly cold grey sky; in one of the top windows was a dull flickering light.

"Oh, make haste!" whispered Isabel frantically. "Make haste!"

They plunged into the dark, decaying shrubs, goaded by an unnameable fear; Compton led them sharply away from the house and in the direction of that former gap in the railings through which he had entered himself, though he recalled grimly enough that escape by that means was now impossible—still he knew of no other way that it was worth while taking—the other side of the house was the mausoleum and acres of a wilderness of park, and he, clear headed as he was, felt a little dazed by that long vigil and its sudden interruption.

"Hark!" whispered Mamie suddenly.

A low howling broke on the grey stillness of the reluctant winter dawn.

"The dogs!" cried Falkland. "Some one has loosened the dogs! They've been shut up these last few nights!"

They had all broken into a run now, for the dogs sounded behind them; and they felt sure that Dobree and Manning, certainly armed, were behind the dogs.

"Shoot the brutes," said Compton as they dodged in and out of the trees in the avenue.

"Can't see them," gasped Beale.

In the avenue indeed it was yet almost dark for many of the trees were evergreen, oak or ilex, and still heavy with sombre leaves; the half lights—vague, grey and dim—the dense shadows were most confusing—they lost each other—they called to each other, they ran backwards and forwards in this treacherous twilight.

Falkland still had, and aways kept on him, the keys he had found in Mathews' cottage, the keys that Manning had not been quite clever enough to snatch away and hide; he now told Compton this as they hurried side by side through the dark.

"Idiot," said Compton, "why didn't you tell me that before? There is a side door in the wall near here——"

They fumbled their way down the avenue, turned out of it and found the door in the high surrounding wall; they had to flounder through a bed of rank nettles and weeds to reach it; but neglected though it thus appeared it was padlocked as securely as the mausoleum had been padlocked. Falkland was lagging behind with Isabel Conway, who, utterly exhausted, could not hasten; Mamie ran back to him to fetch the keys which Compton proceeded to try one after the other, Beale striking matches to help the uncertain light.

Suddenly Beale exclaimed:

"I've dropped my revolver pitching through that undergrowth—"

He turned back, undecided, vexed, his hand to his torn pocket. Compton was absorbed in trying the keys—one did open the padlock. The young man threw wide the door on the hillside and turned back to hasten on the others.

He could not find any one; he plunged down the wrong path; he rushed back to find Beale and Mamie at the open door.

"It's all right, the others have gone ahead!" she cried; the dogs sounded very near; they all three dashed through the door and banged it behind them so that the latch jumped into place, and scrambled over the rough hillside beyond the wall.

The light was now fairly clear, but they could not see Falkland or Isabel Conway.

CHAPTER XXVI

THE little party proceeded across the heath. It looked gloomy and dreary enough in the pallid light of the new day, a slight ground frost gave a bloom of rime to the ground; the clouds were low, dull and threatened rain; it was a gloomy enough prospect.

The two young men were now composed and almost inclined to laugh at their late adventure. There was something in that scramble through the park which was more ludicrous than terrible in the recollection.

They were rather cold, and shivered. The men were without their coats, and Mamie only wore her thick stuff house-dress. She, however, tripped alone cheerfully enough, keeping a sharp look-out for Falkland and Miss Isabel. "They must," she said, "have taken another turn, but it does not matter, as they know where to go."

"What do you mean?" asked Beale: "They know where to go?"

"Well, there was an appointment made," said Mamie, hurrying along through the wet heather.

But Compton interrupted her.

"But are you quite sure they got away?" he asked. "I mean, that they are safely this side of the gate?"

They paused to look round them and listen. They could still hear the baying of the dogs, though this was faint, and with every step farther in the distance.

"Yes," said Mamie, "I am quite sure they got away; I saw them run through the gate. They've happened to take another way, I suppose; but both of them know their way, and Miss Isabel will explain to Mr. Falkland like I'm going to explain to you, sir," she added, as they hurried along over the rough heath—not able to get along very fast, but steadily getting farther away from the house as the light of day brightened.

"This, you see," she added, "is the doing of Miss Sarah Lomax. She arranged it all, though there was no time to tell you about it before, when our one idea was to get away from the house."

"Sarah Lomax?" repeated Beale, in surprise. "What do you mean by that? How could she have arranged this?"

"She arranged it," said Mamie, with a cunning look, "because she is hidden in 'Mockways.' She comes in and out of 'Mockways' just as she likes, sir. Not that she'll tell me quite how—but that doesn't matter from her point of view, sir, does it? And I'm sure I only wish I knew how she does it. But she doesn't trust me that far."

"Oh!" said Beale and Compton, both at once. "That explains a great deal!"

"I suppose Miss Lomax has been this third person hidden in the house, that surprised so many of you with these goings-on? The person who sent the message in the knot of red silk, eh?" said Compton.

"Yes, that's right, sir; she got into touch with me almost at first—that day that Mr. Falkland and Miss Isabel made their escape. She confided in me, but only up to a point. She's a very strong-minded young lady, and not much inclined to confide in any one. But she told me this much——" panted Mamie, trying to keep step with the two men—"that she could get in and out of 'Mockways' just as often as she liked, and that with all them secret rooms and trap doors it wasn't much trouble for her to overhear all that was going on."

"Ah," said Beale, "I suppose that's what made her come and warn me. She saw that Miss Isabel and Falkland were prisoners."

"Yes," said Mamie, "she told me she was going to do that; but she didn't mean you to come to 'Mockways.' She thought that was a silly thing to do; she knew you could do no good there, sir. But still, we seem to have got away now. It was she that suggested this. She said she'd ordered a car to meet us by the cross-roads. I know where they are. We passed them on our way here from 'The Elms,' and I'll just hunt about till I find 'em. It won't take long, I don't suppose."

She was talking rather incoherently in her excitement, and it was not very easy for the two men thoroughly to understand what the girl said.

"Does Miss Isabel know all this?" asked Compton.

"Yes, of course she does; we've talked it over again and again, ever since Miss Lomax told me about it. She said we were to wait till there was the next ghost-sitting, and then to play this trick, whether you two were there or not. And while Dobree and Manning were upstairs, we were all to get out into the park and out of the park some way or other, and so to the cross-roads, where the car will be waiting. Miss Isabel will tell Falkland that. They must be ahead of us somewhere," she added, anxiously, looking round over the brightening landscape. "I don't see them in sight, but it is wonderful how soon any one can get ahead—even a step or two will do it."

"And we've left Miss Lomax behind in 'Mockways,' " remarked Beal. "That doesn't seem quite fair, does it?"

But Mamie only grinned.

"She's quite able to take care of herself, sir, I can tell you."

Mamie now had to sit down on one of the heath-fringed bounders on the hillside; she was exhausted, and no wonder—she had been up all night, waiting for a favourable moment in which to work her trick, and then had come that desperate rush through the park with the dogs behind them.

The two men waited while she recovered herself, taking biscuits from her pocket and munching them.

"What's Mathews' part in all this?" asked Beale. "Is he playing Dobree's game or no?"

"Of course he is," replied Mamie, contemptuously. "He tried to get to warn Mr. Falkland, and then they gave him such a shock that nothing would open his mouth about anything now, and I don't think he really knows very much—only just enough to make him suspicious, and to make them keep him shut up here. I can tell you, sir, it's all a fair tangle to me too. But I know there's no good about it," added the woman, shrewdly; "no good at all. I can tell you that. And I'm fair sorry for Mr. Dobree in a way, for I think Manning's got hold of him. I think he's holding something over his head, to force him to give him Miss Isabel; and if he don't make him marry her I think Manning's going to make it dreadful for Mr. Dobree."

"What makes you think all that?" asked Beale curiously.

She shook her head.

"I don't know, sir; but I've been shut up in that house for a bit, and I've picked up this and that. This listening and being listened to, and watching and being watched, you can't help making some sort of a tale out of it in the end. And that's the tale that I've made out—that Manning's holding something over Mr. Dobree; and though they're putting up this pretence about ghosts, I don't think it's altogether a pretence, as far as Mr. Dobree is concerned: I think he really believes it. The ghosts, I mean—I think he's scared by them."

"Well," said Compton, with a sigh and a yawn, "it all seems to be rather flat as far as I'm concerned. Nothing but a watch in the dark, and a chase in the dark, and nothing happening. I suppose we're clear of 'Mockways' now, and not likely to get into it again. It only remains to get Miss Isabel to her friends, and get all we can out of Falkland. But I doubt if he will have any case against Dobree, considering the man's money and position. We shall have to be quiet about the whole thing, and let it peter out."

"Leave it to Miss Sarah Lomax, you mean," grinned Mamie. "I can tell you, she doesn't mean to give up in a hurry. She's in and out of that place like a rat, watching 'em all the time."

They had now got in sight of the high road along which Miss Isabel and Falkland had escaped before; and there, by the lonely cross-roads, they could see in the grey distance, a large car waiting.

"Miss Lomax told me it would be there," said Mamie, triumphantly, "and there it is. I knew she wouldn't go back on us!"

"Who's in the car?" asked Beale.

"Only a hired man, sir. It's a kind of taxi from the neighbouring town, where she lives, I think, in between her visits to 'Mockways.' She told me she'd hire it, and tell the man to come here and wait—all night, if need be. Of course," she added, anxiously, "we mustn't say anything to him about a queer adventure. It's got to be part of this ghost-hunting business, sir. We must't say anything to reflect on Mr. Dobree or Mr. Manning. Miss Lomax was very careful about that. She impressed that on me, and on Miss Isabel."

" 'Ghost' is the cue, apparently," laughed Compton. "We've all got to talk about ghosts, though none of us has seen or heard anything of them, so far as I know," he added, regretfully.

"But what was the old man?" asked Beale, interestedly. "There certainly was an old man in the window, just as Mamie came in."

"That was old Mathews, dressed up, I expect," said Mamie, contemptuously.

Both the young men thought that it had not been at all like Mathews, but altogether too frail and quavering an outline to have been that of a human being.

They now were nearing the car waiting by the cross-roads.

"I don't see Falkland or Miss Isabel," said Mamie, nervously; "but I suppose they've got inside the car for warmth——" for the morning was certainly raw and chill. The heavy ground-frost still covered the hillside with vapour. They all thought that they, too, would be glad to get into the car: be glad, indeed, to reach the town and have a good breakfast and a good rest.

When they reached the car, they found it was empty. Neither Isabel nor Falkland was there.

CHAPTER XXVII

ISABEL and Falkland had got clear on to the hillside; and then Isabel had missed Mamie, and called out to her in a panic.

Falkland told her not to shout, as it might attract the attention of possible pursuers. She then broke away from him and ran into the park, wringing her hands and looking about for her faithful friend.

In the confusion of the interlacing shadows and dubious lights, she turned down the opposite path from that taken by Mamie, and was soon out of sight of the gate. When Falkland saw that she did not return, he too went back into the grounds of "Mockways," and after her. He chanced to meet her, but could not see any of the others. They called as loud as they dared, and ran about here and there looking and peering through the interlacing boughs and low, dark greenery.

When, at last, they made their way back to the gate, they found this closed on them; and Isabel, in terror, cried:

"We have been caught again!"

But Falkland found the gate was open. It was merely the latch in place; the padlock swung open. He had given his keys to Compton, of course. Compton had got away: this was what he told Isabel. But she would not believe it. She said they were all somewhere in the park, and she could not abandon them. And, weeping hysterically, she refused to escape.

"I can't leave Mamie to it," she said; "I simply can't. They will revenge the whole thing on her. We must go back and face it out."

In vain Falkland tried to persuade her that Mamie had certainly escaped, and no doubt at this moment was looking for her on the hillside.

Isabel was overwrought and unnerved, and would not believe this consolation. She felt, she said, quite incapable of leaving the park while there was any question of the escape of Mamie.

"We must give it up," she said; "we cannot be meant to escape."

She did not tell Falkland about Sarah Lomax and the waiting car on the cross-roads because she was in too much despair to trouble. She sat down and put her face in her hands, disconsolate and weary, among the dead leaves; and Falkland could do nothing but lean against the wall and gaze at her.

He himself believed that the others had got away; but indeed there had been such confusion, and the mingled light and shade of the cold winter dawn was so bewildering that he could not definitely have told what had really happened.

The only thing that was clear was that they were there, a step from liberty, and must not take it.

"Oh, Mamie, Mamie!" lamented Isabel. "She's done all this for me. She's been so wonderful; so good and clever. And I doubted her, I warned you against her: that is what I can't forgive myself! But I have been so confused and bewildered from the first, I really thought that she was one of them—one of those dreadful people!"

And poor Isabel shuddered.

"But she isn't. She's done everything for me! And she's been so clever, too, getting into touch with that Miss Lomax who's hiding in the house."

"Hiding in the house?" asked Falkland, quickly. "Do you mean to say you've got into touch with Miss Lomax, and that she's in the house? You never told me that."

"I didn't have a chance," said Isabel. "When do we get a chance to say a word? I haven't seen Miss Lomax myself. It's been Mamie who's got some kind of signal up with her. There was to be a car waiting for us, at the cross-roads. Miss Lomax managed that, and she suggested the trick Mamie played to-night about the *papier mâché* box."

"A car waiting at the cross-roads?" said Falkland, eagerly. "Then come along. Let's make for it. Even if the others haven't got away, there's no reason why I should not see you into safety. I could always come back for Mamie."

And he held open the door on to the hillside, and again implored the girl to move. But Isabel had taken her resolution. She was convinced that Mamie had not escaped, and she had decided that she could not leave her in "Mockways." Her gratitude and devotion to the poor nurse were unbounded, and it was impossible for her to consider for a moment abandoning her to Manning and Dobree.

"I'd rather go through anything myself," he declared.

And at the very moment when Compton, Beale and Mamie had reached the empty car at the cross-roads, Isabel was abandoning her excellent chance of escape, and turning back, with heroic resolution, to the prison of "Mockways," followed by Falkland, who had, indeed, no choice at all in the matter, but whose soul was full of the most bitter despair at this excellent lost opportunity. He was convinced, in his own mind, that the others had made good their escape, and felt that he must be a fool not to have been able to persuade the girl of this.

"We might, perhaps, find them in the park somewhere," said Isabel, drearily. "They seem to have called the dogs off; I don't hear them any more. We might wander away and perish in the woods," she added, wildly. "That is what I would rather do than go back to the house. And yet there's Mamie to be thought of."

"Not much use in that," said Falkland, dryly. "If you want to stick by Mamie, we'd better go back to the house and see if she is there. After all, it's easy to find some sort of a flimsy excuse for running out into the park. We can say," he added, ironically, "that we saw the ghost; and I certainly did see something, though I suppose it was a trick."

They continued to wander aimlessly through the park, the half-fainting girl hanging on to Falkland's arm. And they had not wandered very far before they saw Manning coming towards them, a couple of large wolfhounds at his heels.

He took off his hat and gave Isabel a mocking bow, and she hung so heavily on Falkland's arm that that young man thought she had fainted.

"Good-evening—or good-morning, Miss Conway," sneered Manning. "Whatever it ought to be. This is becoming rather foolish, don't you think—these wild jaunts with Mr. Falkland. Such a damp, dismal sort of jaunt, this one," he grinned, "a wretched, frosty dawn in winter. I can't think of a more disagreeable time in which to wander in a neglected park."

"We were frightened by the ghost," said Falkland, putting the best face on it that he could. "Or rather, Miss Isabel was frightened."

"What was Miss Isabel doing down in the parlour?" asked Manning.

"She ran down," said Falkland, "when you had gone up to look for the box. She was scared, as she well might have been. You'll be answerable for the consequences, Manning, if she loses her wits through all this. She was scared, and ran down; and we had to run after her: and what's become of the others I don't know."

"Gone away, no doubt," said Manning, "not altogether liking the hospitality of 'Mockways.' And as to the box—that was a lie on the part of your devoted Mamie," he added, looking closely at the girl. "Perhaps on your part, too."

"I know nothing about it," she whispered, in the extreme of terror. "But where's Mamie? What's happened to Mamie?"

"I don't know," said Manning. "I thought she was with you."

And they both knew that he had spoken the truth, and Falkland had the great bitterness of knowing that Mamie really had escaped and that they might have joined her.

Meanwhile, Manning spoke again.

"You had better come back to the house," he purred, in his evil whisper. "Miss Isabel looks quite worn out. I don't think you'd better keep her walking up and down this damp path any longer, Mr. Falkland. I'm sure she will be glad of breakfast and a rest. We must stop this ghost-watching, if this is going to be the result."

"Well," said Falkland, as they turned back towards the house, trying to disguise his heart-sickness, "I think I saw something this time."

"Saw something?" asked Manning, quickly.

"Yes."

"What was it you did see?"

"I don't know—an old man."

"An old man?" ejaculated Manning. "You saw an old man?" And he spoke in such a manner that Falkland was at once convinced that he had not prepared any tricks in those long, dark windows, but that whatever it was that they had all seen, it was not any doing of Manning's.

"I thought I saw an old man," he declared. "The wavery outline of an old man."

"Nonsense!" cried Manning, quickly. "Nonsense! Of course, you didn't see anything of the kind! Hurry along. I'm sure Miss Conway wants to get home and rest: she looks to me quite done for."

Half-dead, indeed, Isabel Conway clung to Falkland's arm, and passed without demur for the second time over the threshold across which she had made two such valiant efforts to escape.

There was now no Mamie to look after her, to console her and succour her. Alone the girl had to go up to her room, and Manning followed her and turned the key in the lock.

"You'd better stop all this folly," he said, coming down to Falkland, who was sitting in an attitude of despair by the dead embers of the fire. "This is twice you have tried this on, and I should think you would see by now that it's quite hopeless. I've means of getting hold of you," he added, "even if you did make a getaway—which you won't. As for Miss Conway, I suppose you know by now that she's engaged to me? She's going to be my wife."

"That's a lie," said Falkland, "and you know it." Manning only smiled.

"I can bear a good deal of that sort of talk," he said. "It doesn't fetch me! At the same time, I should advise you not to indulge in too much of it, Mr. Falkland."

CHAPTER XXVIII

EXHAUSTED, dispirited and disappointed as Falkland was, he was at once roused to take up the challenge in Manning's last words. He rose to his feet and faced the sinister figure the other side of the ember-strewn hearth.

"If you are going to take that tone," he replied, "I may as well take it also; there is no need for disguise, I suppose, any longer. What you are up to—you and your employer—I don't quite know, but you are certainly keeping me and Miss Conway here by force, and, as I suppose you have realised, my friends have got away now, and will soon find means of getting in touch with me again. Your game, whatever it is, is up."

"Oh, is it?" sneered Manning. "My game, as you call it, is certainly not up; and as for your friends, what excuse do you think they will have to return to 'Mockways' again? I believe you'll find that they have had their lesson, and won't be so very keen to get another."

Falkland was silent for a second; he could, indeed, think of no very good reply to this. Casting over in his mind the possible future actions of the two young men and Mamie, he was at a loss to know what they would be likely to do. After all, there was still nothing against either Manning or Dobree except this forcible detention of himself and Miss Conway; and that would be difficult indeed to prove. If he got away from "Mockways" himself to-morrow, he would not know what kind of a charge to make against his late employer and Manning. There was nothing tangible to go on, and the extremely clever disguise of the ghost-hunting would cover up all possible eccentricities and strange behaviour.

Seeing his desperate bewilderment and sullen silence, Manning laughed.

"You see that there is nothing you can do, I suppose?" he remarked. "Therefore, you had better keep civil; you'll stay in 'Mockways' just exactly as long as I choose that you shall stay, and you'll do as you're told, and you won't waste your time trying to communicate with any one outside."

"I'm perfectly well aware," replied Falkland, bitterly, "that all my letters are intercepted and stolen."

"Are you?" said Manning. "A bit of guesswork on your part, then; there's no proof of that, you know, nor of anything else. You've come here to help in investigations about ghosts; this is a haunted house, and we're here to investigate. And meanwhile we are looking for a certain box that an old man—a silly, eccentric old man—hid thirty years ago; a *papier mâché* box with one or two good jewels in it. There's nothing in that, you know, Mr. Falkland; nothing whatever."

Falkland replied, boldly and angrily:

"I think that there is a very great deal in it and I'm not going to rest till I've found out what. That is," he added, "if you insist on keeping me a prisoner here. If you let me go and return Miss Conway to her friends, I, as I told you some time ago, will say nothing about anything. As you said before, it's no business of mine——"

But Manning interrupted fiercely.

"No. No business of yours, but you thrust yourself into it, didn't you? And now you're paying for it."

"I didn't thrust myself into it," retorted Falkland. "I was dragged into it. I happened, most unfortunately for me, to render Mr. Dobree a service; and this was the result."

"You happened," said Manning, "to mention the name of Sarah Lomax, didn't you? And *that's* the result. What do you know about her? What did you mean, saying her name?"

"I knew nothing about her at all," replied Falkland. "I've tried to explain that to you and Mr. Dobree. It was just a chance shot, and if I had happened to guess the consequences——"

Manning took up the words with a sneer.

"I can well understand that if you had happened to know the consequences, you wouldn't have said it. But you did: and here you are!"

"And here she is!" Falkland wanted to say. He would have very much liked to tell Manning what he had heard from Isabel, that Sarah Lomax came in and out of the house, watching them, spying on them, and looking herself for the *papoer mâché* box. Perhaps manning knew this; perhaps, on the other hand, he didn't. Anyhow, Falkland did not feel justified in giving the girl's secret away.

"What do you want to do with me?" he asked, biting his lip. "What's the sense of keeping me shut up here like this? Are you trying to break my nerve down, or drive me crazy? I cannot see the sense of it. You ought to know by now that I am quite innocent of any attempt to spy on you or find out your affairs or those of Mr. Dobree. I am not concerned with any of it; I've told you that again and again," he repeated, violently.

"That may be," sneered Manning; "but your two bright young friends outside have been spending all their time and money trying to find out things about me and Mr. Dobree, and about old Mr. Powell too."

"Well," protested Falkland, "I suppose that was only because they couldn't understand why I was shut up here. That's natural enough, isn't it? And then the strange way you behaved—the trick about Beale in the Bitterne woods, and the trick about Mathews in the shed—all those things make people wonder, you know, Mr. Manning. Sane people, as a rule, don't take all that trouble to play tricks unless there's something behind it."

Manning merely grinned at him.

"Whether there's anything behind it or not," he remarked, "you don't leave 'Mockways,' that's decided. And Miss Conway doesn't leave, either. As I told you just now, she's going to be my wife, and I'm going to look after her properly."

"Look after her properly!" cried Falkland, furiously. "In a place like this! And now without any sort of a nurse or attendant."

"Oh, I'll get her a nurse or an attendant all right," smiled Manning. "There's no difficulty about that, I assure you; and presently, as soon as ever I've found what I'm looking for, Mr. Falkland, I shall take her away. We shall be married," he added, softly, "and go away together. The south of France, I think——somewhere where she'll get a chance to recover from all this."

"She doesn't intend to marry you, and she shan't marry you," retorted Falkland. "This is all just bluff and bullying on your part, and you know it."

"Oh, I do, do I?" said Manning. "Don't you just think you'd better be a little careful? After all, you seem to think I'm a very dangerous character. You might remember that," he jeered, "when you try to provoke me so."

"As I said before," Falkland remarked, as quietly as he could, "you had better, for your own sake, be careful. My friends have got away, and they will have a funny tale to tell, won't they?"

"Will they?" asked Manning, quite unmoved by these veiled threats. "Will they? I don't think so. They were invited to 'Mockways' to join in a ghost-search party. They sat up all night looking for the ghost, and when the ghost came they got scared, and took their heels and ran away, and I suppose are still wandering about the hillside; they're rather cold and hungry, I should think, Mr. Falkland!"

Falkland had a card up his sleeve here in the matter of the car waiting at the cross-roads. He did not mention it, but it gave him considerable satisfaction. He was sure that by now the three of them would be in the cathedral town, enjoying their breakfasts and making their plans. He was convinced that they would not abandon him, and though he could not conceive what the steps would be which they would take towards his liberation, he was quite sure that they would not be slow or idle in his interest.

At the same time, he had a sickening feeling that he could not go on like this; he felt that his nerves and health would break, as no doubt Manning intended they should do.

Useless, of course, to appeal to him; but for the moment Falkland had the impulse to do so. He was so hopeless, so exhausted.

He rose with a groan and turned towards the window, which now let in the light of a grey, winter day.

Manning turned to leave the room. Well he knew that there was no need to lock Falkland in; as long as Isabel Conway was shut up in "Mockways," Falkland was safe not to attempt to leave it. Therefore, he made no attempt to close the windows, or lay any embargo upon the unfortunate young man. He was only too well aware how securely he was tied to the awful house.

Falkland turned wildly over in his distraught mind the possibility of coming to some arrangement with Manning, of bribing him or persuading him to let them go; but it was hopeless, he knew, and with a groan he dismissed the idea. The only thing for him to do was to try to keep his head, control himself, use all the patience he could command in yet another endeavour to get Isabel Conway free from "Mockways."

As he stood still in an attitude of despair by the open window, he heard the door softly close behind him, and, looking round, saw that Dobree was in the tall, gloomy room, looking at him; and looking at him with a new expression.

It seemed to Falkland that this expression was almost one of fear; yes, fear—as if Dobree had been infected by the foul atmosphere of the house.

The heavy man came slowly to the window, and laid his arm on Falkland's shoulder.

"What did you see last night?" he whispered. "In the window, I mean. Did you think you saw something?"

"Yes," said Falkland, briefly, in no mood to be discussing ghosts. "I thought I saw an old man—just the outline of an old man—self-deception, I suppose."

"Not an *old* man?" asked Dobree, anxiously. "Surely you didn't think it was an *old* man?"

"Yes, I did; a wizened old man. But what of it, sir?" he added, wearily. "There's something else to think of, besides ghosts, in this house, it seems to me."

"There is indeed," said Dobree, "a great deal to think of;" and he sighed. "But I hope," he added, "that you didn't see an old man. That's rather dreadful, Mr. Falkland, if there's the ghost of an old man walking about 'Mockways.' "

"I thought you'd seen a good deal yourself, sir," said Falkland, not knowing how to take this, and feeling bewildered to the point of craziness by it all.

"Yes, I've seen a good deal," said Dobree, in an absorbed manner; "and now I want to talk to you, Falkland; I want to talk to you very, very seriously. Will you come into my office—you know, the room next here; but not now, in an hour or so, when you've had some food and rested. What I've got to say requires a very clear head. It is most important."

Falkland felt his spirits leap at this. Anything was better than nothing; any action better than long suspense.

"Very important," repeated Dobree, with another sigh.

CHAPTER XXIX

FALKLAND went about the house without further molestation from Manning. He managed to scribble Isabel a note, bidding her cheer up and trust in him, which he pushed under her door.

Mathews, sullen and hostile, served him with food, and Falkland took some sort of rest. He could not eat, but he forced himself to lie down on his bed and rest.

He was considerably excited by the promised interview with Dobree. There had been something very peculiar in that man's manner which excited the curiosity and even the hope of Falkland. All that heavy, sullen, bullying air had gone; the man seemed frightened—even humble and timid. Perhaps a ruse, a trick, a trap; but Falkland could not turn over in his mind too many of such possibilities. He must try to nourish what hope he could, and there did seem a gleam of hope in Dobree's behaviour.

Perhaps he could get from him the freedom which he had asked for in vain from Manning; perhaps, even, some clue to the mystery or whatever motive was behind all this.

When he went downstairs at the appointed time, he was delighted beyond measure to find Mamie in the parlour, lighting the fire and tidying up the room with a brisk and cheerful air, as if she had been comfortably in bed all night, and not tramping the heath.

She had changed her dress, and looked decent and tidy, as well as placid, and even cheerful.

"So you've come back?" cried Falkland, in his pleasure. "Good, brave Mamie, you've really got back?"

"Of course, I've got back," she answered, contemptuously. "Do you think I'd stay away while Miss Isabel was here? Of course, I came back, and at once. I made them drive me up to the gate, and there I just rung the bell and waited till Mathews let me in; and he was pretty glad to see me, I can tell you. He said it cheered him up a lot to have me back again."

"It cheers me up too," cried Falkland, "and Miss Isabel will be absolutely overjoyed. It makes all the difference in the world to all of us, Mamie, and I feel I owe you an apology——"

She stopped him instantly.

"What are you talking about?" she said, in a loud vice. "A lot of trouble you've put me to this night, scaring Miss Isabel with your ghosts, and letting her run across the park, sending me chasing after her and getting lost. I can tell you, I've had a fair time of it, all through this silly nonsense about ghosts."

Falkland saw at once the cue she wished him to take up. No doubt the clever woman had been able to persuade even the suspicious Manning that she had been making an attempt to recapture Miss Isabel. No doubt, also, she had been able to persuade him that she had not left the park, but had wandered about nearly all night looking for her charge. It was not likely that Mathews would give her away on this point. He was silent, realising that somebody was probably listening—possibly Dobree himself, in the next room.

"Go up to Miss Isabel as soon as you can," he said, anxiously. "She'll want to see you."

Mamie nodded, and went on with her work. Evidently her delay was given with the object of not rousing any doubt as to her stupidity and fidelity to Manning. She did not wish to rush up to Isabel Conway in any manner to show undue devotion to her charge.

Falkland left her, and went into the little office where Dobree had told him to come. He found his employer sitting heavily by the desk, a glass of wine on the dirty, neglected table near him.

His head was sunk on his breast, his arms hung by his side; his whole attitude was one of slackness, almost one of despair.

If this man had not got something terrible on his conscience he could not be quite sane, Falkland thought.

"Sit down, Mr. Falkland," he said, without looking up. "Sit down. But first—" he interrupted himself—"lock the door. I don't wish any one to come in on us; I don't want any one to overhear us."

As Falkland locked the door, he remarked:

"Mamie has come back, sir," and he was sure that his keen scrutiny of Dobree's face was not deceived: a look of relief, even of pleasure, passed over those heavy features.

"Come back!" said Dobree. "I'm glad of that! Has she gone up to Miss Isabel?"

"I don't know, sir; but she's back, and you may be sure she will not easily leave Miss Isabel again."

"Good! good!" said Dobree.

"Well, sir," said Falkland, moved by his evident pleasure in this protection of his ward, "if you feel like that about Miss Isabel, why don't you send her away from this horrible place? This is no house for a young girl to stay in; she'll be ill, sir—perhaps sent out of her wits. Can't you consider that, and let her go?"

Dobree did not answer; his head sank lower on to his breast.

"Good, good," he repeated; "sit down, sit down close to me."

Falkland took the shabby chair on the other side of the neglected desk. He felt his heart beat rapidly. Surely, now, there was going to be some sort of revelation? But first of all he must try to secure some mitigation of the unhappy lot of Isabel Conway, and he continued to urge his plea in an agitated voice.

"Couldn't you send Miss Isabel away, sir?" he urged. "Whatever the trouble is, couldn't you put her right out of it—send her and Mamie away somewhere bright and cheerful, where she could be with her friends? Only do that, sir, and then let everything else settle itself!"

Dobree looked round furtively, and then, in a low voice, replied:

"I can't! I can't!"

"Can't let Miss Conway go?" repeated Falkland, in horror. "Why not, in heaven's name?"

"Because Manning intends that she shall remain," replied Dobree, again looking round.

"And has Manning all this power?" asked Falkland, desperately. "Are you bound to do, sir, as Manning says?"

Dobree did not reply. He gave Falkland a thoughtful look, and rose and began pacing up and down the floor.

"I'm in a dreadful situation," he said, at last, in a low, heavy voice; "a terrible situation, Mr. Falkland; an unspeakable situation. I'm in that man's power. I dare say that seems very odd to you, but that's the truth. I'm in that villain Manning's power."

"How is that possible?" whispered Falkland, overawed by the terrible look that Dobree gave him. "How can you possibly be in his power?"

"I am," said Dobree. "That's what I asked you to come here and listen to—my tale of how I am in Manning's power. And yet I can't tell you," he added, with another sigh of despair. "The whole thing's gone too far. There's no way out; at least, only one way, and that's what we must discuss."

"Any way!" said Falkland, eagerly. "Any way to help Miss Conway and you, sir!"

Dobree stopped deliberately in front of him, and took up his words keenly.

"Any way, did you say?" he repeated. "You would take any way to save Miss Conway?"

"Yes; and yourself, sir," said Falkland, resolutely. "Manning is a villain, of that I am convinced."

"He certainly is a villain," said Dobree, "that I *know*. And he has made me into a villain too. But that's no matter of yours," he added, darkly. "Here I am in Manning's power; here we all three are."

"But," said Falkland, more eagerly still, "if there are the three of us against one, what's the trouble, sir? Why, a man in your position, with your influence——"

Dobree seemed to shudder at these words.

"I tell you, none of that is any good against Manning," he replied.

"Well, he's only a human being, like you and me," urged Falkland. "He's not the devil, I suppose, or any supernatural creature? Surely, whatever it is, it can be met and mastered!"

"No," said Dobree, "it cannot be, it certainly cannot be mastered. Only," he added, with sinister emphasis, "in this one way. Are you, Falkland, prepared to take this one way?"

"Any way, of course," said Falkland, at once. "This life is torture—absolute torture; and I can't stand by and see Miss Isabel forced to marry that loathsome brute. I tell you, Mr. Dobree, I don't ask what your secret is, or what the hold is that Manning has over you: I am prepared to do anything you suggest to help you—and not to ask any questions, either," he added impetuously. "It is no business of mine, any of it. I only want to get Isabel Conway clear, back to her friends, and get away myself to my ordinary life. Just mine." He repeated himself in his desperate attempt to convince Dobree of his sincerity.

"I believe you," replied the older man.

"You said you would take any way," he said, with emphasis. "Isn't that so, Falkland?"

"Yes, sir," replied the young man, resolutely; "of course, I'll do anything—whatever you suggest."

"There is only one way," said Dobree, putting his face close to Falkland's. "Absolutely one way, Falkland. I want you to kill Manning."

CHAPTER XXX

FOR a terrible second, Falkland thought he had to deal with a madman. He gazed, petrified, into the glaring eyes of Dobree, now so close to his own.

"Kill Manning?" he breathed, doubting the evidence of his own senses. "Did you say 'Kill Manning,' sir?"

Of all things, he had not expected this. The horrible words had taken him utterly by surprise.

"Yes, I said 'Kill Manning,' " said Dobree; "kill him at once, quickly, swiftly, without any possibility of escape. Then you and Isabel Conway will be safe, and I," he added, with a deep sigh, "shall be at peace, for the first time in thirty years at least, Mr. Falkland."

The young man recoiled from him, and went and sat down in the chair by the desk. He was shivering all over. Just when he thought there was some way of escape opening to him, some solution of his immense and terrifying difficulties offering, he found himself involved in an even more dreadful situation. Was Dobree mad? Was the suggestion a trap? He could not decide; he could not even speak, but sat there, dumb and shuddering.

Dobree came slowly and heavily towards him, leant on the back of his chair and, bending down, whispered in his ear:

"Kill Manning, I said! Why can't you? I can arrange it all."

"Why," said Falkland, shrinking back, "don't you do it yourself, sir? Why should you put mr on this ghastly business?"

"Do it myself!" muttered Dobree, with a ghastly look; "but I can't! I daren't! If I had dared," he added, "I should have done it years ago; but I can't. Why couldn't you, though? You said you'd do anything—that you'd take any way; and this is the only way."

"But it can't be!" cried Falkland, trying to maintain some reason and balance. "It can't be the only way. I don't know if this suggestion is a test on your part——"

"No, no," said Dobree, hurriedly and impatiently. "Don't bother about that; I'm not testing you—I'm talking to you in desperation. I've about come to the end of things, and so, I suppose, have you. Therefore, I'm giving you this chance. The only alternative is madness, or death, for all of us." And he added, bitterly: "I tell you this: I shan't be able to save that girl upstairs; nor will you."

Falkland shivered to his soul.

"But perhaps you'd tell me something of what all this means," he begged. "Tell me what all this frightful mystery is, sir, and why killing Manning is the only way out."

"Because Manning is a fiend," said Dobree. "Because nothing will move or change him; because he has his mind set on marrying Isabel Conway."

"But why," interrupted Falkland, feverishly, "are you bound to give way to him? The girl is in your charge; she is your ward. Surely you could send her away from this place."

Dobree gave him a diabolical grin.

"Haven't I told you that I'm in his power?" he said. "He has got me in his clutches, and I can't get away."

Dobree's voice sunk to a whisper as he repeated:

"I can't get away. We're rats in a trap, Falkland, you and I—I even more than you. But I can help you to do this. Yes" he muttered, as if communing to himself, "we might do it, you and I, if we were very, very careful."

"Do what?" whispered Falkland, leaning forward.

"Get rid of Manning, of course," replied Dobree, again

furtively glancing round the cold, dreary room. "Get rid of him. Leave 'Mockways,' and leave him in it, Falkland. Clear out—all of us—and enjoy life without any shadow on it."

"Enjoy life!" repeated Falkland, almost hysterical. "Enjoy life, with a murder on our minds?"

At the word "murder," Dobree winced.

"It has been done, I believe," he grinned. "And there would be no great harm in ridding the world of a villain, of a scoundrel, like Manning."

"But," argued Falkland, in great agitation, "if he is such a villain and scoundrel, surely he can be brought to book: he can be denounced and dealt with by the law."

"The law!" cried Dobree, wildly. "You don't suppose that I can bring in the law? If I had been able to do that I should not be where I am now."

"No," said Falkland, slowly, "I suppose that's at the bottom of it all, Mr. Dobree: you've done something yourself—something that put you in the power of Manning."

"Yes, I have," admitted Dobree, sullenly. "But that's neither here nor there, Falkland; it won't help either of us to talk about that now," he added, wildly. "We've got to consider Manning, and get rid of Manning."

But Falkland rose, and said, desperately:

"I can't do it; I don't know whether you're mad or sane. But I can't do it."

"Not even," whispered Dobree, "not even to save Isabel Conway? Couldn't you do it for that?"

Falkland was silent.

"Won't you tell me more?" he cried, frantically.

But Dobree clutched him heavily by the shoulder.

"Don't raise your voice," he whispered, "don't raise your voice! Haven't I said that this is all secret? Any minute we may be spied upon or interrupted. Once Manning knows I've spoken to you——" he stopped abruptly.

Falkland could no longer doubt his sincerity, at least on this point. He was genuinely and deeply terrified of Manning.

"Perhaps I can guess this secret," said Falkland, talking wildly in the dark but trying to force Dobree into some sort of confession. "Perhaps it had to do with old Mr. Powell and young Mr. Vane."

"Ah, then, you *do* know something!" breathed Dobree, softly.

"Who was Sarah Lomax?" he asked. Can you tell me that, sir? Has she to do with Manning or with you?"

"With both of us," said Dobree, sullenly. "With both of us. But we are getting away from the matter in hand," he added advancing closer to Falkland and fixing him with a baleful look. "Will you, or will you not," he added, sinking his voice till it was a mere husky breath, "will you or will you not get rid of Manning for me?"

Falkland, in his frantic desperation, could not decide whether it would be better to accede to this terrible request or not. Surely the best thing to do would be, by some means or other, to gain time.

"I must think it over," he muttered. "I can't say yes all at once to a proposition of murder, you know, Mr. Dobree! However frantic the circumstances!"

"I should have thought," said Dobree, cunningly, "that where Miss Conway was concerned you would have agreed to everything at once. I can tell you," he continued in the lowest possible voice, "she's in the very greatest danger. Manning won't wait much longer. He insists on her marrying him, and one of these fine mornings, Mr. Falkland, there'll be a car at the door and we shall be taken off to the local church; and there you'll see Isabel Conway married to manning. He always carries a special licence in his pocket."

"She will never consent," said Falkland.

"Won't she?" said Dobree. "I can't count on that; neither can you, Falkland. You know well enough that the wretched girl can't resist for ever. She will soon be in such a state that she will do everything Manning tells her; and so, no doubt," he added, desperately, "will even you and I."

"But this is madness," cried Falkland, struggling to throw off the nightmarish atmosphere of the whole ghastly interview. "It really is madness, Mr. Dobree: there must be some way out!"

"I've told you the way out," said Dobree; "I've told it you, and I can't stay any longer to argue the matter with you. Will you or will you not get rid of Manning?"

Falkland shuddered, and parried this fearful question by asking:

"What way did you propose to get rid of Manning, Mr. Dobree?"

"If you agree to it, I'll tell you," replied the older man, grimly. "Not before you do so."

"I can't agree," replied Falkland. "After all, it's risking hanging, you know."

"It's risking nothing!" said Dobree, eagerly. "I can easily arrange that. No one will suspect anything. You don't suppose I haven't thought all that out, do you?"

Falkland shuddered the more to hear this.

Three loud raps on the door interrupted them.

CHAPTER XXXI

"IT'S Manning!" shivered Dobree; and the great, hulking man shivered and cowered where he stood.

"Well, what if it is?" breathed Falkland, though he, too, felt a strong sensation of fear. "We're locked in, aren't we? You needn't answer the door."

"But I must," whispered Dobree; "I must. I've got to let him in. I expect he's been listening—listening to what we've been saying and planning."

"We've been planning nothing," protested Falkland, almost hysterically; "planning nothing. And as for listening—" he added, his nerve seemed to be breaking fast—"as for listening, Mr. Dobree, there's nothing else but listening in 'Mockways'; every one is listening one to the other. We can get out of this room, can't we?" he added, clutching at Dobree's arm. "There's the window: if he's after us we can get out by the window!"

"Of course, he's after us!" smiled Dobree, with a ghastly grin. "Of course, he's after us! Of course, he knows what we've been talking about. He knows everything. But we can thwart him yet, if you'll act—and act quickly!"

"Don't let him in!" said Falkland, again.

But Dobree was already at the door, and had unlocked it.

It was Manning who stood without, in the dark corridor.

"I don't want to disturb you, sir," he said turning to Dobree; "but I was wondering what you were talking about with Falkland. You've been shut in here a good while."

"I wasn't talking of anything of any importance. Nothing

whatever, Manning, I assure you. Mr. Falkland's getting rather tired of 'Mockways' and our ghost search, and thinks it's time things came to an end or a climax; and I must say," he added, with a sideway look at Manning, "I'm beginning to think so, too."

"Oh, you are, are you, sir?" smiled Manning, blocking up the doorway. "You are thinking things ought to come to a climax? Well, I dare say they will!"

"This box, now," said Dobree, heavily, as if oppressed and almost overwhelmed by the power of the other man present. "Suppose we give up looking for it, eh, Manning?" His husky voice held almost an appeal. "Suppose we let it go! A few jewels aren't of much importance, after all. The thing's getting on our nerves—on our brains; we shall go crazy if we keep on searching, searching like this for that *papier mâché* box."

"Certainly," remarked Falkland, trying to bring things on to some sort of a sane and normal level, "it seems to me lunacy to keep on searching like this for a few jewels hidden by a lunatic old man thirty years ago. Why, the whole thing may be a trick—when you find the box it may be empty!"

Dobree laughed dismally.

"If I thought that, Falkland, I'd give up the search. An empty box is no good to us, is it, Manning?"

"Nor a few jewels either, I should have thought," said Falkland, looking carefully from one to the other.

"Nor a few jewels either!" echoed Manning, in a sinister tone. "No, you're quite right, Falkland; a few jewels aren't of much interest to us."

"Then it's something else you're looking for," asked the young man, taking this as a challenge, or perhaps a confession. "You may as well tell me what it is."

"No," said Manning, "I may as well *not* tell you! If you chance to find the box you'll find out for yourself; and if you don't chance to find it, you'll never know—that is, if you don't know now."

"He doesn't," said Dobree, with a sort of eagerness. "I'm convinced of that. We might as well let him go, Manning, for he really knows nothing. The mention of that name," he added, nervously, "the name of Sarah Lomax, you know, was just chance, I'm sure. He really knows nothing of anything at all; he might as well go."

"Of course," agreed Manning, quietly. "Mr. Falkland can go whenever he likes. The way is open; let him leave 'Mockways' to-day, if he wishes. I'm sure, sir, you will quite easily be able to find some other secretary." And he smiled evilly at Falkland, knowing what held the young man to "Mockways"; knowing that he would not leave the dreadful house while Isabel Conway was a prisoner there.

Falkland hung his head.

"Well," said Dobree, with a certain eagerness, turning towards him, "do you hear that? You hear Manning's suggestion and advice—you can go. Go, if you like."

"I'd rather stay," said Falkland, sullenly. "And both of you know why, don't you?"

Dobree did not reply to this, but he said immediately:

"I'm glad; I'd much rather you did stay, Falkland; very much rather, indeed."

Falkland made a desperate effort to break that sense of spell that Manning's presence gave him—a spell that he was sure that Dobree felt also. He straightened himself up, and, facing that formidable, sinister creature, said:

"But I agree with Mr. Dobree that things ought to be brought to a conclusion—to some sort of a climax. Here we all are, waiting and searching—for no purpose as far as I know. And we can't go on. I can't go on. Miss Conway can't go on, and I don't think," he added, with meaning, "Mr. Dobree wants to go on either. Do you, sir?"

"No," said Dobree, heavily, "no. I think, Manning, we had all of us better leave 'Mockways,' and leave it quite soon."

As he spoke, he looked at Manning in a challenging way. It was a defiance that was instantly taken up. Manning advanced into the room, and assumed the air of a master.

"We don't leave 'Mockways' till I choose, Mr. Dobree," he said. "And when I shall choose I don't know. It won't be just at present, I don't think. Now I'm here—now I've come back, after thirty years—there's one or two things I want to find out; one or two accounts I want to settle. When that's done we can leave—and not before."

Falkland looked apprehensively at Dobree, thinking he would surely fall on Manning for this insolence. But Dobree did not. With a long shudder that shook his great hulking body, he turned away.

Manning shot a long, evil glance at Falkland, and turned to leave the room.

"We'll have another ghost sitting to-night," he remarked, as he went through the door. "Till then, I think you can enjoy plenty of leisure, Mr. Falkland. No doubt you would like a rest, after your adventure last night."

He did not see either Manning or Dobree for the rest of that day. He was allowed to wander about unmolested. Manning knew well enough that he would not try to escape. He might go out as he pleased into the dank, wet park—by the mausoleum down to Mathews' cottage, round the walls; he might peer through the gates.

As he did this, he reflected bitterly that Compton had gone off with his precious bunch of keys. He was without even that small aid now—the possible chance of the use of those keys which had proved so useful on the day they had nearly escaped.

In the afternoon, he went upstairs to the top storey, and looked into the two rooms occupied by Beale and Compton for such a short time. Their two valises stood on the floor, and their few clothes were put about in the wardrobe. He noticed that there was nothing there but clothes, and surmised that anything else they might have brought had been taken from them during their absence at supper.

From there he went to look at the room which had always fascinated him—the old forge—with the dirty shreds of two or three crude wallpapers hanging in strips from the plaster, which was full of holes and cracks; the room where Mamie had declared she saw the *papier mâché* box, resting on the old anvil.

There was certainly nothing there now; and though Falkland made another restless, almost mechanical search among the rubbish accumulated there, he again found nothing.

Wandering dismally downstairs, he entered the room which he had occupied the first few nights he had been at "Mockways," and tried another search before the secret door which Mathews had entered. He could not find it, and Mathews was now far too terrorised ever to give him any information about anything. He resolutely refused to enter into any communication with Falkland whatever. Evidently he had been very badly frightened indeed.

The horrible emptiness of the house oppressed him dreadfully; he felt his nerves all ajar, his limbs shivering. At the least sound he started.

Manning and Dobree had disappeared. For all he knew, they were chasing each other with murderous intent through the dismal chambers of this foul house.

This pause was more dreadful than any activity, and Falkland, wandering from one to another of the atrocious rooms illuminated only by the ghostly light of the short winter day, began to turn over horribly in his distraught mind the ghastly proposals that Dobree had made to him—the proposals of getting rid of Manning.

To such a pass had he come from his residence in "Mockways" that now he was considering—actually considering murder!

He paused in one of the large ground-floor back rooms—a room that seemed once to have been used as a drawing-room, for the few pieces of tarnished furniture bore the remains of tattered satin covers—covers that were now faded to a dismal red like old bloodstains.

Here Falkland sat down and gazed through the long, uncurtained windows into the dank, dreary tangle of green beyond. One portrait still hung on the discoloured walls, which no doubt, had once been gay with many pictures; and Falkland found himself idly staring at it, while these horrible thoughts raced through his agitated brain. It was the picture of a woman, and as Falkland gazed at the dark dirty canvas he noticed the portrait wore a locket with the letters "S. L.", and he thought of the name "*Sarah Lomax*."

CHAPTER XXXII

AS soon as the meaning—or the possible meaning of those two letters "S. L." on the locket penetrated to Falkland's receptive mind, the portrait became to him of supreme interest, and fixed itself in his brain as being the most important object in the dilapidated room—perhaps in the whole hateful house.

He stared at it for a moment fascinated; it was a picture painted, probably, about the 'nineties; an indifferent performance, already darkened from bad varnish and dirt. It represented a pale, long-faced woman in a rather clumsy evening dress, leaning forward and gazing out of the picture in a conventional attitude; wearing no ornament but this one locket, which was at first almost indistinguishable in the dark folds of the bodice.

Falkland approached the picture, which hung some way above his head. When he was close he could see, even in the indifferent light, the form of the ornament, which very distinctly showed the letters "S. L."

Several times since his enforced stay in "Mockways" he had been through this gloomy room, but had never noticed this picture, which was insignificant enough, and one well in tone with the gloomy wall on which it hung.

He now took one of the chairs which stood about, and, mounting it, took hold of the picture. With a little effort he was able to detach it from the hooks, and lift it to the floor.

Turning it round, he saw written on the frame of the canvas: "Sarah Lomax, afterwards Mrs. Powell."

The blood leaped quickly in his veins. Here, if not a clue, was at least one definite fact: Mrs. Powell had been a Miss Sarah Lomax. Quite what that had to do with the mystery, or what amount of enlightenment it would throw on it, he did not know; but at least it was a definite fact, and one that had not occurred either to him or to Beale or Compton; indeed, when these two last had looked up the will of old Mr. Powell, it had never occurred to them to look up his marriage, or some time ago they would have discovered what Falkland had discovered now by this odd chance: that the name "Sarah Lomax," which seemed to mean so much, which seemed, indeed, the key to everything, was that of old Mr. Powell's wife. "And this girl," thought Falkland at once, "is probably some descendant. Daughter she can't be; but granddaughter she may be, and it is some wrong done to this woman that she is trying to avenge, I've no doubt."

He turned the picture round again, and stared long at the dingy canvas from which the plain, conventional face looked so blankly out, giving no indication whatever of what manner of woman this Mrs. Powell had been—this original Sarah Lomax whose name had come to mean all that was sinister and dreadful to Falkland.

The young man tried to fumble his way into some sort of solution of the mystery while he stared at the painted face, which seemed to gaze at him with a certain wistful plaintiveness.

Falkland went over in his mind the last dreadful interview with Dobree, when Dobree had spoken of being in the power of Manning. He could not doubt the sincerity with which Dobree, moved and agitated to the last degree, had spoken. There could be no doubt whatever that there was some dreadful secret, and that, whatever it was, Sarah Lomax was connected with it. But it could have nothing to do with the property of old Mr. Powell, since that was worthless.

Falkland leant against the wall feeling disheartened, agitated and baffled. He turned the picture round again and this time he observed, sticking into the frame, a small, filthy envelope, coated with dust and cobwebs.

Eagerly he took this out and unfolded it. Probably it was only some note left by the painter or frame-maker, but Falkland unfolded it with trembling eagerness, nevertheless. In his atrocious situation, shut up in this dreadful house, every trivial incident had come to take on a portentous meaning. The atmosphere of tension, of this perpetual search, the thought of the girl shut up, a prisoner in the room above, were all breaking his nerve down; and he opened the faded, stiff paper with trembling hands.

There were some lines of writing on it, half effaced with age, in faded ink; and Falkland could not at once decipher it. Turning it over, he took it to the window, which looked upon the back of the house, and as he did this he was aware of Dobree entering the room.

Falkland could not control himself.

"Don't keep following me about!" he almost screamed. "Don't keep coming behind me like this! Don't keep spying on me and watching me!"

Dobree looked at him fixedly.

"It seems to me that I've got to keep a watch on you," he muttered. "What are you doing here? And why have you taken that picture down?"

"Why shouldn't I take it down?" cried Falkland, furiously. "I've got to do something, haven't I? You keep me shut up here like this, wandering round these detestable, dilapidated rooms. I only wonder I didn't see the picture before, because I find it's one of Sarah Lomax, and she seems rather an important person in our concern."

Dobree took no notice of any of this.

"What's that you've got in your hand?" he asked with a snarl, advancing on the young man. "What's that you're trying to conceal from me?"

"Only a scrap of paper," said Falkland, putting his hand behind his back.

"Yes—something you've found," exclaimed Dobree. "Something that may be a clue, for all I know."

"A clue to what?" asked Falkland, violently.

"A clue to the *papier mâché* box, of course!" said Dobree, stepping nearer to him.

With a sudden, nervous laugh, Falkland held out the paper.

"Here—take it," he said. "I don't care what's on it. Read it, whatever it is—rubbish, I suppose."

Dobree snatched the paper and unfolded it. He seemed able to read it at once, and with the greatest ease.

To Falkland's surprise, he at once held it out to him, and told him to read it aloud.

Falkland did so, but only with some difficulty, and with Dobree helping him with a word here and there.

The message ran:

"I have found a secure place in which to hide what I wish to hide. Those who find it will be very clever or very lucky. When they do they will know the truth. I am afraid it will be a long time before this truth comes to light, but there it is hidden away, and when it is found everything will be cleared up. In that will be my message, my instructions, my wishes. I charge whoever may find it to act on these as they value their immortal souls. I am being watched and spied upon; I shall never be allowed to communicate with the outside world again; I have not very long to live. But I have managed to get the better of them in this—that I have written and hidden a full account of everything *and they know it*." (Signed) "James Powell."

These last lines "*and they know it* " were underlined. What Falkland had taken to be but a few lines turned out to be several, for the paper was folder over and over again in an intricate manner so as to form a sort of pellet which could be wedged in the frame.

"Queer I should have overlooked that," muttered Dobree, who seemed to have forgotten Falkland. "Queer with all this searching up and down I should never have thought of that picture—never thought of looking behind it. That'll be the same with the final hiding-place. I expect we pass it every day and never think of looking."

"This refers, I suppose," asked Falkland, "to the *papier mâché* box?"

And Dobree nodded his head sullenly.

"Yes, you see, the old villain hid it away somewhere. That was his only means of revenge: to hide it away and let us know he'd hidden it. I dare say he's left several little notes like this," added Dobree, with an evil grin, "trying to put people on the track."

"It doesn't help much, does it?" said Falkland. "Can't you tell me what it's all about, Mr. Dobree?"

"Can't you," asked Dobree, with some violence, "get rid of Manning for me? And then it will never matter what it's all about."

Though Falkland shrank, shuddering, away from all this, he could not lose sight of the fact that Dobree was far more useful as an evil friend than as a foe. His one chance seemed to be an ally of Dobree, so he tried to receive this monstrous suggestion quietly.

"If I am to help you in any way against Manning," he suggested, "then you must tell me all there is to tell."

"That I can't!" said Dobree, grimly. "If I were to tell you that would be to give yet another one power over me. And that I won't do. No, I won't!" he repeated, advancing on Falkland. "I won't tell you anything; and I'll see you don't find out anything."

He stuffed the paper in his pocket, and strode up and down the gloomy room. Falkland put his hand to his aching head. To gain time seemed the only thing to do.

"How would you suggest," he asked, "that we should 'get rid' of Manning, as you call it?"

"I'll show you," said Dobree, instantly. "Come with me, Falkland, and I'll show you."

He turned and left the room, and Falkland, as if fascinated, followed him.

CHAPTER XXXIII

FALKLAND followed Dobree upstairs past the room where the forge was kept.

Dobree led him on, through the ramifications of the old rooms which had so many times been rebuilt, altered and readjusted, till they seemed a mere warren, without plan or consequence; and finally, taking a key from his pocket, he unlocked a door in a part of the house where Falkland had never been before, because it had seemed so dark, gloomy, shut away and dust-choked; and told Falkland to follow him into his room.

Falkland did so, and could not resist an involuntary start of surprise and horror.

He thought at first he had come into the company of a lot of horrible human beings—lunatics or deformities; but a second glance showed him that he was in the presence of the waxworks which he had heard about, and which Beale had told him he also had heard about from the old man in the cathedral town.

The room was large and unfurnished: only these waxworks occupied it. Some of them were seated; some standing; there were about a dozen in all, all differently clothed. These clothes were moth and rat eaten, and tattered; but, more than that, the waxworks had been partially destroyed. They were ripped open—their arms and legs pulled off, their garments torn from their backs, their wigs cast down, in many cases their faces battered and cracked. Straw and tow and other stuffings were scattered about the dirty floor, and fragments of lace and silk flung here and there on the floor.

"What a ghastly sight!" muttered Falkland.

"Yes, it isn't pretty," agreed Dobree, with a horrible grin. "It isn't pretty at all. This was one of the fancies of old Mr. Powell. When I was in his employment," he added, in an absorbed manner, "I used to have to look after the waxworks."

Falkland passed in through the miserable wreckage.

"What happened to them?" he asked. "Some one has broken them up—tried to destroy them—haven't they?"

"Manning," answered Dobree, briefly; "Manning. But there's something here that even Manning doesn't know about," he added, with a look of ferocity; "something that will come in very useful for you and me, Mr. Falkland."

"Ah," said Falkland, "you, then, have your secrets from Mr. Manning?"

"I've got this one," whispered Dobree, touching him lightly on the arm—"just this one. But we'll have to be very careful, I assure you." And, moving back, he locked the door.

Falkland shivered to find himself shut in with Dobree and these ghostly waxworks; in this lonely, dismal room, which was only lit by one window, and from that the daylight was almost blotted out by a curtain of rusty and decaying ivy and the shadow of the cedar beyond. If Dobree chose to turn round on him here and murder him, he would not have much chance of escape, nor even of defence. No doubt, he reflected, biting his lips, Dobree was heavily armed, while he had nothing. Even the razor, which at first he had cherished, had been stolen. Manning, with a sneer, had long since provided him with a safety razor.

Falkland thought of this with a sort of hysteria, and leaning against the wall, laughed weakly. Dobree looked at him and began to laugh too, and the laughter of the two men quavered up, higher and higher, in the awful chamber.

"I'm going crazy," thought Falkland, "I'm surely going crazy! I must hang on to things—to real, normal things."

And, controlling himself with a great effort, he asked:

"Take care, Mr. Dobree, take care; Manning will hear us."

Dobree stopped laughing.

"Yes, we must be careful," he whispered, "or Manning will hear us."

"Who are these waxworks?" asked Falkland, moving among them and turning over wax limbs and heaps of stuffing. "Why has Manning destroyed them? I should have thought he might have found them useful," added Falkland, thinking of the trick with Mathews.

"Yes, I dare say," said Dobree, ferociously, "he would find them very useful but he has slashed them up and knocked them about looking for the box, Falkland; don't you understand? He thought this would be the very place in which Mr. Powell would hide the box; for this was his special room, and here he used to like to come and sit and talk with his friends, as he used to call them. This one," added Dobree, standing over a figure which still remained seated in the skeleton of an arm-chair from which all the stuffing had been ripped, "this one was his wife, Sarah Lomax. Let me present you, Mr. Falkland, to the original Sarah Lomax."

And with a start of genuine horror, Falkland found himself gazing at a ghastly figure of a woman, still wrapped in the remnants of a tattered black evening gown, her hair hanging down on her shoulders and her gaunt face staring out blankly, while her arms had been pulled off and lay across her lap.

There was a likeness to the picture downstairs, and even, Falkland thought, a likeness to the girl who had spoken to him in Bitterne woods.

"This was his fancy, you see," continued Dobree; "to have these things up here and come up and sit with them—all his old friends, he used to call them; people who had been kind to him once; people whom he had lost, or who were dead. You see, he trusted nobody; he didn't want to see anybody. He was just happy with these. "And that"—Dobree touched with his foot the remains of another figure like a gigantic doll, with a crude, pink-and-white face and a mass of yellow hair—"that was supposed to be his daughter, whom he treated cruelly and never would see. And yet he used to come up here and stare at this image of her. What do you make of that, Falkland?"

"His daughter?" said Falkland. "I didn't know he had any children."

"Yes," said Dobree, "he had a daughter. Now," he added, lowering his voice and coming close to Falkland, "Manning has an idea, a fixed idea, that the box is hidden here. I don't know why—perhaps from something the old man said, or just from some idea he has in his head, he is convinced that some where in this room the box will be found. Now, I think I could get him up here for another search."

"Well, and if you did?" asked Falkland, fiercely.

"Well, if I did," smiled Dobree, lowering his voice still more, "you and I could contrive that he never came out again; and that would be the end of all the trouble for you and me, Mr. Falkland."

"Oh, would it?" said Falkland. "I'm to murder your enemy for you, I suppose—the man who seems to be blackmailing you—and then, when we get out, you can denounce me. Is that the idea—eh?"

"No, no," said Dobree, quickly, "of course not. I shall stand by you through everything."

"Why don't you do it yourself?" suggested Falkland. "That would be a good deal easier, I should think."

But Dobree shook his head and sighed.

"There's a reason for it," he muttered; "a very good reason. Now, don't let's waste time; I expect that scoundrel will be following us. He'll be up here soon. He's watching us, I can tell you! He or that wretched Mathews—whom he has quite terrorised."

"What does Mathews know?" whispered Falkland, furiously. "You both of you seem a bit afraid of Mathews."

"Mathews doesn't know anything very important," muttered Dobree, "but he does know just a little bit that might be dangerous. Don't stand staring at those waxworks, Falkland," he added impatiently. "To-morrow we can make a bonfire of the lot—even a bonfire of the whole house, if you like! Yes," he added, as if this idea gave him fiendish delight, "that wouldn't be bad, would it, Falkland?—make a bonfire of 'Mockways' and all that's in 'Mockways'—eh?"

Falkland moved cautiously between the waxworks, unable to resist a fascinated gaze at their staring faces, yellowed and faded in some cases, cracked and distorted in others, but all with that look of inanimate life—a kind of petrified and evil humanity.

Dobree had now removed the damaged figures of two old men in the remains of Victorian clothes, and showed that there was a large chest behind them.

"Manning has been over this again and again," he said, "but there is one thing about it which he did not notice." He opened the lid of the chest, and Falkland peered fearfully within. It was quite empty. Dobree ran his hand round it.

"Quite empty," he remarked; "you see there is nothing in it?"

"Certainly," said Falkland, "there is nothing in it. What do you mean?"

Dobree put his hand in again, and touched some sort of

a spring, for the bottom of the chest slid back, and Falkland found himself looking into blackness—into what seemed to be a fathomless well.

"There's a drop there," said Dobree, bringing his yellowish face close to that of the young man, "right to the bottom of 'Mockways'—one long shaft; rather useful, don't you think? Any one could easily fall down there, Falkland, saying they were searching and prying: looking for something. Looking for a *papier mâché* box, for instance! Head first into this! Two other men could push him down—don't you think?—and then there would be an end of all the trouble. We could slide the lid back, put the waxworks on top; and who should know any better than that Mr. Manning is away on a holiday? A long holiday! A holiday for you and me too, I think, Falkland!" And he peered down, long and earnestly, into the blackness revealed at the bottom of the shaft while Falkland stared at him in fascinated horror.

CHAPTER XXXIV

"DON'T talk like that," said Falkland, turning away, sick and giddy, "whatever Manning's done, it's not for you and me to bring him to justice. There must be another way out, Mr. Dobree. This way lunacy lies—don't let's talk about it any more!"

And then he added, frantically:

"But why did you want to bring *me* into it? Couldn't you settle scores with Manning without bringing me into it?" And he cast a frantic glance round the horrid room, filled with those rifled and dishevelled waxworks. The whole thing was like the setting of a nightmare, and he felt his spirit fall.

Dobree, leaning on the open chest, continued to gaze as if fascinated, down the blackness of the shaft.

It was a large hole, quite sufficient for a big and heavy man to fall down. It must have been made—Falkland thought—with some very sinister intent. Perhaps it dated back to the first building of the house, and was some means of getting rid of possible prisoners. Perhaps the existence of this ominous shaft had something to do with the horrid reputation of "Mockways"; he wished that Dobree had not shown it to him, and suggested that they should now leave the room, which he felt he could not endure much longer; adding, in frantic persuasion, the argument which he thought most affected Dobree:

"Better come away, or Manning will see us! He'll certainly find us out. He won't lose sight of us both for very long, I'm sure. Hadn't we better come away if you want to preserve that secret?"

At this Dobree moved instantly, and sliding the false bottom into position, slammed down the lid of the chest.

"Yes, we'll come away," he repeated, quickly, "we'll come away. And we'll find a means of getting him up here. He'll come if he thinks we've found the place where the *papier mâché* box may be."

Falkland did not answer. He went to the door, waiting impatiently for Dobree to open it. He felt that he could not with sanity have endured another moment of the company of these waxworks and that awful shaft. If this went on much longer he would himself have had to jump down that black hole, and end the strain, the tension and the suspense that way.

They went down the dingy stairs, each looking fearfully round for Manning. It was horrible and alarming, the way that Manning impressed them both. Even when they could not see or hear him they were thinking of him. He seemed to be there always—like a shadow behind them; like an echo in the wall; like a step on the stair beside them.

"He's more than a mere man, surely!" muttered Falkland; "he's something more than human."

"He's an embodiment of evil," replied Dobree. "You're right; he's something more and something less than a man. I'm going to find him now," said Dobree, in the lowest of cautious whispers. "I'm going to begin to work him up with an account of that room. I'm going to tell him that I've found something that may lead to discovering the box. He doesn't want me to find it, and he'll be up there himself, I can tell you; and then will come our chance." Chuckling to himself, Dobree left Falkland and shambled away down the dusty corridor, and the young man, with a shudder of relief, went in the opposite direction.

He was fortunate enough—at least to him it seemed fortunate—to meet Isabel. She, by Mamie's advice, had left her room, and was walking up and down the corridors for a little exercise and change of air. She knew that it would be quite impossible for her to attempt to leave "Mockways," and she no longer had the spirit or energy to wish to do so. But she was trying to preserve some health and sanity by this pathetic exercise up and down the passage outside her room, and in and out those other empty rooms beside her own.

When she saw Falkland she advanced at once to meet him, but exclaimed at his haggard looks.

"What has happened?" she asked. "You seem dreadfully upset. What's the matter, Mr. Falkland? Oh, don't say some other terrible thing has happened!"

Falkland did not know that his inward terrors and apprehensions betrayed themselves so clearly. He tried to reassure her, but felt that his words rang hollow.

"Everything is all right," he tried to say; "nothing whatever has happened!"

But she shook her head.

"It seems to me," she murmured, "that everything is far from all right. I think we shall all go mad. Would it not be better for me to say that I would marry Mr. Manning?" she added, wildly, sinking her voice to a trembling whisper, "and get us all out of this? It seems to me that is the only way!"

"No," cried Falkland, with soft violence; "that is not the only way." And he thought of the gruesome alternative suggested by Dobree himself, and thought of it with relief. Sooner that, whatever the consequences to himself, than this most awful sacrifice of Isabel. "You must not think of any such thing. There is no need to despair: Dobree is coming round to our side—he is almost an ally.

You may expect some protection from him. As for Manning, he stands alone, and it will go ill with me if I can't defeat him."

The girl looked at him anxiously, and seemed to derive some courage from these brave words, so much braver than she knew; for Falkland was speaking from the extremity of fear and despair. He knew that if he could save the girl it would probably only be in the ghastly manner Dobree had indicated, and, though he would not, in an extremity, shrink from doing this, it was a ghastly prospect.

"Mathews is getting very frightened," said Isabel; "he has tried to talk to Mamie. They've scared him rather badly, I think. He won't stand much more. They keep terrifying him until he is half-crazy. If you tried, I think you might perhaps get something out of him, not very much, perhaps, but all he knows."

Here she looked fearfully round, and, imagining that she heard a footstep crept away back to her room, shutting her door behind her.

Falkland at once took advantage of her hint, and went downstairs to find Mathews. He was fortunate enough to discover him attending to the fire in the first-floor parlour, where the grim travesty of afternoon tea was already on the table. The sight of the cups and saucers, indeed, of the whole dismal equipage, gave Falkland the desire to laugh hysterically.

He approached Mathews, who indeed looked shaken and shrunken, and who was muttering to himself as if his mind was unhinged, while his trembling hands replenished the fire, piling up limps of coal on the dismal iron grate.

"Look here, Mathews," whispered Falkland, quickly, "Miss Isabel has just told me that they're going too far with you. That we are all in rather a desperate plight, I can't disguise; but couldn't you tell me what you know? It might help."

Mathews looked up at him suspiciously out of his little bleary eyes.

"What I know ain't much," he whispered, nervously, "but I dare say they'd wring my neck if they found out I'd spoken."

"I dare say," replied Falkland grimly, "they'll wring your neck even if you don't speak, so you may as well tell me, Mathews."

Mathews sighed and shivered, and again went on his hands and knees before the hearth, carefully picking up bits of coal and cinders, and piling them on to the central blaze, which now sent a grotesque, red leaping light round the dreary room. It was getting on to late afternoon again, and "Mockways," always a place of shadows, was once more full of them—all the crossing shadows of approaching evening.

Falkland shivered and drew nearer the fire, holding out his hands.

"Won't you tell me what you know, Mathews?" he urged, desperately. "Maybe it would be something that will clear up what baffles me. I've found out that Mr. Powell had a wife, that her name was Sarah Lomax, that she had a daughter. I think that Dobree and Manning wronged these, but I can't find out how this could have been, since Mr. Powell left nothing."

"Left nothing," said Mathews, quietly, gazing into the fire; "that's just it, sir; that's just where you've hit it. Mr. Powell did leave something: he left a very big sum—all the means which Mr. Dobree has built up his fortune on."

"No, he didn't," said Falkland; "my friends found out his will. He left nothing but this house and its contents."

"And its contents; that's just it," said Mathews, with a cunning intonation. "And you don't know what the contents of 'Mockways' was—do you, sir?"

"You mean—" asked Falkland, anxiously and eagerly "—you mean there is something hidden here; something no one knew about?"

"Something Mr. Manning and Mr. Dobree knew about," breathed Mathews, so faintly that Falkland, though bending close to him, could hardly catch the words; "something that I knew about; and that's why they had to pay me to keep quiet. I found out, sir, you see; and I was the only one who did."

There was a silence, while the wretched Mathews tried to pluck up courage to speak. That he wished to say something important was clear to Falkland, who waited with what patience he could. At last, still crouching down before the fire, and whispering in the lowest tones, Mathews said:

"You've seen that room with the forge, sir, upstairs—the room with all them torn shreds of wallpaper?"

"Yes, yes," cried Falkland, impatiently; "I've seen it."

"Hush, sir! Lower your voice, please—don't talk so loud! But, as you say, probably we'll all get our necks wrung anyhow, so here goes:

"Well, sir, behind that wallpaper was sheets of gold, and holes where all kinds of jewels was poked away. That's what was up there!"

This sounded to Falkland like joking or raving.

"What you say is impossible," he said, almost angry in his disappointment; "it's no good trying to tell me a tale like that."

"Tale like that or not, sir," retorted Mathews, bitterly, "it's the truth. Mr. Powell used to have all his money brought up in sovereigns, and he used to beat it flat on that anvil and then pin these sheets and strips up on the wall and have them papered over. In between, he used to make holes and stick diamonds into the plaster. That was his form of madness, sir, and no one knew it but Manning and Dobree."

CHAPTER XXXV

MATHEWS rose; and, as Falkland bent over him, continued his story in a quick, hurried whisper.

"This is what I wanted to tell you before, sir—what I meant to tell you that day I made an appointment in the kennels; but I never dared. It don't seem to matter much now."

"Hush!" said Falkland. "They may come in upon us at any moment. Hadn't we better wait—be a little careful?"

But Mathews, though fluttering with fright, seemed desperate.

"It don't seem to matter much," he repeated, "whether they know or whether they don't know. As you said just now, sir, I expect we'll get our necks wrung anyhow. And besides," he added, "I don't think they'll come listening after us." He gave an evil chuckle. "They are too busy chasing each other, sir—chasing each other up and down and in and out of the house, looking for that there *papier mâché* box—looking for a chance to wring *each other's necks*, perhaps."

Falkland shivered. Had Mathews possibly overheard the fearsome conversation of Dobree with himself?

But Mathews evidently was not thinking of this, but of something else, for he added, in a horrid whisper:

"Do you know what Mr. Manning's been after me for, sir? Trying to sort of mesmerise me into getting rid of Mr. Dobree—getting rid of you! Wants me to do it and take the blame, I dare say." And the little man shivered and shuddered, while the teeth clicked in his head.

Falkland could have laughed in ironic despair. The two men were, then, double-crossing each other! While Dobree was trying to get him to put Manning out of the way, Manning was trying to get Mathews to put them both out of the way! Perhaps even by the same means: for all he knew, Manning might also be aware of that ghastly trap in the waxwork room—of that deathly shaft running down the side of the house by the black cedar tree.

Everything he heard and every turn the adventure took made it all the more bewildering and the more horrible. It seemed that they could not all live a day more in this house without there being murder. Murder was the word that Mathews breathed, leaning on to Falkland and peering up to whisper into his face.

"Murder, sir," he murmured—"murder! That's what they're out for: trying to murder each other. That's what it's come to. What else could you expect, shut up in this house, knowing what they know, thinking all the time of old Mr. Powell—seeing his ghost, no doubt hanging about and urging 'em on. Oh, I can tell you, I've fair had enough of it. If they put me out of the way quickly I don't care."

"Ssh, ssh," whispered Falkland; "we may get the better of them yet. You and I must keep together, Mathews. We at least are sane, and have nothing on our consciences. I don't think you could say the same for either of them. Come, now, what was that you were telling me about old Mr. Powell, and the way he used to hide his money? It sounds fantastic."

But Mathews assured him that he had only spoken the truth.

"The old miser didn't trust any one or anything long before he came to 'Mockways'; and his one intention was to hide his hoard so that no one could possibly find it. He despised crude and easy methods as hiding it in chests or burying it in the ground, and thought out this scheme, which he congratulated himself upon as being likely to baffle the shrewdest.

"But he didn't baffle them long," continued Mathews, "as you can understand, sir; and even me, hanging about the house I got wind of it, though I don't think the other two servants ever knew what he was up to.

"He put all his money into jewels, sir—at least, nearly all of it—and the rest he used to take out of the bank in sovereigns; you could get sovereigns in them days: real gold, sir. He used to get it up there and beat it out on that forge and plaster it up on the wall; and he knew something about jewels, too—he used to put his money into fine stones, and then he'd stick them into the plaster up there with the sheets of gold and have wallpaper put all over it. He used to do that himself, sir—I had to fetch the rolls of paper and the paste and leave them at the door. And then, when he'd papered over one lot, he'd stick some more and put some more paper, thinking all the while that no one knew anything about it. Just a hobby of his, he said, that forge was, like the waxworks. But I can tell you that it wasn't long before Mr. Dobree knew better. Yes—and Mr. Manning too. You see, he had to trust some one because he got so old and ill he couldn't leave the house. By that time Mr. Dobree had been with him a good while, and he was trained up to know something about jewels, and used to be sent up to London to buy them—all the good ones, whose value wouldn't go down. And it was up in London he met Mr. Manning, I think. Mr. Manning's something to do with that trade, he gave up doctoring for it—and not in a very honest way either, young as he was then; and he got in with him and sold him some jewels, and then he came down here to value them. And then he saw the game the old man was up to—it was finished for all of them, I can tell you, once Mr. Manning came on the scene."

"Did he let Mr. Powell know that he had discovered this hoard?" asked Falkland at the end of this breathless recital.

"Not he, sir—he was too cunning for that! He just pretended he didn't see anything; but all the time he knew. He knew it was worth while digging himself in here in 'Mockways'; worth while waiting; worth while going through anything! I tell you it was a big fortune the old man stuck behind the walls in this house."

Mathews paused, shivering, and glanced furtively and yet with a certain defiance round the room.

"There, now, sir, I've told you, and you can make the best of that you can, remembering that 'Mockways' and contents—*and contents*, sir!—were left to Mr. Dobree; and the contents included what was behind the wallpaper in the old forge room. Now perhaps, sir, you can see a bit o' daylight. When your friends went and looked up Mr. Powell's will that's what they found," he repeated. " 'Mockways' *and contents*. And now, sir, you know what part of that *contents* was—something worth taking a bit of trouble for, wasn't it?"

"If you're sure of what you say," sighed Falkland, in a low voice, "it certainly was. And that's why there was this grievance with the wife and daughter, I suppose? They were cut out of all that money that the old man was sticking up on the walls of that room. I think I do begin to see things a bit clearer."

"As for the wife and daughter, sir," said Mathews, sullenly, "I don't know anything about them. Mr. Powell had quarrelled with them pretty long ago; some sort of trouble and grievance there was, but I don't know who was in the right or who was in the wrong of it. But you may be sure that when the old feller got into the clutches of Mr. Dobree there wouldn't be any pickings or any leavings for any one else."

"And you don't know what became of them?" asked Falkland,

cautiously. "You don't know who this present Sarah Lomax is?"

"The present Sarah Lomax?" said the old man, fearfully. "I don't know of any present Sarah Lomax. There ain't one as far as I know, sir."

"But there is," said Falkland, cautiously, "some one about the place. You remarked on it yourself. Don't you remember the first night, when I came here, you came flying out to the gate in a panic because of some one you'd seen up a tree? Who was that?"

"Well, sir," admitted Mathews, reluctantly, "I thought that was Sarah Lomax—the old one—come back like she used to be when she was a girl. There used to be pictures of her about—photographs in the old man's time—standing round; though they've all disappeared since he died. I remember her; and that's what she looked like—up in a tree. She wouldn't have been up in a tree if she'd been an ordinary human being—she wouldn't have been in 'Mockways' at all. I'd been worrying about it and thinking about it, shut away here; and when I saw that face looking down out of that tree——"

"Ssh! Nonsense!" said Falkland. "Just an ordinary girl; and she'd climbed up into 'Mockways' that way—got hold of some of the branches, I suppose, and swung herself up. I saw a motor cycle outside. There *is* a present Sarah Lomax—she's on the track of Mr. Dobree and Mr. Manning."

"Well, good luck to her if there is!" sighed Mathews, incredulously; "but I don't believe so: I believe it's just a spirit, sir—a spirit come here to haunt Mr. Manning. That's what I think, sir. I never heard tell of no Sarah Lomax living now," he said, shaking his head. "If there is anybody about this place, it's a ghost."

"Ghost!" said Falkland. "The only ghost I've seen seemed to me the ghost of an old man."

"Ghost of an old man?" asked Mathews, at once.

"Yes—it was you dressed up, I suppose," said Falkland, irritably. "So much fooling goes on here one doesn't know where one is."

"It wasn't me dressed up, sir," said Mathews, obstinately. "If you saw an old man I expect you saw old Mr. Powell. He's come back, hunting for those papers himself. Isn't it enough to bring him," he added, on a note of rising hysteria, "—all this searching, up and down and in and out and through and round, for something what he hid thirty years ago: something that was pretty important to him? Isn't that enough to bring his ghost back?"

"I dare say," said Falkland; "I certainly thought I saw a shape in the window that night."

"Well, that's him, you may be sure—it's always thinking of him that's enough to bring him back. I wish he'd point out where them papers are," he added; "that'd put an end to anything."

"I don't quite see that it would," said Falkland; "and even if we get hold of them—what should we do with them? Where should we go with them? We can't get out of 'Mockways,' either of us."

"Well, they don't seem to put many obstacles in your way, sir."

"That's because they Know I can't leave Miss Conway. While that unfortunate girl's shut up here how can I get away from the house?"

"I don't see what good you do by staying," said Mathews. "Why don't you get off, sir, and see if you can get some help from outside?"

"What help can I get?" asked Falkland, desperately; "the whole thing is still moonshine, still in the air—even that fantastic story of yours about the forge, and the hidden jewels behind the wallpaper. It sounds like a fairy tale—whom am I going to get to believe it? And if I *did* get some one to believe it—what could they do? They couldn't go and break into 'Mockways' on that excuse! The thing's not proved, and probably never will be."

"It might be proved if you found the papers, sir," said Mathews.

"Yes; if I could find the papers and get away with them, there might be something in that; but it doesn't seem to me very likely I *shall* find the papers. We shall all be dead, or crazy, or murdered, long before we find any papers."

"There's your two friends outside, sir—can't they do something? They seem energetic young men."

"They're in the same state as I should be," said Falkland, helplessly. "What can they do? They can't very well make a noise and a scandal: begin saying things about Mr. Dobree, who's got nothing against him; and also against Mr. Manning, who also seems to have quite a good reputation and record. What on earth *can* they do? They can't bring police and detectives round about 'Mockways!' If they were to tell any one that I and Miss Conway are prisoners here, they wouldn't be believed. And even if they *did* get any one to believe it, as I say, what sort of action could be taken? They couldn't have the place forced, could they? No, Mathews, we are in a trap, I can tell you, and it's only our own wits can get us out. Look here!" he added, sharply: "do they know that you know the secret of the forge?"

"Well, sir, they do and they don't. I never dared tell 'em that I knew it, but they thought I did; and that's why they kept me here. They sacked the other two—that they were sure knew nothing; but me they kept on, calling me the caretaker. And I was old and hadn't got any other work; I didn't mind settling down in the cottage, with the dogs. Pretty high they paid me, I can tell you! A little bit *too* high for an honest bit of work. What was I getting all that money for—just living in that cottage and doing nothing, year after year?"

"You've been there thirty years?" said Falkland, incredulously.

"Thirty years, sir! I was a youngish man too, at the time; and I'm getting old now. I don't say that I haven't liked the post. A bit solitary, but I didn't mind that. I used to get out, cycling about and seeing things, and I forgot all this, until lately, when they came down—coming in here; and I saw that creature in the tree, began to hear movements in and out of the house: then it all came back to me. I don't say they haven't paid me well—but what have they paid me for? Not looking after 'Mockways,' but for keeping quiet about what was up in that room, the forge room."

Falkland asked him if he remembered old Clement, the gardener.

He said yes, he remembered him quite well.

"But he doesn't know anything, sir; he was always working outside, in the garden. He wouldn't know."

"People heard this rumour about jewels," said Falkland. "I thought the old fellow was in his dotage, or babbling, but according to you it's quite true. He thought there were jewels hidden in that box."

"Yes, I know," grinned Mathews; "that's what they told all of us. Jewels! They didn't want to go looking for jewels hidden in a box when they'd got all them jewels plastered into the walls; and sheets of gold, too. There was something else they was looking for, I can tell you! The old fellow was terrorised—just like they've got me terrorised now. He couldn't get away from them; he couldn't get out. Manning was supposed to be a kind of doctor, looking after him. He wouldn't let him move, even when he did have the strength to get out of bed. He used to write, and hide it away, hoping somebody would find it, some day."

"Yes, I know," said Falkland, thinking of the envelope he had found tucked into the frame of the picture. "At the same time it may all have been a delusion. You know what people are when they are ill and half senile: he may have thought he'd written something and never done it. And what had he got to write about. His secret of the money, I suppose—his secret as to where he'd hidden all his money away: was that it?"

Mathews looked obstinate and stared down at the ground.

"Well, I think I know what it was, sir, but I'm getting away from what I *know*, now, and only into what I guess, sir; and I'd rather not speak."

"Well," said Falkland, "you seem to me to have said quite enough: you might say a bit more. What is it you think?"

"I'm not going to tell," said Mathews; "I've said quite enough. I've told you all I know," he repeated, obstinately, "and I'm not going on with any guesswork. As you said yourself, sir, it seems to me we're in a trap, and I don't see who's to help us—unless we do something desperate ourselves." And he looked furtively at the young man as he spoke. His suggestion, though put so differently, was no doubt the same as the suggestion made by Dobree—to get rid of Manning.

CHAPTER XXXVI

FALKLAND felt that things were getting very near to a climax—perhaps a terrible climax. Certainly things could not go on as they were: the tension was more than unbearable; it was absolutely insupportable. Something must happen soon.

One of the men would, in time, turn on the other. He could not think quite which it would be. He cast over in his mind whether Dobree would fall on Manning, or Manning on Dobree, or Mathews on either of them, or he on any of them: and he laughed hysterically and desperately at the picture this conjured up.

All these people shut up in this atrocious house, chasing each other, pursuing each other, suspecting each other; ready, almost, to murder each other.

Not "almost," in some cases. For he knew that Dobree was perfectly ready to murder Manning, just as Manning, no doubt, was perfectly ready to murder Dobree, himself and Mathews. He thought of Manning as a wholesale criminal, and was prepared to believe anything of him, so much had the man's sinister and powerful personality impressed him.

"And I shall be drawn into it, too," he thought, frantically. "They'll make a murderer of me. It seems to me I must murder or be murdered." And he began to play with the gruesome idea of acceding to Dobree's request and getting rid of Manning.

After all, might they not call it an accident? Wouldn't it be an accident, if they got Manning to look down into that awful chest, and they pushed him down the shaft? Dobree would be on his side, and he would support the tale. There would be no other witness. Mathews certainly would not accuse them for the sake of Manning! Mathews detested and feared Manning.

Falkland tried to shake off this dreadful temptation; but when he thought of Isabel Conway, shut up there, and the fate before her, he did not find it so easy to shake off.

His distraught mind turned to Sarah Lomax. Where had she been lately? He had seen no trace nor heard any sound of her in "Mockways." Had her secret way in and out been discovered by Manning or Dobree? Had she given up the task? He did not think that likely; but perhaps some misfortune had overtaken her. Anyhow, he could not think that she was any longer coming in and out of the house. There had not been a sound—ghostlike or human; nor in any of the gloomy rooms into which he wandered had he seen any trace of her. Perhaps Manning had discovered how she got into "Mockways" and had blocked up the entrance: and Falkland had a horrible picture of the girl, perhaps locked away for ever in some subterranean passage—shut away in a cellar, beating and striking in vain against some door or some obstacle which Manning had placed. Her high adventure, undertaken at least with a great deal of skill, gallantry and ability had come, perhaps, to this gruesome end.

This thought was too ghastly to be endured. Falkland flung himself from the house, and walked up and down the drive; then across the neglected lawn, and directed his steps towards the pagoda where he made his futile attempt at escape with Isabel Conway.

Gaunt and blank in the dismal winter afternoon the tower rose up through the leafless trees, and to Falkland's surprise he found the door open. Probably there was now no need to lock it, since Manning would have taken all precautions against any escape by this means.

Falkland peered aimlessly into the empty tower, which rose up, one long, straight shaft, very much like that other dark, sinister shaft by the side of "Mockways." Here, he thought, was another way for some one to meet their death, falling from the top of that tower! Then he laughed at his own craziness, feeling his brain was going: for, without stairs, how could any one get to the top of the tower?

As he reflected this, he walked out and looked around, and saw, to his surprise, that there were small notches and footholds in the outside of the tower by which means it would be possible to get to the top.

He wished he had asked Mathews about this tower: perhaps he could have told him something of it. It seemed an extraordinary building, without purpose, and certainly without any beauty. Was it merely the cloak and shield for that underground passage, built, perhaps, by Mr. Powell?"

He wandered round and round, more or less listlessly, trying to distract himself by wondering the purpose of this horrible-looking tower; but he could find nothing.

Walking round by the kennels, he found Mathews there feeding the dogs, and asked him about the tower. Mathews did not answer at once.

"They seem to allow you a good deal of liberty," he said, suspiciously. "You'd better look out, sir."

"Well, I can't stay in that house, listening to Miss Isabel pacing up and down her room," said Falkland, nervously. "I thought I'd rather take a turn about the grounds, to keep myself more or less steady. They'll be up to something soon, I've no doubt—probably to-night. And I've been looking at that old tower—the one where we nearly made our getaway. We might have tried it again, but I expect the passage has been blocked up. I shouldn't care to risk it now, though the door is open."

"That there old tower," said Mathews, reflectively; "yes, it is a queer place, isn't it, sir? Old Mr. Powell had it built: it was supposed to be a sort of watch tower."

"Whatever for?" asked Falkland. "The man must indeed have been a lunatic!"

"Lunatic or not, sir, he had that built for a watch tower. There was the idea that you could get up to the top of that and see who was entering the grounds. You can see all over the grounds, sir."

Falkland remembered that he had had this idea when he had first seen the tower. It had seemed to him a wonderful vantage ground to look all over the park of "Mockways."

"There aren't any stairs inside," he remarked.

"Well, there's some kind of steps or stairs outside," said Mathews, "or used to be. I don't know whether they've decayed away now, sir. It's not so high as that—only just above the tree tops. Old Mr. Powell was always fidgeting with that tower. I remember, the year before he died, he had the workmen in, making a new parapet to it: a kind of seat, or outlook place, where you could climb up and then stand and look round."

"I should rather like to get to the top myself," said Falkland. "One might see something—some way out—some possible escape."

Mathews shook his head:

"That ain't very likely, sir; there ain't no way of escape they've overlooked, you may be sure!"

Falkland wandered back to the house, hoping against hope that at the midday meal he might possibly see Isabel Conway. The meal was laid in the dreary parlour, but there was no sign of the girl—not even her footsteps overhead, now.

Mamie was laying the table with her usual cheerfulness, and Dobree was sitting by the fire with such a look on his face that Falkland felt his blood run cold, and for the first time the idea occurred to him that he ought to warn Manning. That seemed a grotesque thought; but was he not in honour bound to warn Manning? If ever a man's face meant murder, surely Dobree's face meant it now! And Falkland's sympathies were with Dobree—with the blackmailed; not with the blackmailer: with the man who was trying to put up some sort of feeble defence for Isabel Conway; not with the man who was persecuting her to the last extremity.

"Mr. Manning," said Dobree, with sinister softness, "is still looking for the *papier mâché* box: a very patient searcher, is he not, Mr. Falkland?"

"Where's he looking?" asked Falkland, tersely.

"He's looking upstairs," said Dobree, "—raking round the attics again. I shouldn't be a bit surprised if he went into the waxwork room."

"You've put him on the trail, I suppose," thought Falkland. "You're trying to get him to look down that chest!" And again a struggle went on in his mind whether or no he should rouse the suspicions of Manning. He tried to console himself by thinking that probably Manning already knew that Dobree was set against him, that he had gone too far in his life-long persecution of Dobree, and now the moment had come when the victim had turned.

Whatever it was he knew against Dobree, he had held it over his head for a very long while, and surely the time had come when Dobree had the right to defend himself!

Falkland had the sensation, as he stood there and looked at the heavy figure and white face of the man sitting by the fire, that whatever he had done he had surely paid for it!

They had their meal together in silence, and Mamie took up food to Miss Conway, taking the opportunity to remark that Miss Conway was quite well and happy, and that there was no need for either of them, she said, with meaning, to worry about her.

"Quite well and happy!" said Falkland. "That sounds ironic enough, doesn't it?"—and he looked at Mr. Dobree.

Dobree gave one of his queer, heavy sighs. He ate a little food, drank a glass of wine, and then rose from the table.

"We won't have any more ghost searches," he said; "we won't have any more hunts for the *papier mâché* box, Falkland. We will go away from here, all of us."

Falkland looked at him in horror. What did his words mean—where was Manning? Had he already seen to the end of Manning? Had he already secured his freedom? Falkland could not help feeling a leap of joy at this thought. As long as he had no hand in the getting rid of Manning he could scarcely expend any sorrow at any fate that might overtake that scoundrel.

"Why doesn't Manning come down to dinner?" he asked. "Where is he?"

And Dobree gave a ghastly grin.

"Hunting for the box," he said; "he isn't tired of the search, though we are!"

Falkland could eat nothing. He felt the food choke in his throat, so heavy was the air with dread and tension.

"I should not stay in the house," suggested Dobree, softly. "Why don't you take another walk in the park?"

Falkland did not answer. Was this meant as a hint to him to keep clear while Dobree worked his will with Manning? In that case, if this was so meant, what was he to do? Was it his duty to interfere—to try and warn the victim? He could not think so.

Whatever the matter there was between these two men was no concern of his. He had been dragged unwillingly into the whole terrible affair, and had nothing to do but to think of the safety of the defenceless girl also involved, and then his own. So he thought: "Well, I may as well take the hint and clear out. As long as he doesn't ask me to do anything active, let them settle it between them. It will be better for Isabel Conway to be in the power of Dobree, even if he proves himself a murderer, than in the power of Manning."

It was raining—a flat, grey drizzle blotted out the park, but Falkland threw on his coat and plunged out into the wet. There was a certain satisfaction in the cold sting of the rain on his face—in tramping over the wet leaves and under the bare trees.

Relaxing of physical tension was refreshing after this long nervous tension, but he could not help continually looking back over his shoulder at the blank, dark, ugly shape of "Mockways" which now rose up so sharp against the winter sky; there being no leaves on the trees near by save the black blot of the cedar which leant against that horrible wall which hid the shaft.

He thought wildly:

"I couldn't help Manning if I wanted to; I've got no weapons. Manning himself has seen to that. Mathews couldn't help him, either."

He remembered that Mathews was down by the kennels; he would not be able to come if he wished to; and Falkland thought ironically that he was not at all likely to wish to. If Dobree intended to come to issues with Manning, he certainly had the field clear.

To give some sort of direction to his nervous walking, Falkland returned to the tower, which fascinated him from its curious sinister aspect, and from having been the scene of his abortive attempt at escape.

This time he began to mount the outside by means of the iron loops and notches in the stone. It was not, after all, a very difficult ascent: the tower was not high, and the steps were firm and neatly placed together; with a little scramble, Falkland got to the top, where there was a platform and a sort of seat built out, just as Mathews had described.

There had been a weather-vane, and this was lying, broken, on the roof.

CHAPTER XXXVII

FROM the top of the tower, Falkland could just see above the trees across the park, and as there was not any longer any foliage, he had a very good view of the domain of "Mockways," stretching right to the high wall in one direction and to the ditch and railings in the other, which shut out the estate from the bare hillside.

He gazed on this forlorn prospect with a feeling of gloom and apprehension. Gaunt and hideous, the house rose up in the midst; very clearly he could see the shape of it, against the blank, rainy sky; and his thoughts were with what was being enacted there: Isabel and Mamie shut in their room, Dobree and Manning pursuing each other, watching each other, up and down, in and out the rooms. For all he knew, murdering each other.

He felt that he should not have left the two women to this; that he ought to return. He wondered how it was he could have gone from "Mockways" at such a moment; he had not thought about the two women shut up there—only of getting out of the way, while Dobree and Manning came to grips. But though he knew that he could not do much, still he thought that he ought to go back for the sake of Isabel Conway.

He turned to descend the tower, and in doing so, struck against the vane, which, rotting from age and neglect, had fallen across the tiles. Two or three of these same tiles were loose, and Falkland noticed with curiosity that the displacing of these tiles had revealed an iron ring, rusty from age and neglect.

He leant forward across the roof and pulled at this. After a little effort, he found that it raised a small stone under the tiles, and disclosed an aperture in the roof, carefully lined with concrete. In this aperture was an iron box.

Falkland felt his heart thrill with excitement.

With trembling fingers he drew the box out. It was not very large; like a smallish, old-fashioned cash-box. Nor was it locked. He opened it and found there was something inside, wrapped round and round with stout waxed paper.

Without stopping to examine inside, he began the descent from the tower, and after only scratching his hands a little against the rough walls, found himself once more on the ground. To be out of the rain, which might deface or soil any possible treasure there was in the little cash-box, Falkland stepped into the tower, and there unwrapped his prize.

He saw what he had, in his excitement, expected to see: inside the cash-box was another one . . . small, *papier mâché* box, painted with a view of Windsor—a little box, such as women used a few generations ago to put trinkets in.

This box was locked; but the lock was so frail that Falkland had no apprehension that he would not be able to break it. He stared at the thing in a fascinated silence. So there *was* a *papier mâché* box, and the old man had taken that extraordinary place to hide it! What a remarkable precaution! There must indeed be some vital secret inside this little trinket-box, for Mr. Powell to have taken all that trouble to hide it.

And what an odd chance that his attention should have been directed to it by the fall of the vane across the roof which had displaced the tiles!

Falkland tried to think how old Mr. Powell could have hidden it there. He must have told one of the workmen to put it in there when he had had the vane and the seat put up. It was odd how he could have got the men to keep the secret, but probably they did not know what was in the little cash-box; probably he told them it was some plan or calculation to impress future generations, in the same spirit that people would put Bradshaws or time-tables underneath new buildings.

Well, anyhow, here it was, and Falkland gloated over it. After all these days and nights of feverish and desperate searching, he was the person who had found the prize at last: not Sarah Lomax; not Manning, not Dobree—but he, himself. And whatever power went with this secret, that power was his.

He felt so excited, and his hand trembled so that he could scarcely force the lock. He began to turn over in his mind what he should do with the secret when he knew it. After all—his heart sank again as the reflection came to him—after all it would not be very much use, whatever it was, unless he could get clear of "Mockways." It might even drive Manning to frantic desperation if he knew he was in possession of the secret at last. Therefore, Falkland decided to be very cautious, and not breathe to any save to Isabel, if he had a chance to speak to her, the information that he held the precious prize.

He left the tower, and hid the cash-box and rolls of waxed sealed paper in the hedge, digging them deeply into the litter of rotting leaves and the soft ground; then he tried again to force the lid of the *papier mâché* box. But, trifling as this looked, it was stronger than he had thought; and as he had no weapons of any kind on him, not so much as a pen-knife, he could not succeed. He would, then, have to take it to the house and smuggle a knife from the dinner-table or the kitchen.

He could tell Mamie, he thought; yes, he could trust Mamie. And she would be able, no doubt, to give him something, if only a pair of scissors, with which to open the *papier mâché* box.

It was so small; he had never thought of it as small as that, but as being large-sized. But here it was, small enough to go into his outer pocket.

Hardly able to contain himself for excitement, he hastened back towards the house. He had to pass the stables and kennels; and as he did so, he stopped to speak to Mathews, who was still pottering about with the dogs.

"I've been to the top of the tower," he said, trying to control his voice; "there's quite a good view from there, as you said—a view of the whole park. But I don't quite see the object of the thing! Did Mr. Powell ever go up it himself?"

"Lord, no! sir," replied Mathews; "how on earth could he get up there—and he bedridden for years; unable to lave his room at least—besides, Mr. Manning would have taken care that he didn't get up that tower, or get up to any pranks like that. Old Mr. Powell thought a lot of that tower," added Mathews; "he even had an account of it written, and buried up in the roof—hidden away in one of them tin cash-boxes: I dare say you'd find that, sir, if you was to poke about. I remember him giving it to one of the workmen. One of his crazy ideas, it was.

" 'The tower's unique,' he said. 'Here's an account of it! You must stick that up in the roof, underneath the vane.' And I think there was some joke about that, sir—Vane being Mr. Dobree's name in those days. Some sort of feeling about the vane; I don't know what, sir, but that's the way he spoke—as if there was more to it than just the word."

So that was how the old miser had deceived the two men who were watching and spying on him, was it? reflected Falkland. He had had the cleverness to hit upon this bold expedient—openly to give this cash-box, which was supposed to contain an account of the re-building of the odd old tower, and tell the workman to hide it in the roof. A very clever idea indeed, and one that had thrown the other two men off the scent. For evidently he had told them his secret was hidden in a *papier mâché* box when he had put this same box in an outer one of tin and hidden it in the roof in the park. The workman would put it in there unsuspecting, no doubt, taking it merely to be the whim of an eccentric, half crazy old man, and so, for thirty years, Mr. Powell's secret had been safely hidden under the vane of the old tower.

"Yes, I dare say it's still there," remarked Falkland, as quietly as he could; "but I didn't see anything. The vane's blown down and some of the tiles are loose. I dare say the box has been destroyed by now."

"I dare say, sir," replied Mathews, indifferently. "Are you going back in the house?" he asked.

"Yes," said Falkland, "I'm going back now: it seems to me that matters have now about come to a head, and it's my job to be as near to Miss Isabel as possible."

All was quiet when he returned to the house; he could see Isabel sitting at her window, and trying to amuse herself with a little sewing. She smiled down at him, but he dared not say anything to her; he felt that "Mockways" was all eyes, and he did not know who might be staring from any of the windows.

He therefore merely returned her smile and passed into the parlour, which was as familiar and dreadful as a place visited many times in a nightmare.

He looked at once round the room for something with which to open the *papier mâché* box, which lay, light and snug, in his pocket. There was nothing: Manning was always very careful not to leave any kind of weapons about—not as much as a penknife.

Falkland wrenched at the box with his bare fingers, but it would not give. Though the thing was little more than a toy—just a trinket for a lady's table—it was very strongly made. Though he did not wish to do so for fear of injury to the contents, Falkland saw that he would have to smash the thing.

Then he thought of Isabel and her sewing, and went out again into the rain. She was still there with her white, wistful but brave face, gazing out across the park. The window was slightly open at the bottom.

"Can you throw me down a pair of scissors?" said Falkland. "I've torn my nail."

She at once threw him out a pair of embroidery scissors, suspecting far more than he said; for he had tried to throw meaning into his words.

It was not a very difficult matter, with the little scissors, to prise the lock open. There was, as he had suspected, a roll of papers inside, very carefully tied and sealed. They were little odd scraps of paper, closely written on, some in red, and some in black ink, some even in pencil—evidently scribbles put down at odd moments, furtively and secretly.

Falkland, with one eye on the door, turned them over hastily in the dull glow of the firelight, trying to find beginning or end to them—for they were not numbered, and seemed to be put together incoherently. Here and there a sentence of big, spidery writing was clear to his anxious glance.

"No one knows where I've hidden it: they will never find it. No one will ever guess." It was repeated again and again, till it seemed to Falkland that he was merely about to read the babblings of some one in delirium.

Then another line caught his eye:

"All I possess, all there is in 'Mockways,' to my wife and daughter absolutely. Everything to them. I have charged them on their honour, on their oath, to see that this is done." This paper was signed "James Powell."

"Ah," thought Falkland, "I begin to see to the bottom of the whole thing." And again he fingered the pitiful little slips on which were written:

"I'm spied on—I'm being watched. They won't let me out; they won't let me write; they won't let me send for her. I've had to sign the will—they won't know where to find this though."

And then again, on another strip, which seemed torn out of a book:

"Whoever finds this will know I accuse *them*, both of them of murder."

CHAPTER XXXVIII

FALKLAND heard a step, and the creak of the door, and instinctively pushed the worn red cushion of the chair over the bundle of scraps of paper and the small *papier mâché* box.

It was, as he had expected it would be, Dobree who entered. Where was Manning? It was always Dobree now, creeping round the house. It was quite a long time since he had seen Manning.

Falkland felt a thrill—a sense of deliverance—from this absence of Manning, and even from the discovery of the *papier mâché* box.

Dobree looked at him askance, came to the fire, took the chair opposite, and, propping his heavy head in his hands, gazed at him steadily and with a faint smile.

Falkland was forced to ask, almost against his will and in a fascinated manner:

"Where is Manning? Where is Mr. Manning?"

"Manning is still looking for the *papier mâché* box," smiled Dobree. "That's what Manning's doing! Don't you know by now that that is what every one is doing—hunting for a *papier mâché* box? Miss Sarah Lomax," he added, with a queer intonation, "is doing that too. She is here, searching for a *papier mâché* box."

"Have you found her?" asked Falkland on a note of dread.

"I've seen her," said Dobree; "I saw her just now. Creeping in and out of my house like a thief! Well, she is a thief, isn't she—looking for property of mine? for," he added, with a cunning look, " 'Mockways' was left to me by old Powell, you know! 'Mockways' and all that was in it. And if the *papier mâché* box is hidden here, then it's mine, isn't it?"

"Don't bother about the *papier mâché* box," replied Falkland. "I shouldn't trouble about that any more; I don't think it's in the house, anyhow. What about Mr. Manning and Miss Lomax—have you let her go?"

He wondered if the man before him was sane—if what he said might be believed and taken as coherent sense; or whether it was the mere babbling of one whose brain has collapsed. Had he really seen Sarah Lomax? Had that resolute, energetic young woman allowed herself to be caught at last?"

"I came upon her just now," said Dobree, softly, "walking through the passage she's always used. Of course, I've known for a long time that she used it, but I haven't troubled about it very much. It wasn't likely, was it, that she, creeping in and out of the house like that, would be able to find what we've been looking for so long?"

And again Falkland asked:

"Where is Manning?"

This time Dobree did not reply. He signed and stared into the fire.

"I think you can leave 'Mockways,' " he said, at last. "You and Miss Conway, and that Mamie creature. You may as well go—tired of this place, aren't you?"

"Yes, we want to go," replied Falkland; "but what do you mean quite by letting us go like this? What'll Mr. Manning say?"

"Never mind, Mr. Falkland, about Manning: it doesn't matter any more about what he says."

Falkland leant forward and whispered, hoarsely:

"What have you done with him, Mr. Dobree?"

Dobree grinned, and made no reply.

Falkland rose, and walked up and down the room. He was

still bewildered. He held in his hand what should have been the trump card, but he did not know how to play it. He had found the box; he had got the papers, and he knew the dreadful things those papers said; but how to use all this knowledge? How to use this powerful weapon? He was in the power of Dobree—in the power of Manning, for all he knew. Surely it were better to try some other means of getting away from "Mockways," and from a safe distance use the papers.

Dobree, in an absorbed voice, as if he hardly realised there was any one else in the room, said:

"The ghost of an old man—that's what there is in 'Mockways'; the ghost of old Mr. Powell."

"I dare say," replied Falkland, "you think by now you see that—after being shut up here——"

"Yes," replied Dobree, with a sigh, "I do think I see it—the ghost of an old man." He seemed to shake himself, as if to try to throw off the burden of some nightmarish reflection. "I see it, Mr. Falkland—and not only in 'Mockways.' I've been seeing it for thirty years. One of these days I knew it would lure me back to this house; and I knew that here we should meet, face to face, at last."

"Can't we stop talking about these things?" asked Falkland, in an awe-stricken voice. "It's all very terrible, Mr. Dobree, and no affair of mine. As I said so often before, let us go, and I will have no more to say or to do in your business."

"It doesn't matter," answered Dobree, in a queer voice, "what any one has to say or do with my business, for I think my business had come to an end now."

Falkland moved a step away from him. He believed that he had by himself "got rid" of Manning, as he termed it—that he was looking at a man who was twice a murderer; for what had those pathetic scraps of paper in the *papier mâché* box revealed?

He could no longer contain himself. Moving away towards the window with a shrinking gesture, he said in a low, quivering voice:

"Mr. Dobree, I may as well tell you after all: I've found the *papier mâché* box."

To his astonishment, Dobree seemed to take no notice of this—to be not in the least impressed by this momentous declaration. He sighed, and, shifting his heavy head from side to side:

"Oh, you have, have you?" he replied. "And what was in it after all? Just a few scraps of paper, I suppose, with the old man's babblings on them."

"Just a few scraps of paper," said Falkland, advancing to the chair where these were hidden, "but they are quite enough, I'm afraid, Mr. Dobree. The old man put on them his final charge."

"His final charge to whom?" asked Dobree.

"His final charge to posterity—to any one who found them—to see justice done."

"Justice, justice, justice!" repeated Dobree, dully. "Yes, that was what he was after—justice—wasn't it? A queer-sounding word, when you come to think of it. Mr. Falkland: justice!" And again he lapsed into a heavy silence, staring into the sinking fire.

"He said that he wished to leave his property to his wife and child," whispered Falkland, "that he was prevented from doing this, that he was terrorised by two men."

"Yes," said Dobree, "by myself and Manning—principally by that scoundrel Manning."

"You kept him here," pursued Falkland, "shut away; he was old—almost senile. You prevented his wife and daughter from coming near him. He made a will in their favour—this is the story as I take it—and you destroyed or hid or in some way made away with that will; and you forced him to make another, leaving everything to you."

"Rather a commonplace sort of story, isn't it?" said Dobree, quietly, as if these words did not refer to himself at all.

"And you succeeded in all this villainy, and the poor old man had no means of letting any one know what was happening to him. You and Manning terrorised him, just like Manning has terrorised you ever since, Mr. Dobree."

"Well? Go on, Mr. Falkland—you seem to know the whole tale."

"Yes, I know it now," replied Falkland. "I tell you I've found the *papier mâché* box, and everything fits in quite well. Just an ordinary, commonplace story after all, Mr. Dobree—but not a very pleasant one."

"No, Mr. Falkland, not at all pleasant," said Dobree, in a mechanical voice.

"You knew that there was something in 'Mockways' besides the rotten furniture and the few, wretched sticks, didn't you?" said Falkland. "You knew that the old man, half lunatic, had been plastering gold and diamonds behind the paper in the forge room. All his fortune, whatever it was, had gone into those jewels and those sovereigns that you and Manning used to bring into 'Mockways' for him. You knew what he'd done with them."

"Yes," said Dobree, "we knew what he'd done with them. It wasn't likely that he'd be able to fool us."

"No; but he thought he had. Yet he knew himself outwitted, too, when he made that will leaving you 'Mockways' and all its contents; and all he could do was to write it down on little, odd scraps of paper as he got time and opportunity."

"An where did he hide them?" asked Dobree, turning slowly and heavily in his seat. "That's curious—he used to keep taunting me with a *papier mâché* box in which he'd written everything, in which he'd put down about his wife, and the property, and what we were doing to him: and now you say you've found it! Curious, Mr. Falkland—curious!"

"He put it in an ordinary little tin cash-box," replied Falkland, "and when he had that crazy old tower repaired he gave it to a workman and told him to put it at the top—under the tiles—under the vane. Vane was your name in those days, wasn't it, Mr. Dobree? Well, that's what he did. Said there was an account of the tower in this little box, and the workman was to put it there. And there he put it very safely, in a little aperture of concrete, where wind and rain couldn't get at it for a whole thirty years, Mr. Dobree. There, by just a fantastic chance, I found it to-day."

"A fantastic chance," repeated Dobree. "And what, after all, is in those papers, Falkland—just what you told me: about being shut up here, and two young men taking advantage of him? About a crazy old lunatic of a miser, who used to beat out sovereigns and plaster them on to the wall; and putting money into diamonds, to stick them into that same plaster? Is that all there is in that paper?"

"There's just something else," said Falkland; "but since we've come to issues like this, I don't know——" he hesitated, and turned away. "There's something else, Mr. Dobree."

"And what might that be?" asked Dobree, softly.

"I think," Falkland stopped, and gathered up the papers from behind the shabby red cushion, and pushed them into his pocket. As he did so, he revealed the small *papier mâché* box, and he saw Dobree's eyes turn to it.

"That box! Yes, I remember. He used to have it in his room. It was something he'd given to his wife, years before . . . just a little trifle for her to keep her trinkets in. And so that was where he put his secrets at last. Do you know," he added, in an impersonal tone, "I was never thinking of that box. I thought of something large—never of that silly little box Sarah Lomax used to keep her trinkets in."

"I don't know," replied Falkland, "whether there's any need for me to say any more, Mr. Dobree. It seems to me I'm still in your power——"

"Yes," said Dobree, slowly, "I suppose you are, in a way. You needn't leave 'Mockways' if I didn't choose you should. But you can go, if you like—out into the world; anywhere."

"With this secret?" asked Falkland. "You don't care if I go away with this secret? It's rather a dangerous one, you know, Mr. Dobree—a bit more dangerous than I have yet told you."

"You haven't told me the whole thing?" muttered Dobree. "There's something else, is there—something else the old man wrote on those scraps of paper?" And his eye glanced over Falkland's hand, which lay upon his pocket where the papers were hidden. "Well, you mustn't believe all he wrote, you know—he was very old and very queer. And as for his wife—he'd never been happy with her; and she was a very great deal younger than he was, and they quarrelled long ago. It wasn't altogether my fault—or even the fault of Manning—that he quarrelled with his wife, Mr. Falkland."

"No; but it was your fault that they were cut out of everything—that they were left penniless, to struggle along somehow. But they didn't forget, you see; the daughter handed the story on to *her* daughter, and it's she, the granddaughter Sarah Lomax, who's coming in and out of 'Mockways' now, looking for the *papier mâché* box."

"Well, well," said Dobree, "it seems to me a tale that's told; the whole thing's over, isn't it? Not such a very terrific mystery, after all,

Mr. Falkland—not anything so very wonderful. Suppose we don't talk about it any more? Supposing we let the whole matter come to an end? I dare say Sarah Lomax will find herself provided for, after all."

"I dare say," replied Falkland; "but it's rather difficult for you to make amends now, you know, Mr. Dobree: your fortune was built up on what was practically stolen money. You and Manning between you robbed the old man, and his wife, and his daughter. And it's not a thing you can easily make good; or one that will be lightly forgiven."

"I don't ask to be forgiven," said Dobree, sullenly. "I don't ask anything."

Falkland could not understand this new, quiet demeanour on the part of Dobree. He had now played his last card by revealing that he had found the *papier mâché* box and knew the secret. He did not know how Dobree would take this. It seemed impossible that he would let him go now. The only thing was to over-awe him and bear him down. The time for subterfuge and concealment was over—it was impossible for them to take up any game of pretence again. And meanwhile, where was Manning? Falkland rather shuddered as he thought there was still Manning to be faced.

Dobree rose, and seemed to stretch himself. He looked at Falkland with a long, dull gaze.

"Tell me," he asked, "what else was there in that paper. There's something else, you know; something besides the fact that we robbed the old man."

"Yes, there is," said Falkland, goaded: "there's the fact that you murdered him. He says there that he knew you were going to murder him; and you did murder him!"

CHAPTER XXXIX

DOBREE leant forward. He seemed to peer into Falkland's face as if he was extremely curious and no more.

"Murder?" he said, softly. "Yes, that's the right word. And the old fellow knew it, did he—that's rather dreadful! He knew he'd got no chance?"

"I'm afraid he did," whispered Falkland. "He's written it here—that you were tired of waiting, and that you meant to murder him.

"He might have lived, you see, quite a long time. He might have managed to get in touch with somebody outside. It wasn't so easy for you to keep him shut up here, old and feeble as he was. There were the servants: you were rather afraid of them, weren't you. And there was the wife and the daughter outside. They might have managed to communicate with him, for all your care; and so you thought you'd make an end of it, and you murdered the old man—when you'd safely got the will out of him."

"So you've got the whole story at last," said Dobree, with a smile. "Yes, that's quite correct, Falkland. We murdered him. Or, rather, *I* murdered him and Manning stood by; Manning was far too cunning to do anything himself. He made me do it. And therefore, he was the worse criminal," added Dobree.

"He made you do it that he might hold it over you afterwards, just the same as you wanted me to murder *him*, Mr. Dobree, that you might hold it over *me* afterwards."

Dobree shook his ponderous head.

"No; no," he repeated. "That's not true. I wanted you to murder Manning because I didn't know that I'd got the courage to do it myself. Not a second time," he added, with a sigh.

He moved away heavily, muttering to himself:

"The old man didn't suffer: he'd got no use for the money, and I knew what to do with it—I knew what it would mean; power, influence, everything in the world I could get with that money. But what did *he* do with it? He was a lunatic, hammering it out there on that anvil, pasting it up on the wall, just one thought: to keep it hidden from people; his mind going round and round like a rat in a trap as to how he was to keep that stuff hidden. How do you think that a man like myself, full of ambition and youth, was going to stand by and see that? And the moment I set foot in 'Mockways,' Falkland, I made up my mind to get that money."

"And Manning, I suppose," replied Falkland, "made up his mind to get *you*; and each of you got what you wanted. You had the money and Manning had you. He stood by, like the devil himself, and saw you do murder, and from that moment your soul wasn't in your own keeping, was it, Mr. Dobree?"

"You're quite right," said Dobree, dully. "From that moment my soul wasn't my own. I had to keep Manning with me always. He was always there, standing beside me; he never spoke of it and I couldn't look at him without thinking of it: and that was my punishment, Mr. Falkland, for thirty years."

"Punishment enough, I should think," said Falkland; and he felt an impulse to cast those papers into the fire. The crime was over now, and it hardly seemed to be his place to avenge the old miser. Dobree had surely paid. And as for Manning——

Looking at Dobree, he believe that Manning had paid too.

"I prospered," muttered Dobree, thoughtfully, as if talking to himself; "everything went well with me—I made money, more and more money, and sometimes I quite forgot where it all came from—sometimes when Manning wasn't there. Manning had his share, you may be sure. He had no sense of making money himself, but he got all he wanted from me. But he seemed to want more than money—he seemed to want to torture me."

"The sense of power," muttered Falkland; "the sense of power—that's what appeals to characters like Manning. He'd got you like you got your money, and he wanted you to know it, just like you wanted other people to know that you'd got money."

"It kept me away from people," said Dobree, reflectively. "I couldn't get married; I couldn't make friends; I was always moving about. Heaps of acquaintances, you understand, Mr. Falkland, but no friends. But I began to cease to be afraid. The years went on, and it seemed so long ago; and I began to have a certain affection for Isabel Conway. It seemed to me as if she might have been my own daughter—and Manning began to have an affection for her, too. And there was the trouble, Falkland—there was the trouble.

"Then it began, my torment; I was fond of the girl, and sorry for the girl, yet I'd got to give her to Manning—a brute like Manning—a murderer like Manning. Manning became violent—he demanded his price, nothing else; for he was capable of telling the whole tale, hanging himself to hang me."

And Dobree's lips curled in a horrible sneer.

"He was willing to bring himself down to blast me sooner than give up the girl."

"Well, she's safe now," murmured Falkland. "You didn't quite do it, Mr. Dobree."

"No," answered the old man heavily. "I've always got that consolation; I didn't quite do it. I kept her away from him; I did try to save her, if only by a compromise."

A dull and heavy silence fell; the twilight was invading the room. An awful gloom fell over the whole prospect. The short winter day was drawing to an end, the rain was falling heavily against the frame of the tall windows."

"And what now?" asked Falkland, putting his hand to his aching head. "What now, Mr. Dobree? Shall I throw the whole thing into the fire and say nothing more about it?"

"If you did," smiled Dobree, "you'd still *know*, wouldn't you? Manning had no *written* evidence; but that didn't help me."

"You don't think," asked Falkland, "that I'm a blackmailer like Manning, do you?"

"I don't know," said Dobree; "but you'd always have my secret, wouldn't you?"

"And what's the way out?" breathed Falkland.

"Well," muttered Dobree, "the way out is pretty clear. Not both of us can go on living. I can't endure life with some one knowing all that—all that you know, Falkland. I've had thirty years of it."

Falkland wondered if this meant that he was after all going to get rid of him by foul means. After his talk of escape, of letting him and Isabel Conway go, was he, after all, going to dispose of him now? Everything seemed possible, and Dobree a murderer, even if a murderer under provocation; even if for thirty years he had committed no crime. He was capable of murder, and Falkland stood in his power; and if once he disposed of him, what about the unfortunate women overhead, whose footsteps he could again hear, pacing to and fro in the chamber that was their prison?

Useless to appeal to Dobree—that Falkland knew. What he had resolved upon to do he would do without any possibility of his being turned aside by what any one else might say. Falkland folded his arms, looking with a frown down on the dingy floor.

Dobree's story was out—a story pitiful and commonplace, only rendered grotesque by the eccentricity of the old miser, all was now clear. He could understand the quest of Sarah Lomax, how the story had been handed to her from her grandmother and her mother, and how, goaded by disappointment and poverty and the consciousness that they had been deeply wronged, she had endeavoured to discover the secret of old Mr. Powell.

Somehow or other it had leaked out—probably through the talk of servants—that the secret lay in the *papier mâché* box: and he could understand how the high-spirited and resolute girl had set out on the search.

"What are you going to do about Sarah Lomax?" he asked." Are you going to render any justice to her? After all, she ought to be the heiress of 'Mockways,' and all it contains."

"She and Isabel Conway," replied Dobree, softly, "will divide my fortune between them. That is sufficient reparation, I think; to those two dead women I can offer nothing. To her, half my fortune. For," he added, with a sneer, "it's all about money, isn't it? It's just money she wanted, so she'll get it; and rather more than her grandfather left. After all there wasn't so much underneath that wallpaper, you know; nothing like as much as I made of it. The old fool wasted his means in those stupid vagaries; he knew how to hoard, but he didn't know how to make money."

"That is reparation enough for the future, I think," said Falkland; "but you are a young man yet, Mr. Dobree. What about the present? Are these two women to be provided for, and how is Miss Conway to be saved from the persecutions of Manning?"

Dobree grinned, and did not answer.

"Where is Sarah Lomax?" urged Falkland. "Won't you let her go, if you have her shut up somewhere? It's absolutely getting on my nerves—these women shut up in this house."

"They may go," replied Dobree, "whenever they like."

"Have you told Sarah Lomax what you are doing for her?"

"No," said Dobree; "it was scarcely worth while. I told her she could stay in 'Mockways' and look for the *papier mâché* box, and that there was no need to use these secret entrances. She could come in and out as freely as she liked. No need," he added, with a sneer, "for masks and disguises, and messages hidden in knots of red silk. 'Mockways' is hers from now on. She can have it and do what she likes with it. Yes, in my will I've left 'Mockways' and all it contains——" and here his sneer deepened into a diabolical ferocity—"to Sarah Lomax, as she calls herself."

"But the contents of 'Mockways,' " said Falkland, wondering what was meant by this, "are worth nothing now, and I should think Miss Lomax would be glad not ever to see the place again. It seems to me," he added, with a shudder, "that if this place were burnt to the ground it would be a good thing for every one. The place is nothing but a nightmare; it is full of horror."

"Burn it," said Dobree, heavily; "burn it, if you like."

"And these with it?" asked Falkland, holding out the pathetic packet of scraps of old paper on which the wretched miser had written his last wishes, his terror and his fears and his prophecy of his dreadful doom. "Shall I burn these with them, Mr. Dobree? They are of no use to me."

"You mean you do not intend to use them?" asked Dobree. "Is that it? Well, you can do as you wish about that."

"Justice is not in my hands," said Falkland. He took the papers and advanced to the fire. He could see no use in keeping them: after all, they were not definite proof. He did not know that in a court of law they would stand as any evidence whatever against either Dobree or Manning, and he hated the thought of being burdened with another man's secret, of trying in any way to hold a threat over Dobree. "If I cast these into the fire," he asked, "will you let me and Miss Conway go?"

"You will in any case go," said Dobree, "whether you burn them or not."

Falkland, with an impulse that he could not altogether account for, threw the scraps of paper and the *papier mâché* box into the fire, where the low embers caught them and smouldered them into charcoal at once.

Dobree watched them burn into black cinders.

"You can go whenever you like," he said. "I have nothing more to say. You will find my money divided between those two women—I can't do any more."

"No," said Falkland, "no; but what about Manning?'

"Manning," smiled Dobree, "has met with an accident."

CHAPTER XL

SARAH Lomax stood hesitant in the big room at 'Mockways'—the room where the portrait of her grandmother had hung, where it now stood resting against the discoloured wall. She was at a loss. After years of absorption in one subject, after the most painful and strenuous endeavours, after the greatest daring in pursuing her ends, everything had come to an abrupt, and to her, miserable conclusion.

Mr. Dobree, whom she regarded as the man who had defrauded her, her mother and grandmother before her, had met her, told her coolly that she was free of the house and might search for the *papier mâché* box as much and as openly as she wished.

The resolute and energetic young woman did not know quite what to do. All the zest had gone out of the pursuit. She saw her pretences, subterfuges and disguises seen through. Dobree had spoken to her almost with contempt.

She decided, and decided with bitter reluctance, that she must give up the search. If there was anything against Dobree, it was not to be given to her to find out. Now that she was free to search "Mockways," all sense had gone out of that same search.

Bitterly she supposed that Dobree's permission meant that he had himself found the box or else had good evidence to know that no such thing had ever existed.

Perhaps it was all a delusion, those tales she had heard from her mother during their long, bitter poverty—tales of the mythical fortune left by her grandfather which should have been hers and which she had been cheated of through the machinations of

Dobree and Manning. Tales of the *papier mâché* box which had leaked out through servants: no doubt old Clement, the gardener, had mentioned to Mrs. Powell, when she had tried to get some information from him, that the old man had been heard to mutter that all his secrets were in a *papier mâché* box.

Now all this had appeared to Sarah Lomax so much fable.

All her weapons were taken out of her hands; she did not know what to do, and she felt fearful for the safety of that other woman shut up there, and of that of the young man whom she had involve in all this.

She resolved to make one attempt to get into communication with Isabel Conway and then to give the whole thing up in despair. Dobree had looked at her so scornfully, and at the same time so queerly that she wanted to get away from "Mockways": the long search had broken down even her hard nerves.

She turned and left the room, where the twilight was gathering fast, and going upstairs, knocked on the door where she knew Isabel Conway was confined. First, she had listened over the banisters and heard Dobree and Falkland talking to each other in the front parlour. Where Manning was she did not know; it was some hours since she had seen him.

Mamie answered the knock. Sarah Lomax stood outside without any disguise now, and asked for Miss Conway. Isabel came at once; she was amazed to see in this place a person who had been to her just a name, almost a ghost.

"It's all over," said Sarah Lomax, sullenly. "I've nothing more to do here."

"He's found it himself!" exclaimed Mamie; "that's what it is. He or Manning have found it themselves."

"Or perhaps," said Sarah Lomax, "there was nothing to find.

After all, it was only a tale, something handed down. But somehow it impressed me, got hold of me; I could not get rid of it. And I thought I was so clever—pursuing and frightening him."

"You frightened him all right," said Mamie.

"Yes, I frightened him too much—frightened him into something desperate—frightened him down here into shutting you up," confessed the girl, bitterly; "and now I don't know how to get you out."

"Perhaps if he lets you go free," said Isabel, hopefully, "he'll let me go too—me and Mr. Falkland. I always thought there was something not so bad about Mr. Dobree. It's more that he's in Manning's power."

"And there's Manning still to reckon with," said Sarah Lomax.

"Where is he?" asked both the other women. "We've been watching from the window and listening at the door, and we haven't seen or heard anything of him all day, since quite early this morning when he went upstairs."

"Perhaps," said Sarah Lomax, "he is upstairs now. I'll go and look," she added, with a flash of her old spirit.

The other two women tried to hold her back.

"What do you want to go upstairs for looking for him? Leave him alone."

"Well, I should just like to face him before I leave 'Mockways' for ever. Mr. Dobree and Mr. Falkland are talking down in the parlour, and I'll just go and see—just make a last attempt; perhaps I'll charge him with having found the box, and accuse him of what I believe he did."

"And what was that?" whispered Isabel, fearfully.

"You know, I believe, what I think it was. I think there was foul play: I think old Mr. Powell was done to death."

Sarah Lomax turned away and went resolutely up the darkening stairs. She really was determined to face Manning. She had a bold, firm courage, and did not wish to leave "Mockways" without seeing him.

The rooms were getting dark and the lamps had not yet been lit. She looked from one to another, turned into the two rooms occupied by Beale and Compton for those few hours, and in which their few clothes still hung.

At last she came into the room where the forge still stood, where the shreds of paper hung from the walls in dismal rags and tatters. And there, on the floor, she saw Manning stretched out, with his head near the forge and his brains dashed out by one of the heavy hammers. He had been done to death violently, brutally and, no doubt, suddenly. The girl sprang back in an access of terror, and closed the door violently. She stood for a moment unable to speak, scarcely to think. Murdered! Manning had been murdered! And by whom? There was only one person of whom she could think—Dobree.

Inspired by terror, the girl dashed downstairs and again knocked on the door of Isabel Conway and Mamie.

"Make haste!" she said. "Let's get away; let's get out of this house anyhow. There's my secret passage: we'll go through that."

Alarmed by her white face and frantic words, they pressed her with questions.

"But we are watched: can we do it?"

"Never mind all that," she said. "Mr. Dobree is down there talking to Mr. Falkland."

"But what," asked Mamie, "about Mr. Manning?"

"Never mind," shuddered Sarah Lomax, "about Mr. Manning. He won't follow us."

The women, in nameless agitation, tiptoed down the stairs. Sarah Lomax, shaken with great shuddering, the others bewildered and terrified.

They did not walk so lightly, however, that Dobree did not hear them. He opened the parlour door as they were about to pass it and find the entrance which led to that long, black shaft which opened from the waxwork room. That was Sarah Lomax's secret way. Dobree, holding the door open, looked at the three women, and behind him, Falkland gazed at them all.

"So you're leaving 'Mockways' " asked Dobree, softly.

None of the women had the courage to answer. Even Sarah Lomax's boldness had left her. What she had seen in the forge room was too vividly before her eyes. She felt faint and sick.

"Aren't you afraid?" asked Dobree, glancing from one to another. "Aren't you afraid of trying to get away from 'Mockways?' "

"No," said Mamie, summoning a little courage; "We're not afraid, Mr. Dobree—we're more afraid of staying here. You've no right to keep us."

"That's quite true," muttered Dobree; "I've no right to keep you, and I want you to go away. There'll be no obstacle in your way," he added, with a queer look, "and you might as well take Mathews with you. Mathews isn't a bad sort."

"And what about you?" breathed Falkland. "What about you, Mr. Dobree? Do you intend to remain behind in this house?"

"Yes; I'll remain behind."

"And what about Manning?" asked Falkland.

"Manning, too, will remain behind," smiled Dobree.

And Sarah Lomax could not repress a shuddering exclamation.

"Of course, Mr. Manning will never leave 'Mockways,' " she cried, hysterically. "Don't trouble about him, Mr. Falkland."

"Oh! So you know he'll never leave 'Mockways,' do you?" smiled Dobree. "Now, where have you been to find that out?"

"I've been upstairs," breathed Sarah Lomax, through white lips; "I've been in the forge room."

"Ah, you have, have you?" smiled Dobree, with an even more cunning look. "Well then, you know all there is to know. There's pretty well an end to everything, I think, as far as I'm concerned. Matters will go on for you, and, Miss Lomax, there is some provision made for you; some sort of justice. Justice, Falkland—isn't that the word?"

"I don't know whether you call it justice or atonement," said Falkland. "Mr. Dobree," he added, to the two shrinking women, "has left you provided for; he's going to divide his money between you."

"What's this talk of money?" cried Sarah Lomax, hysterically; "I don't want the money. I don't want anything; let's get away."

"Yes, let's get away!" echoed Isabel.

Dobree stepped back and pointed to the windows, opened on the rainy evening.

"Go, then!" he said. "Go at once! Don't stop for anything. Pick up Mathews by the cottages. There's a car there; you'll be able to drive it, I suppose?" He looked gravely at Falkland. "Clear out, all of you. Go, quickly!"

There was something in his look and gestures which made them obey him immediately. The three women scurried and cowered across the room, and out on to the bleak lawn where the evening drizzle was falling with dull greyness. Falkland was after them.

"Better get away—get away and ask no questions."

Dobree pointed to the means of escape and looked after them. Without another word, they left.

They did not even stop to discuss things among themselves.

Sarah Lomax did not even mention the horrible thing she had seen in the forge room. They fled, with feet winged with terror, down to the cottages, and called Mathews, bidding him at once get the car ready.

While he was doing this, too scared to ask questions, they stood looking back at "Mockways," seen gaunt and grim against the darkening sky; and then they heard a shot ring out—a shot that seemed to come from one of the upper rooms.

"I guessed it!" cried Sarah Lomax. "There's an end of both of them!"

None of the others spoke. They looked at the sinister outline of the horrible house and presently they saw a red light appear in the lower windows; a light that spread, that surged out through the window frames in clouds of smoke.

"He's fired the house!" cried Falkland. "We only got out in time. I expect he did that long ago, perhaps meaning to consume us all."

"Don't say that," whispered Isabel. "Give him the benefit of the doubt! Only let us get away: I don't want to hear any more about him." But even she could not at once withdraw her gaze. The three women and the two men stood for a fascinated moment or two, watching the flames get hold of the cursed fabric of "Mockways."

Then they turned, and went out, through the park and on to the road which led to freedom and safety.

"No need to say what happened to any one," said Falkland. "There was an accident, and the house was burnt down with those two men in it. That will be enough, I think. There is an end of 'Mockways!' "

www.ingramcontent.com/pod-product-compliance
Lightning Source LLC
Chambersburg PA
CBHW020933310726
48980CB00007B/753/J

* 9 7 8 1 9 1 7 1 1 3 0 9 0 *